ABSOLUTELY GALÁPAGOS

DAVID FLETCHER

Matador
9 Priory Business Park,
Wistow Road, Kibworth Beauchamp,
Leicestershire. LE8 0RX
Tel: 0116 279 2299
Email: books@troubador.co.uk
Web: www.troubador.co.uk/matador
Twitter: @matadorbooks

ISBN 9781788035071

British Library Cataloguing in Publication Data.
A catalogue record for this book is available from the British Library.

Printed and bound in the UK by TJ International, Padstow, Cornwall
Typeset in 11pt Aldine by Troubador Publishing Ltd, Leicester, UK

Matador is an imprint of Troubador Publishing Ltd

For Caroline

2016

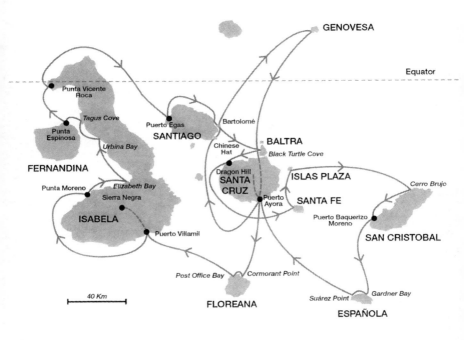

GENOVESA

Equator

Punta Vicente
Roca

Tagus Cove

Puerto Egas

Bartolomé

BALTRA

Punta
Espinosa

Urbina Bay

SANTIAGO

*Chinese
Hat*

Black Turtle Cove

FERNANDINA

Dragon Hill

SANTA
CRUZ

ISLAS PLAZA

Cerro Brujo

Punta Moreno

Elizabeth Bay

Sierra Negra

Puerto
Ayora

SANTA FE

ISABELA

Puerto Baquerizo
Moreno

SAN CRISTOBAL

Puerto Villamil

Post Office Bay

Cormorant Point

40 Km

Gardner Bay

Suárez Point

FLOREANA

ESPAÑOLA

1.

The Hilton Colon Hotel in Quito wasn't anything like its name might suggest. In fact, it was very pleasant indeed, and the only thing that was crappy was Brian's knowledge of Spanish. Sandra's was better, and it was she who pointed out to Brian that the Spanish version of the anglicised 'Christopher Columbus' is, of course, 'Cristóbal Colón', and that for their two-night stop in Quito, prior to their travelling to the Galápagos archipelago, they had been installed in the Hilton *Columbus* Hotel. This revelation brought embarrassment and relief to Brian in almost equal measure, but he also knew that from now on, however hard he tried, he would never be able to contemplate a certain hidden body part – and a certain not very desirable medical procedure – without also bringing to mind that famous explorer from the past. It was just the way he was and he could do nothing about it.

Anyway, it was now the evening of their second day in the Colon Hotel, and Brian and Sandra were in bed, both eager to shed the remains of their jet lag and so be in tip-top form for their journey tomorrow. Because tomorrow would see them flying off to their Galápagos destination, and there embarking on a two-week voyage around its 'enchanted isles'. However, Sandra was still wide awake, and was now reading a book, and Brian was still wide awake – and reviewing their experiences so far.

These had kicked off yesterday when they had flown into Quito in the late afternoon (Quito time), and had thereafter just managed some alcoholic resuscitation before succumbing to sleep. Their experiences then recommenced about twelve hours later in the form of a city tour in the company of their fellow 'Nature-seekers', a dozen other souls who, like themselves, had booked a comprehensive circumnavigation of the Galápagos Islands – and did not necessarily have an intense interest in Spanish colonial architecture. Even if, in Quito, it was so good and so well preserved that it constituted a World Heritage Site. And quite right too. It was pretty impressive, albeit that under a clear blue sky (and at an altitude of 9,000ft), walking around it did entail a perilous exposure of certain sparsely covered scalps to the attention of an unrelenting tropical sun. Furthermore, there was also an exposure to the rather heavy-handed history of Catholicism in this land, probably at its worst in the gold-embellished interior of the *Iglesia de la Compañia de Jesús,* a 'house of God' that, despite God's inclusive credentials, had originally been out of bounds to all but the upper-crustiest of Quito's very Spanish establishment.

Understandably – at least from Brian's perspective – it was something of a relief to abandon the cultural delights of the city in favour of its concentrated natural delights, in the form of Quito's botanical gardens. Here was spent a pleasurable afternoon looking at all things botanical (and especially at a collection of orchids that must rank amongst the best in the world) – as well as witnessing nature in the raw. This episode of rawness was in the shape of a large blue wasp dragging off an enormous (paralysed) spider to its burrow, there presumably to use it as a living larder for its larvae, and in this way illustrate not the inclusive nature of God but his/her/its indifference to all forms of cruelty and suffering.

It was at this stage of his musings – when Brian realised that he'd been sidetracked into 'philosophy' – that he decided to abandon his brief review of his and Sandra's time in Quito, and instead turn his attention to where they would soon be going. Yes, it was time to give some considered thought to the Galápagos Islands, and to start with, how they had come about – in geological terms.

Well, the first thing to bear in mind, he remembered, was that the Galápagos Islands had never been part of the South American continent. They sit about 1,000 kilometres off its coast, but they and the continent have never even been introduced to each other, let alone been joined in any way. This, of course, is because they are the result of volcanic activity and are largely the tips of vast submarine volcanoes – together with the occasional slab of basaltic rock uplifted from the ocean floor.

But that is to gloss over their genesis, and Brian thought that such is the remarkable nature of this genesis, that it warranted a rather more detailed exposition, starting with the fact that the Galápagos Islands are located at the 'Galápagos Triple Junction'.

This is nothing to do with some double bifurcation of the East Coast Mainline outside Banbury, but all to do with the confluence of three of the Earth's tectonic plates: the Pacific Plate, the Cocos Plate and the Nazca Plate. Now, as all those who have not been subjected to the worst of faith schooling will know, tectonic plates are huge slabs of the Earth's crust that are floating on a bed of liquid rock – or magma. Well, at the Galápagos Triple Junction, the Nazca Plate is on the move – east/south-eastwards – at a rate of just two centimetres a year (meaning that in Brian's lifetime it had shifted east/south-east by a distance equivalent to just the length of his chest-waders – if one ignored the shoulder straps). However, as well as this movement – and intimately associated with it – there is a lot of heat. And this is because below the northern edge of the Nazca Plate is a 'hotspot'. Nothing to do with Galápagos night-life but everything to do with a point in the Earth's crust where the superheated magma beneath it is able to pierce its way through – and, in doing so, form massive volcanoes.

Right. Well, this hotspot is stationary. The 'mantle plume' that causes it is a fixed point in the Earth. So... if the plate above it is moving east/south-eastwards – albeit very slowly – then it follows that the volcanic islands created on it will themselves move – west/north-westwards – on a sort of geological 'conveyer belt'. And this is exactly what is observed. (Although, as a human observer, you would be hard put to notice any movement, given that mere chest-waders-length shift in a lifetime.)

What can be observed, however, is that, of all the

islands making up the present-day Galápagos Islands, those in the east are the oldest and those in the west the youngest. So, the south-eastern-most island, Española, is the great granddaddy of the ensemble, whereas Fernandina, to the west, is the real whippersnapper of the group at just 700,000 years old. So… to reinforce this location and age connection – in Brian's tired mind – we have a collection of islands that began to be formed possibly eight million years ago (and are still being formed), where the more east they are the older they are, and the more distant they are from volcanic activity the more eroded they are. In fact, the old hotspot has probably been at it a lot longer than eight million years, with evidence in the form of undersea mountains and ridges to the east of the existing islands, which indicate that it may have been pushing out volcanic material for as much as the last ninety million years. That is to say, that 'lost' Galápagos islands emerged much earlier than those that still exist, and were then either eroded away entirely or found themselves underwater through the action of a (still observable) sagging in the Earth's crust. And although it will take an interminably long time, the same fate awaits even those young thrusting islands to the west – such as Fernandina – whose presently sharply defined features will one day be smoothed down and then submerged beneath the waves.

At this point, Brian had a thought. And his thought was that if this hotspot kept up the good work for a few more hundreds of millions of years, the westward drift of the (above-water) Galápagos islands would eventually see them turning up in somewhere like Borneo. Or if they drifted off slightly southwards, then maybe they'd end up somewhere between Brisbane and Cairns, having first breached the Great Barrier Reef and the Australians' confidence in their border controls. Or maybe, there again, the situation and action of other tectonic plates, of which Brian had no knowledge whatsoever, might just scupper that outcome, and the Galápagos might instead simply end up going around in circles – as he often did when he was jet-lagged but not quite tired enough to sleep.

Yes, perhaps it was time to abandon the challenge of geology and all that scientific sort of thinking, and focus instead on the history of the Galápagos Islands. And first their pre-human history, and in particular how exuded molten rock in the middle of an ocean can possibly end up with any form of life on it, especially when it is so remote from any established landmass.

Well, the short answer is, with the help of ocean currents, a constantly restless atmosphere, birds and rafts of vegetation. The longer answer is... well, longer, and it requires, thought Brian, a distinction between the islands' flora and their fauna – and, to start with, a consideration of how the first plants managed to arrive and then survive in such an unpromising environment as a field of bare lava.

Fortunately, this is far from being a real mystery, because the process is still extant and it can be observed on the very young islands. For here, on what are really little more than expanses of cooled, barren lava, can be seen such pioneering plants as cacti, which, when given the time and just enough precipitation, will ultimately create the right conditions to allow other plants to thrive. And these plants, like those original pioneers, will have arrived on these essentially sterile islands as just tiny seeds, either carried by the sea or the wind – or stuck to the feet or feathers of birds – or even deposited in their droppings. The result: the creation of a mix of environments within which fauna can then make a home.

Now, this process is a little more difficult. Because, although birds can fly and can either arrive in the Galápagos intentionally or, by being blown off course, accidentally, most other animals can definitely not fly and neither can they do 1,000 kilometres of breaststroke, even with the aid of inflatable armbands. So how the heck did they turn up?

Well, the answer is to be found in mainland South America, where, even now, during the wet season, huge clumps of vegetation and whole trees are ripped from the banks of rivers in flood and washed out to sea – in the general direction of the Galápagos Islands. Needless to say, the invertebrates and the small mammals and reptiles who together were just minding their own business in this riverside flora – but who now find themselves pressganged into maritime service – can only hang on desperately and hope. Yes, they can hope that their vessel is one of that tiny minority that doesn't sink or break up and that eventually, after a somewhat challenging voyage, manages to cast them up on a no less challenging Galápagos shore. Of course, very few of these rafts of vegetation would have done this. But enough would to constitute the basis for what we observe as the distinctive – and varied – Galápagos wildlife of today.

Of course, this raft process would be just a little bit selective. Certain creepy-crawlies could survive such a crossing, and certain rodents and reptiles could just about cope with the inevitable dehydration and starvation. But no way could any amphibians have joined the party. Neither could giant tortoises, come to that. But in their case they probably arrived as much smaller species and may even have floated to the Galápagos Islands on their backs – either as a dare or as an act of rebellion while they were still very young. That said, they wouldn't have been small enough to achieve this dare/act of rebellion by drifting through the air – on their backs or otherwise. That option was only open to critters such as spider hatchlings and various absolutely minute insects that together drift constantly on air currents thousands of metres in the air and can end up landing on any piece of the planet, including the Galápagos archipelago. Then, of course, there are bats, kept awake by incessant fiestas on mainland South America, and looking for somewhere quieter to live...

Umm, Brian was clearly getting more tired – and more 'fanciful' by the minute, a fact he confirmed by trying to imagine himself as one of those early reptiles or mammals who had endured an extended nightmare at sea, only to discover that he or she had made it to the safety of a great lump of rock. And on this rock are none of those delicacies one used to enjoy so much at home – like earthworms, avocadoes, roaches and flies – and one is either going to have to learn to eat lichen or risk a faceful of cactus spines every friggin' day. And then there's the threat of sunstroke, to say nothing of the likelihood of clinical depression...

OK. That, decided Brian, was enough of the natural history of the Galápagos – for now. Maybe, as a preparation for some much needed sleep, he should instead turn his diminishing attention to its human history. This had the advantage of being short, fairly uncomplicated and marginally interesting – when compared to the activities of those pioneering cacti.

It began in 1535, when the Bishop of Panama, one Fray Tomás de Berlanga, was on his way to Peru to arbitrate some dispute (maybe involving what tonnage of gold was required in the building of a new church?) and he got blown off course. That is to say, his ship got blown off course, not the bishop in his capacious vestments – or, at least, as far as is known. Anyway, when he finally made it back to his Spanish homeland, he reported on the conditions he found on the islands and on some of the animals there. What he didn't report, because it wasn't discovered until much later, was that the islands did contain evidence of earlier visits – by indigenous South Americans – in the form of various artefacts. But none of these artefacts included ceremonial vessels and there were no graves anywhere, which strongly suggested that there were never any permanent settlements on the islands. Those early South American visitors must have been just tourists or people out and about looking for a new picnic site – or, more likely, they were well on their way to a watery and distinctly terminal end somewhere in the endless Pacific.

So, King Carlos of Spain was informed that he had yet more real estate, but, from what Brian could remember, he seemed to be entirely underwhelmed, and his new property got filed away under 'boring' and was essentially ignored entirely. Indeed, it wasn't until 1570 that the islands were included on any map – when they were (separately) by the two Flemish mapmakers, Gerardus Mercator and Abraham Ortelius. They were named 'Insulae de los Galopegos (Islands of the Tortoises) in reference to the giant tortoises that were found there. (They were not, incidentally, named after 'saddles'. The Spanish for 'saddle' is *'silla de montar'*, and the erroneous attribution of the islands' name (to saddles) arises because there used to be a form of saddle in Spain called a *'galapagos'* – in reference to its tortoise shape. And if Brian could get his head around that distinction in his still jet-lagged, weary state, then surely, he thought, everybody else should be able to as well.)

He then thought he should move on to when the first English sea captain, a certain Richard Hawkins, visited the Galápagos – which was in 1593. Because this marked the first active human use of these islands, which was as a refuge for English pirates. Yes, rather than being exploited by the Spanish, they were used by their sworn enemies to conduct a drawn-out pilfering campaign on all those Spanish galleons carrying gold and silver out of South America and off to their homeland.

This English tenancy even extended to the drawing up of accurate navigation charts of the islands. This was done by a guy called James Colnett, who was an officer in the Royal Navy, with a sideline as a maritime fur trader. In fact, he was really bad news – for the wildlife of the Galápagos. This was because he was the first to suggest that the Galápagos would make a wonderful base for whaling in the Pacific, and in due course the whalers came – and killed and captured thousands of tortoises for consumption and for their fat. Then fur-seal hunters arrived and made matters even worse. So much so that the population of tortoises was greatly diminished and certain of their species were eliminated entirely.

Well, this horrible history must have made the arrival of the first human resident on the Galápagos Islands something of a relief for the local fauna – in that he was on his own. This chap was not Spanish and nor was he English. He was, in fact, Irish. He was a fellow by the name of Patrick Watkins and he was a sailor by profession who, by accident, had found himself marooned on one of the Galápagos islands called Floreana. He managed to survive there for two years – between 1807 and 1809 – and he did this by hunting, growing his own veg and trading with visiting whalers. He was clearly a resourceful sort of chap, and he was even able to bring his one-man colonisation of the islands to an end by stealing an open boat from one of the whaling ships and navigating himself back to the South American mainland. There, he probably swore never to go near any tectonic plate boundary ever again, and certainly not one that was associated with an all too active hotspot.

OK. Brian now moved on – to 1832, which was when Ecuador finally got around to annexing the Galápagos Islands and finally restoring that original connection with the Spanish Empire – in a way, at least. The first governor of the islands was a fellow called General José de Villamil, who took over from where Mr Watkins had first made a mark, by, in 1832, taking a group of convicts to Floreana who were joined later that same year by a group of farmers and artisans. However, their venture there cannot, in all honesty, be said to have made the same impact as a brief visit made just three years later – by yet more Englishmen, this time in a ship called the *Beagle*...

Yes, on 15 September 1835, the *Beagle* arrived to survey approaches to natural harbours. The captain of the ship (and one Charles Darwin), as well as conducting this survey work, made observations on the geology and the biology of a number of the Galápagos islands before they left on 20 October. They were assisted in these observations by the acting governor of the Galápagos at the time, and when this chap met the *Beagle* people (on what was then not yet Floreana but Charles Island), he happened to mention to Charles Darwin that the giant tortoises varied in appearance from island to island. With this pointer and with his own observations of mockingbirds, which he'd noticed also varied from island to island, our Charles, towards the end of the *Beagle*'s voyage, speculated that these variations might 'undermine the stability of species'.

Well, the rest is history. Although that history did have to wait until specimens of the birds he'd captured in the islands were analysed back in England, where he discovered that what he'd originally thought were different kinds of birds were, in fact, various species of finches – all of which were unique to different islands. With this further insight into the natural world, Mr Darwin developed his theory of natural selection that set out the principles underlying evolution and which were eventually presented in his world-shaking *On the Origin of Species*. This was nothing less than a giant step in mankind's own development as a species, and its genesis is no better described than in a quote that Brian had seen only quite recently, which was: 'the best idea anybody has ever had'.

Anyway, despite enlightenment arriving back in England, the mundane continued in the Galápagos – with another attempt to kindle some sort of commercial activity on the islands. This was the formation of a new colony, this time based on the exploitation of lichen… Well, even Brian wouldn't have thought up something that dumb. And he probably wouldn't have then tried his luck with sugar cane either. Needless to say, no great success was achieved in any of these enterprises, and in the early part of the twentieth century, right up until 1929, cash-strapped Ecuador spent more time looking for a buyer for the islands than it did embarking on any more dismal and disastrous new schemes.

Incredibly (in retrospect) nobody wanted to buy the Galápagos Islands. Accordingly, Ecuador offered twenty hectares of land (for nothing) to all those who were prepared to settle on its unwanted possession – along with the granting of a tax holiday for ten years, the right to hunt and fish on all the uninhabited islands and the right to retain their citizenship. This offer clearly had some appeal to a number of people fed up with the weather in Europe and fearful of a future in the European Union, and amongst the first to take up the offer were some Scandinavians. These guys were followed shortly thereafter by a number of Americans who had experienced a vision of Donald Trump as President by eating magic mushrooms.

Well, Brian was beginning to think that some of these historical facts were maybe a bit suspect, to say the least. But although he was now feeling extremely tired he had nearly concluded his potted history of those islands in the Pacific. So why not continue to the end?

Quite. And anyway, he could now jump forward to the era of the Second World War, when Ecuador authorised the US to build a naval base on one of the islands and to set up some radio stations in other strategic locations. With these facilities, the US was able to patrol the Pacific for submarines and to protect the Panama Canal. After the war, they were then able to gift these facilities to the Ecuadorean government, and what then became an official Ecuadorean military base was possibly the most significant human presence on the islands right up until the 1960s. In fact, the Galápagos Islands were still seen then as very much a pristine environment and definitely worthy of some heavy duty protection. This had first been put in place by the Ecuadorean government as far back as 1935 (the centenary of Darwin's visit) and it was later reinforced by declaring the islands a national park and recruiting the support of both the Charles Darwin Foundation for the Galápagos Islands and the Ecuadorian National Parks Service.

However, in the first place, all those pirates, whalers, fur traders and hapless colonists had left a legacy of introduced invasive species, in the form of goats, pigs, donkeys, cats, dogs, fire ants, cockroaches, possibly unicorns and certainly a whole list of unwelcome plants such as blackberries and even elephant grass – but no elephants. So, even without too many humans, it wasn't quite as pristine as one would have liked. And in the second place, it must have been known forty-five years ago that in our crowded, impoverished world, the 2,000 or so humans that then called the Galápagos their home would soon swell to a much larger number and inevitably constitute a new series of threats to these precious islands. As indeed they now do.

Nevertheless, Brian knew he was now moving from history into current affairs. And the only thing current in his mind at the moment was the need to abandon his musings on tomorrow's destination and get down to some serious zeds. Sandra already had, with her book still in her lap. Brian would now do the same – immediately – not with a book in his lap, but with a resolve to learn some more Spanish. Enough, anyway, to learn whether Cristóbal Colón, as the initiator of the annexation and settling of South America by Spain and Portugal, was also the initiator of the word '*colon*-isation'. Unlikely, thought Brian. But one could never be sure…

2.

*Q*uito isn't all World Heritage standard. Brian had observed this on his way in from Quito's airport two days before. But now, in today's early-morning rush hour, his observation was being confirmed in spades – and in an all too visible haze of diesel fumes. Much of 'new' Quito is shabby, ugly, higgledy-piggledy and bathed in car fumes – and so too is much of its barely moving traffic. In fact, whoever had decided to build Quito in such a dramatic, elevated position had clearly not given any thought to the consequences of urban sprawl in what is a decidedly precipitous mountain situation – or to the needs and emissions of modern-day traffic. The result is a somewhat incongruous metropolitan 'stain' on an otherwise dramatic environment – bathed for most of the time in a greyish-brown fug. No surprise then that Brian was fairly relieved when the Nature-seekers' minibus arrived at Quito's Mariscal Sucre International Airport and all he had to do was endure a fug of bureaucracy rather than one of fumes.

Yes, when controlling the passage of visitors to the Galápagos, Ecuador takes its responsibilities very seriously indeed, and winging one's way to this archipelago involves a number of checks, forms and vouchers that certainly wouldn't be encountered if one was winging one's way to Ibiza, say. And who can blame it for taking such a stringent approach? After all, the Galápagos archipelago is precious and it deserves to be protected at all costs. Whereas, Ibiza… well, you get the general idea.

Anyway, eventually the vetting and fretting process led to the boarding of an aeroplane, and the first surprise of the day for Brian. Because whilst he'd thought that the flight to the Galápagos might entail some sort of diminutive aircraft, what he ended up sitting on was a sizable Airbus A320, operated by TAME, the flag carrier and principal airline in the country. And, of course, this sort of aircraft was vital, as it wasn't carrying just a clutch of foreign visitors to that archipelago in the Pacific, but also a large contingent of its residents, people returning to the Galápagos after a funeral/ wedding/shopping binge/secret tryst or whatever else had caused them to travel to mainland Ecuador in the first place. And they came in all sorts and at all volumes – from the essentially silent oldies to the unremittingly raucous toddlers, who unfortunately didn't desist from their boisterous behaviour even when the A320 made a not brief enough stopover at Ecuador's second city of Guayaquil. Brian was therefore forced to distract himself with a consideration of (a) the paddy fields that seemed to surround Guayaquil – and (b) the insuperable difficulties that surrounded even a reasonable stab at this city's correct pronunciation. Oh, and then, of course, there was the prospect of flying out over the Pacific and actually arriving in the Galápagos.

Well, an hour after taking off from Guayaquil, this arrival... arrived. The A320 touched down at the principal airport of the Galápagos, which is situated on the tiny island of Baltra. This island, which sits just to the north of the much larger island of Santa Cruz, is the one on which the Americans built their military base in WWII days and the one that still serves as an Ecuadorian military base to this day. It is best described as nondescript – but, for the passengers of an aeroplane in need of a long runway, also very reassuring.

The airport building, Brian observed, was very new – as was the covered walkway from the runway to the building, which was topped with solar panels and went some way to shielding Brian and his fellow travellers from the heat of the midday sun. It was remarkably hot, and only a tiny bit cooler in the air-conditioned terminal. This was a little unfortunate because more of those rigorous entry procedures needed to be dealt with here, and this led to the sort of queues one now sees only in Caracas – for luxuries such as toilet paper. That, incidentally, was Brian's thought as he stood stewing in the queue and which, in retrospect, he considered to be a gross exaggeration of the situation in the terminal as well as being highly disrespectful to the people of Venezuela. But, there again, he had never claimed to be perfect.

OK. He and the rest of the party were now through all the entry procedures and were waiting for their transport to their 'maritime vessel', which, rumour had it, was awaiting them in a nearby bay. The transport (a bus operated by a company that apparently exploited the lack of bus competition on Baltra Island to its huge financial advantage) finally arrived, and the Nature-seekers boarded it. Three minutes later they unboarded it and found themselves at the shore of the bay, under both a covered landing stage and the distinct impression that they would soon be making the acquaintance of an inflatable *panga* (two of which were moored just below them).

This was because their guide for the next two weeks had joined them at the airport, had accompanied them on the bus, and was now handing out lifejackets. He was a forty-something Ecuadorian and his name was Darwin… (It really was, as he had apparently been born on the anniversary of the other Darwin's birthday and had been named accordingly.) But, anyway, the live Darwin, having handed out the lifejackets, was now about to embark on what would prove to be one of his most popular pastimes: that of delivering briefings…

This first one was on the perils of stepping into an inflatable dinghy (one of the aforementioned pangas), and how to avoid these perils by stepping carefully – and by adopting the all-important 'panga handhold'. This wasn't such a bad idea. Because one did need to steady oneself when one was abandoning reassuringly solid land in favour of a not necessarily steady, pliable platform. And how one steadied oneself, as explained by Darwin, was not by grabbing the offered hand of the panga driver as one stepped onto and into his vessel, but by grabbing his forearm, and thus enabling him to grab yours. This way the two parties to the hand/arm-hold would become locked together – entirely platonically – and the embarking party could successfully avoid all those panga-associated perils and thereby stay dry. Of course, a similarly arid outcome could be achieved by employing this same robust handhold when one was *disembarking* the panga – either onto solid land or onto something like, say, a swaying gangway. So, all in all, the panga handhold was a really very good idea indeed.

Anyway, when both pangas, in accordance with these instructions, had been safely loaded with their cargo of Nature-seekers, they together set off from the landing stage and made for a boat, a boat that until now had been obscured by another. But soon, it was unobscured and then there it was: the *M/Y Beluga*, a stunning, literally ship-shaped motor yacht that would be the Nature-seekers' home for the next two weeks. It was a beaut: a sleek vessel of the sea, over one hundred feet long and rendered in true nautical white, save for an elegant black stripe just beneath its main deck. And it had a proper bridge, and canopies above its upper deck, and portholes and everything... Brian was really quite excited. So too was Sandra. She told him.

It wasn't long before all its passengers were aboard it, all of them having avoided any mishaps in the transfer between the pangas and the *Beluga*'s gangway, slung from its side. It also wasn't long before Brian and Sandra were exploring their cabin and agreeing that they had certainly made the right decision in not bringing a cat – or even a kitten. Yes, nothing could have been swung in their compact accommodation, other than maybe one leg over the other as, sitting on their beds, they took in their cabin's bijou charm.

It was pretty small, but it was also pretty, full stop. It

had two narrow beds occupying most of its floor – with just two feet between them – and, off it, a bathroom that had been modelled on a corridor – and then shrunk. Indeed, it seemed to offer the possibility of shaving while seated on the loo and there was clearly no risk whatsoever of falling over in the shower. There simply wasn't enough room. However, to return to the cabin proper – and why it had such charm and why, indeed, Brian and Sandra had chosen it in preference to other slightly larger cabins on this boat. And this was because, with a sister cabin, it was at the stern of the boat on its main deck – just off the boat's bar area – and unlike all the cabins down below, it had no portholes but just two picture windows that made up two of its four sides (at the back and at the side of the boat – obviously). It was, indeed, a cabin with a panoramic view – and, of course, it had that easy access to the bar. Hell, what could be better? Well, maybe contemplating the charm of one's cabin with a drink in one's hand and the prospect of the first proper meal of the day.

Well, in the event, this contemplation had to be put on hold, because Darwin had another briefing to deliver – on the disposition of various amenities on the boat. And even after what proved to be a splendid lunch, contemplation again had to be deferred because there was now a briefing by Darwin on the dos and don'ts of being in the Galápagos National Park. Oh, and then a briefing on the intricacies of 'wet landings' from the panga as opposed to dry landings – which would need to be borne in mind for one of tomorrow's expeditions. But not for today's. Yes, while the Nature-seekers had been feeding themselves and listening to Darwin, the captain of the *Beluga* had taken it from that Baltra Island bay, along the north coast of Santa Cruz and had now parked it off the north-west of this much larger island at a site called Dragon Hill. Just three hours into their nautical adventure and the Nature-seekers were about to go on their first proper excursion. Great!

Now, at this stage it is worth pointing out that Darwin's briefing on the dos and don'ts of the national park had underlined the severe restrictions imposed on all those visiting the park. That is to say that by paying one's US$100 entry fee to the Galápagos, one was not then able to go anywhere one wanted. In the first place one would, in all likelihood, be on a boat, and the operators of that (licensed) boat would have agreed an itinerary with the park authorities from which it could not vary and which was intended to ensure that none of the Galápagos' 'visitor sites' became overwhelmed by a flotilla of boats all arriving at the same time. Furthermore, those 'visitor sites' were very important, as they were the only sites on virtually all the islands where visitors were allowed to set foot. And when they'd set foot on these sites, they'd have to make quite sure that they didn't deviate from clearly marked paths. All these restrictions might be regarded as overly onerous but they were clearly essential if the Galápagos archipelago was not to be completely ruined and its wildlife destroyed. Even so, they did mean that Brian and Sandra were embarking on the sort of controlled 'expedition' that was the antithesis of the sort of free-roaming experience they often enjoyed in places such as Namibia and Botswana. And they would certainly never set eyes on a Land Cruiser here.

Anyway, they had known about this necessary regimentation before they had embarked on this modest odyssey and in no way would it be distracting from the excitement of their first taste of the real Galápagos. Nor would the prospect of their first 'dry landing'.

In the *Beluga*'s two pangas, the fourteen Nature-seekers had abandoned their mother ship and had motored gently towards a rocky promontory composed of 'irregular' rocks. They looked as though they might provide a bit of a challenge in the disembarking stakes, particularly as there was a noticeable swell in the sea and the rocks looked as though they were all slicked with algae. They were. And it *was* something of a challenge. But eventually, Darwin had all his charges on terra firma, and the only moisture about their persons was not as a result of accidental immersion but instead as a result of copious perspiration. It was furiously hot, and the sun was so intense that even Brian gave not a second's thought to donning a hat. Indeed, anybody who found themselves standing on a beach, listening to the first of scores of lectures to be delivered by Darwin over the next fortnight, would not have given it a second's thought, although he or she might have considered the wisdom of these open-air addresses...

It was very difficult. Darwin had a great deal of knowledge on every aspect of the Galápagos archipelago, whether concerning its geology, its flora, its fauna or its conservation, and he also had a desire to impart as much of this information to his guests as possible – irrespective of the power of the sun. Furthermore, as would become apparent over the next two weeks, most of the trails on the visitor sites are not overlong, and without stopping for lectures on the way, they would be completed in far less than the two or so hours that they were designed to take. So, it would be grossly unfair to find any genuine fault with Darwin's frequent didactic pauses – other than they often seemed to ignore what was going on around him. Because, as will be reported, Galápagos wildlife is extremely unfazed by the presence of humans and is therefore often in sight or almost underfoot. But even when birds and animals were no more than feet away – and being entirely fascinating – Darwin seemed reluctant to even interrupt his address. It was a little, thought Brian, like visiting some wonderful art gallery, with a guide who was eager to impart all he knew about a series of famous artists – but who was somewhat unconcerned with their works on display. There again, in Darwin's situation, Brian would probably have done the same, albeit he might have set up his soapbox in a location where his audience could have found just a little bit of shade. Not that this would have been easy on his first pitch...

This was the beach, where there was no prospect of shade whatsoever, and where, because of the reflecting power of the sand, the heat was 'excessive to fierce' and at risk of becoming 'extreme'. Brian simply streamed as he stood and listened to Darwin's dissertation on fish, and he wanted nothing more than to at least get off the sand. But that wasn't going to happen any time soon, and in the meantime he decided to study what was a great deal easier to see than any of those translucent fish in the shallows, and this was the first (for him) real-life manifestation of marine iguanas!

They weren't around in large numbers, but they were around and obvious, and they all had a very distinct demeanour, one that somehow put Brian in mind of Karl Lagerfeld, that well-known doyen of the fashion world. It wasn't, of course, that these largely black and grey sea-going lizards had a great deal in common, physically, with Mr Lagerfeld – other than possibly in the mouth department – but there was just something about them that prompted their unlikely connection with that particular designer of frocks. Brian never really worked it out, but it could have been something to do with the iguanas' stiffness, their lack of a discernible expression, their apparent indifference to the world around them and their... well, their slightly 'alien aura'. Anyway, they were quite a thing, and they took Brian's mind off his melting right up until it was time to leave the beach and head off inland.

This inland was an expanse of scrub-covered Santa Cruz, rising, in the distance, to the 'Dragon Hill' itself, a modest scrub-covered hillock that Brian was already hoping would be out of bounds and therefore not part of their peregrination. Walking on level ground in this heat, he could cope with. Anything involving an upward incline might be more of a problem.

Well, in the event, he had to cope with only a gentle climb and Dragon Hill remained safely in the distance. In fact, the only challenges on the Nature-seekers' two-hour expedition – other than the incessant heat – were a few puddles as they skirted an inland lagoon and what would become a common feature of their Galápagos rambles: the unevenness of the paths. These challenges, they could easily cope with, and they could thereby devote all the time they needed to observing the waders and waterbirds that were on the lagoon – and the Galápagos 'specials' that were close to the path. Included in these were some incredibly unbothered (Galápagos) flycatchers and some even more unbothered (Galápagos) mockingbirds. In fact, these mockingbirds were so unbothered – and so audacious – that, if one stood still for just a little time, they were quite likely to peck at one's shoes in search of something to eat. They were like starlings on speed.

They certainly made themselves obvious on Darwin's third lecture spot (or was it his fourth?). Here they hopped around between the Nature-seekers – as a number of the Nature-seekers, in search of some relief from the sun, half-crouched beneath some tallish scrub. And again there were the distractions, this time in the form of even more mockingbirds, more flycatchers (sometimes just inches away) – and then the ponderous approach of a couple of *land* iguanas.

These guys, unlike the marine iguanas, did not put Brian in mind of any representative of the fashion industry – probably because they were the antithesis of 'thin'. At more than three feet long and weighing maybe twenty pounds, these rather corpulent yellow-brown lizards were more reminiscent of overfed Labradors than they were of skeletal designers and models, and they certainly didn't have a catwalk gait. Instead, they waddled and quite often they didn't move at all. In fact, it took them an inordinate amount of time to get from any A to any B, and any C was simply out of the question. This, combined with their obvious 'limited intellect', made Brian think that he would never live to witness a 'guide-land-iguanas for the blind appeal'. Not only would these creatures find even the rudiments of guiding the blind well beyond them, but unlike all those Labradors who could guide their owners to the local Greggs within minutes, they, even if they ever learnt how to, would take several weeks to do it. That said, they were pretty impressive, and they certainly looked at home in their Galápagos environment. Which is more than could be said for a still-sweating Brian. Yes, it was becoming quite clear. 'Glowing' and mild perspiration would both be a rare experience on these Galápagos hikes, and copious sweating – together with constituting an incongruous sight in this archipelago's unique environment – would be the order of the day.

There were, of course, other features of this Dragon Hill excursion, including erudite expositions on the flora, but in all honesty, towards its end, Brian's focus on Darwin and on what was around him was rather overtaken by his thoughts concerning the quite admirable skills of brewers, and particularly of those who specialised in the brewing of lager. It was no less than heresy, really, but Brian couldn't help himself. He was hot, tired and in need of a drink, and when the Dragon Hill path led his party back to the beach, he was definitely not that enthusiastic for another of Darwin's lectures…

However, this one proved to be very short. It merely concerned a warning about the perils of boarding the pangas again, and an announcement. And this announcement was that when all the Nature-seekers were back on board the *Beluga*, there would be a safety drill. This would involve the sounding of the boat's alarm just five minutes after their return to the vessel, whereupon all the boat's passengers would be required to collect the emergency lifejackets that were stowed in their cabins and then immediately gather at the front of the vessel (on the main deck where it narrowed to a point), there to receive further instructions. And quite right too, thought Brian. No point in not knowing where to spend one's final minutes in the event of an unscheduled sinking...

So... when, back on board, the alarm went off as scheduled, and Brian and Sandra grabbed their lifejackets and made off immediately for the *Beluga*'s prow, and when they arrived there, so too did an almost full complement of the *Beluga*'s passengers and crew. But only an almost full complement, not a completely full complement. Because two of the Nature-seekers were missing.

They were still missing after a full minute, and still missing after a full three minutes, and incredibly still after a full five minutes. And their identity was not a secret. It was Rick and Delia, a married couple who had been friends of Brian and Sandra for years and who now occupied that other window-abundant cabin on the main deck, next to their own. Why they hadn't arrived with the others was a complete mystery. Were they, pondered Brian, the subjects of an alien abduction? Had they perhaps been kidnapped by (long-range) Somali pirates? Or had they suffered an unexpected attack of agoraphobia, which meant they now couldn't countenance leaving their bijou accommodation? Or just possibly, had they completely forgotten about the safety drill, returned to their cabin and there engaged in the noisy process of showering and so failed to hear the alarm?

Well, as reported by Delia, when she finally made it to the assembly point, it was this latter reason. Indeed Rick was still in the shower, which is why it was a full ten minutes after the alarm had been sounded before he had joined his fellow sinking friends – there to receive a round of applause. That said, he would have been there a little sooner had he not met one of the crew on his first departure from his cabin, who had suggested to him that as it was just a drill and not the real thing, his appearance on the prow would be more welcome in a full set of clothes than it would be with just a towel around his waist. When this was made known to the gathering, nobody, including Delia, disagreed.

Well, unintentionally, Rick and Delia had now earned themselves the 'slightly disorganised but essentially nice' designation on the *Beluga*. Which meant that Brian would have to consider which designation he and Sandra should seek. He did this over that first longed-for lager in the bar, and he briefly considered the 'opinionated but receptive', the 'reserved but approachable', the 'incisive but humorous' and the 'cool but not that cool'. However, he could not come to a decision, and he would just have to see where this first evening meal on the *Beluga* took him – and essentially play it by ear.

It took him – and Sandra – nowhere. Because at

their table of six (with eight others on the other table), they had for company just Rick and Delia and Bill and Andrea. And Bill and Andrea were themselves busy going for the designation of 'the odd ones out'. A little cruel this, but Andrea spoke only in spurts – and with giggles – and her husband, Bill (a retired submariner), spoke not in spurts or with giggles, but essentially without any sound. It was quite remarkable, but when he uttered any words, nothing much made it into the audible spectrum. It was as though he'd spent his life talking to dogs at some inaudible frequency or that he was now saving his larynx in case of some unspecified emergency. Like when he needed to attract the attention of a passing ship when the *Beluga* went down. Anyway, he and his wife were rather hard work, and whatever Brian and Sandra had done at the table, they could never have established for themselves anything as distinct as that 'slightly disorganised but essentially nice' classification that their friends had won so easily and without really trying.

Brian and Sandra agreed on this outcome when they were finally back in their cabin, after which Brian sought Sandra's agreement on another matter, and this matter was the nature of her daily (intellectual) entertainment. He began this quest for her agreement by reminding her – casually – that on past holidays he had enlivened her evenings with such things as a review of the failings of certain countries and the merits of the Seven Deadly Sins, and then just as casually asking her whether 'various interesting facts about the nations of South America' might be a suitable choice for their current expedition.

'What!?' screeched Sandra, at a volume that must have been audible in the engine room. 'You want…'

'Well, I thought…'

'You never think, Brian. You just do. I mean…'

'So that's OK then? And I thought, as we're in the Galápagos, I'd start with Ecuador…'

Sandra looked livid. Or was that exasperation? Well, whatever it was, it seemed to make her Bill-like, and she failed with any further words. And before she could rectify this absence of a protest, Brian was onto his first pitch, talking about Ecuador's president and the colour of his politics…

'… yes, this chap, Rafael Correa, is definitely a little *pink*. He was one of Chavez's buddies and he came to power promising to introduce popular social programmes at the expense of servicing debts, and well… at the expense of playing by international norms. So, for example, he declared the country's international debt illegitimate and, by doing this, he did actually reduce the price of outstanding bonds by 60%…'

'Outstanding,' interjected Sandra.

'Ah, but like all these lefties in charge of South American countries, he failed to understand real-world economics, something that you simply can't afford to do when your economy is dependent on commodities, and particularly on oil. So even when you've mortgaged your country to the Chinese, by granting three million hectares of your Amazon rainforest to Chinese oil companies, you still get bitten in the bum – when the price of oil and of other commodities falls off a cliff. The result: the economy in a tailspin, up to three million Ecuadorians seeking work overseas, a systematic and hostile campaign against the country's free press to silence dissent and the fall-back position of blaming the States for all your ills. In fact, the only funny thing that this guy has ever said is something that reflects his phobia of the US. And this was: "The only country in the world that won't ever have a *coup d'état* is the US – as there is no US embassy in the US."

'Funny that, isn't it?'

'Not really,' responded Sandra. 'And neither is this lecture. You know, I think I've already had quite enough lectures for today.'

'OK,' conceded Brian. 'But I want to make just one further point about this ever-so-virtuous president of Ecuador, and it's one that's not funny in the least…'

'Which is?' encouraged Sandra plaintively.

'Which is that he fairly recently overturned a ban on the sale of shark fins. Although, of course, he went to great pains to stipulate that the only shark fins that could be sold were those caught 'accidentally' by artisan fishermen – without dwelling too long on how the authorities could possibly determine whether a shark had been caught deliberately or "accidentally".'

'You mean he is an absolute bastard who should be put against a wall and shot?'

'Well,' stuttered Brian, 'I suppose you could put it like that. I was just going to say that, as far as I'm concerned, he's the pits. As is anybody who conducts, condones or conspires in the killing of millions of sharks – just for their fins and just for all those execrable Chinese soup-drinkers, all of whom I sincerely hope end up choking to death on their fucking soup.'

'Good,' said Sandra. 'It seems we're agreed. And that presumably means you've done "Ecuador" and I can now get some sleep. And you can either go to sleep as well or you can contemplate the wisdom of regaling me with any more facts about the nations of South America, no matter how "interesting" they might be.'

This announcement drew to a conclusion this first day afloat, but sadly for Sandra it did nothing to dissuade Brian from his planned programme of 'entertainments'. In fact, it did quite the contrary. Heck, Sandra had actually responded to his first brief dissertation, and without the use of a single profanity. It was a clear signal, he thought, that she was prepared, if not eager, for more of the same – in just about the same way that it is always crystal clear when a marine iguana is feeling a little bit on edge or even really rather tense…

3.

*B*rian and Sandra's first night aboard the *Beluga* had been… illuminating. They had retired shortly after their evening meal, and as soon as they had settled down, the master of the *Beluga* had set off for their next destination, a small island to the south-east of Santa Cruz by the name of Santa Fe. This was to become standard practice: undertaking the longer elements of the journey around the Galápagos in the hours of darkness, thereby enabling the *Beluga*'s passengers to sleep and then to wake to find themselves at the site of their next on-shore expedition. Now, in this instance, the trip to Santa Fe took nearly three hours, and the *Beluga* was in position off the island just after one o'clock in the morning. Brian knew this because he had been awake for much of the voyage, and although he did finally get to sleep, he had then been awoken by the noise of the boat's arrival at its mooring, involving, as it did, the dropping of an anchor and the shutting down of its engine.

Now, what had kept both Brian and Sandra awake initially was a combination of the boat's engine noise whilst underway – and the boat's motion. This could not be ignored, because the boat rolled. Not, fortunately, through 360 degrees, or even worse, through 180 degrees, but 'nautically' to and fro along its bow-to-stern axis. Which meant that if one's bed was on this same axis – as Brian and Sandra's were – one rolled as well. And not just a little, but a lot. In a way, Brian had found it quite a pleasant sensation, but not one that his body would willingly recognise as conducive to sleep. Consequently, like Sandra, his body had needed to become acutely tired before it would willingly ignore both the motion of the vessel and the noise of its engine, and finally nod off. Until, that is, the motion and the noise both came to a halt…

Maybe Brian's body would adapt. Maybe Sandra's would as well. And soon they would both be sleeping through the *Beluga*'s gyrations and the dancing of its pistons without being aware of a thing. But right now, on this first morning after the first night, neither of them could claim to have had a peaceful night and 'weary' would be the entry in their log, along with 'might as well get up and savour our situation' – which is exactly what they did. And the first aspect of their situation that they savoured was the *Beluga* itself. Nobody else was up, so they had decided to have a proper look round.

The deck below theirs was essentially out of bounds, as this contained the five portholed passenger cabins, the engine room and the cramped crew's quarters. So when they left their stern cabin they inspected just the bar area, with its padded seating and its table for eight, before moving through to the dining room, with its other table for eight and its coffee station. Beyond this was an extremely modest galley, and beyond that, a small map room and the bridge (with a closet at its rear that served as the captain's cabin). Stairs at the side of the galley led to the upper deck, which hosted one further cabin – amidships and to one side – but which was otherwise open, as a sundeck at the rear and as a covered 'flying bridge' at the front. It was from here that Brian and Sandra now turned their attention from the boat itself to where the boat was moored. Because it was moored in heaven. And if it wasn't heaven, then it was some corner of paradise or an outpost of dreamland. It was truly superb.

What stirred these thoughts in Brian's mind was the clear blue sky above and the clear turquoise sea all about – and the *Beluga*'s situation in a beautiful sheltered bay, with, for company, just one other *Beluga*-sized boat. It really was as though the captain had found his way to Nirvana – and Nirvana wasn't even crowded. In fact, it was pretty well deserted as well as being stunningly gorgeous.

Well, there was only one thing to do. And this was to go downstairs and wait for breakfast – and when breakfast arrived, to contemplate how many pounds would be added to one's frame if this really was the smallest of the three full meals to be served each day. Nevertheless, those thoughts were transitory and were soon overtaken by the anticipation of what would be the Nature-seekers' first 'wet landing'. As promised in Darwin's final briefing of the previous evening, the pangas would soon be loaded with their complements of 'wet virgins' and they would then make their way to a white sandy beach at the end of the enclosed bay and there deposit their loads – in the foam.

This wasn't as bad as it sounds. When the pangas were close to the beach, by using their outboard motors, the panga drivers were able to hold them in position – their fronts nearest the sand – and the virgins could disembark. And all this entailed was one pair of virgins at a time – on either side of a panga and starting with those nearest the front – swinging their legs over the panga's inflated sides and then standing up in the surf – preferably barefoot. Oh, and then not falling over, not dropping their rucksacks or their cameras, and remembering that they then had to wade to the shore.

Observing what proved to be an entirely successful landing by all the Nature-seekers was a Galápagos hawk. He – and, from his colouring and size, it was a he – was perched on a rock well above the bay, and was no doubt confirming the fact that this island was one of the few remaining hotspots for this rarest of rare birds. Because, whilst this brownish-black raptor does occur on other islands, its habit of snacking on anything it can find – including domestic chickens – has guaranteed its persecution and consequently its preference for uninhabited islands such as Santa Fe.

Throughout the Galápagos archipelago, there are only 400 to 800 individual hawks (depending on what reference work one chooses), and within this tiny number there are probably no more than 150 breeding pairs. This means that there are only 150 breeding pairs in the whole world, and this, of course, earns this bird the classification of 'vulnerable'. It is just as well, then, that the females of the species have developed a very successful breeding strategy, one that is guaranteed to optimise their chances of producing a new crop of hawks. This strategy is called cooperative polyandry –

and it does exactly what it says on the tin. That is to say that one female Galápagos hawk will have it off with up to seven male hawks, and these males will then help out with the subsequent incubation work and even with the rearing of the young. It's a great idea, and it certainly helps the survival of the Galápagos hawk as a species. However, Brian doubted that it would ever catch on in the human world. After all, whilst many men would no doubt buy into the first part of the deal, they would probably all baulk at its associated service commitments. And, furthermore, there is very little doubt that most women would find it very difficult to believe that there were as many as seven suitable and worthy males in the whole bloody world.

Anyway, this Galápagos hawk on the rock was a welcome sight, and what would really constitute icing on the cake would be its now landing on a Nature-seeker head. Unlikely, but not impossible. Because these birds, as well as being largely fearless of man, are irrepressibly inquisitive, and they have actually been known to land on people's heads. In fact, even Darwin (the nineteenth-century dead one) remarked on their audacious behaviour, when he wrote 'A gun here is almost superfluous; for with the muzzle I pushed a hawk out of the branch of a tree...'

Well, this one didn't even approach the Nature-seekers, but instead he flew off inland (no doubt looking for something tasty – in any sense of the word) and Brian and his fellow shipmates were left to turn their attention to the other very obvious occupants of the beach: a score of basking sea lions.

They were, inevitably, Galápagos sea lions, of which there is a fluctuating population of between twenty and fifty-thousand, often being towards the low end of that range as the result of the effects of El Niño (on their food source). This morning, on this beach, it has to be said that none of the lolling lions looked as though they'd ever given a second's thought to the effects of El Niño, probably because they never had, and possibly because thinking and worrying weren't high on their agenda. What was clearly more important was their lolling about, their caring for their pups (they were all females), and their exercising of their *thigmotactic* behaviour. Yes, Brian had learned a new word, thigmotactic, which simply means the seeking of body contact with others, and which, for sea lions, manifests itself in their desire to loaf around in piles – and which, for certain humans, manifests itself in a way that can easily result in their being arrested and then charged with indecent behaviour.

They were delightful – the sea lions, that is – and the pups were especially charming, albeit a little directionless as they flopped around the beach. They were all, as advertised, entirely unbothered by their new human companions, whom they must have regarded as neither a threat nor an object of interest. Brian liked to think it was more the latter. Anything that reminded humans that they were of intense interest only to themselves was a 'good thing' in his book, and this wasn't the first time he'd thought this. He'd encountered too many other animals who displayed this same indifference to the presence of *Homo sapiens*, not least a number of resting lion-lions, who all appeared to have as much interest in all those ubiquitous people as they did in the size of Uranus.

Anyway, Brian had now been distracted from his observations of the sea lions – and their insouciance – not by Darwin's current beach lecture, but by a gang of mockingbirds. They were just a few feet away, having obviously had their insatiable curiosity in all things, including Nature-seekers, overcome by their uncontainable opportunism. Yes, there was clearly something to eat or to steal or to make off with, and there was a full-scale squabble going on to decide which bird would have it – if another opportunistic mockingbird hadn't had it already. They were fascinating: a gaggle of rather scrawny-looking chancers, squawking and chattering, and seemingly achieving nothing other than the successful entertainment of a small clutch of visitors (all of whom had plainly lost the thread of their leader's dissertation). And these birds were so engrossing that this same group of truants almost failed to notice that their leader was now on the move and, with his party of better-behaved pupils, was heading to the back of the beach. It was time to go, and time to explore more of Santa Fe's gems.

There were quite a few, and they were all observed from a surprisingly short track that climbed gently upwards towards some coastal cliffs and then back down again to finish at the far end of the beach. To start with, there were more birds: big ones like smooth-billed anis (a bird introduced by Galápagos farmers in the 1960s in the mistaken belief that it would remove ticks from their cattle, and not constitute another threat to the established wildlife), and small ones like yellow warblers, Galápagos doves and Darwin's finches. Brian studied them all as best he could – other than the Darwin's finches. These, he knew, would be one or more of the fourteen species of Darwin's finches that lived on the Galápagos, just as he knew that it would take him much longer than the two weeks he was spending on this archipelago to tell one species of finch from another. There *are* physical differences between the different species – reflecting the adaption of these birds to the different environments on the different islands and that had been so critical in Darwin's understanding of natural selection – but these differences are principally in beak size and shape. Furthermore, they are so subtle that Brian would have needed a micrometer screw gauge, a protractor, a chart of beak illustrations and a dead finch in order to identify with any degree of confidence which dead finch he had in his hand. And if the finch was alive and in a bush, forget it – or wait for (the current) Darwin to tell you what it was. And generally Darwin would only know what it was because of the bird's particular location. Yes, all the species of (the other) Darwin's finches are essentially dark brown or black, and are as difficult to tell apart as most modern pop songs. Albeit they are generally more tuneful than most modern pop songs – of course…

There were lava lizards here as well (much smaller and much livelier reptiles than their iguana cousins) – and land iguanas, very similar to those seen only yesterday at Dragon Hill. They looked just as corpulent and just as unenergetic as those seen at Dragon Hill, but that didn't stop them having a significant impact on the local vegetation and, in particular, on the local variety of *opuntia*. This is otherwise known as giant prickly pear cactus, and it occurs throughout the Galápagos as six different species divided into fourteen varieties. Which doesn't sound terribly interesting until one understands that this isn't the sort of cactus that one would grow in a pot in the conservatory, but the sort that can grow up to twelve metres tall and thereby assume the appearance of a tree. Well, it seems reasonable to suspect that it developed these lofty credentials in response to a competition for light and as a protection from predators. Principally giant tortoises. However, light is abundant in Santa Fe and there are no tortoises on the island. It therefore seems likely that here there was another nibbling predator it was seeking to avoid – and that this chap must undoubtedly have been the local land iguana. Yes, this bumbling creature, all on its own, has given rise to a small 'forest' of *Opuntia echios var barringtonensis* (named in honour of the British admiral, S. Barrington, of course), a cactus that is amongst the tallest in the archipelago and that has a massive, straight trunk, which is quite capable of preventing even the most nimble of land iguanas from eating its prickly pads. And by golly, these cacti were tall – and above that massive trunk, very prickly and certainly not conducive to the building of tree houses, even by boys with prick-proof, chrome-leather gloves. Not that there were any boys here or were ever likely to be. Instead there were just middle-aged Nature-seekers who were back on the beach – and getting another briefing from Darwin…

This one concerned the importance of avoiding cross-contamination between the various Galápagos islands, a contamination that could easily occur if a band of careless visitors were to transfer soil or sand between these islands. And as they would all be unshoeing themselves in readiness for a 'wet boarding' of a panga and would thereby be equipping their feet with a cargo of beach, it was vital that this cargo was ditched before their feet were within the panga. So... Darwin explained how they would all need to waggle their feet in the water when they were sitting on the side of the panga and before they'd swung their legs aboard – and how, when they arrived back on the *Beluga*, they would then be required to rinse both their feet and their shoes in a small tank of water that had been prepared for this purpose. Fortunately, they were not required to disrobe completely, shake out their underwear and then undergo any sort of intimate screening. Which was not just very welcome news for Brian but also a reflection of his unreasonable impatience with what were no more than entirely sensible and completely reasonable measures to protect a unique and precious environment.

In fact, as soon as he was back on board, he became aware of his unreasonable impatience – and of the imminence of yet another Darwin briefing!

This one proved to be a brief briefing and a useful briefing – in that it concerned the choice, adjustment, preparation, use and care of a snorkel. So, the seven Nature-seekers (including Brian) who had opted for some snorkelling recreation before lunch, listened intently – and then went off to the front of the boat, where the snorkelling gear was kept, and readied themselves as advised.

And then... well, wow! Because, within minutes, the snorkelling seven – with Darwin in attendance – had been taken in one of the pangas to the rocky wall of the bay, and there they had entered the water. Had they all been wearing socks, there would now have been fourteen of these floating away in the current, because without a doubt they would all have been blown off – at speed. It was simply magical: crystal-clear water, full of all sorts of colourful fish, the odd ray, a few white-tipped reef sharks and even a couple of juvenile sea lions – and a complete sense of wonder. The sea lions, in particular, were captivating; clumsy on land, but here, in the water, supple, streamlined, sinuous and sublime – and friendly. (Yes, it wasn't until much later that Brian discovered that whilst it would be unusual to have an unfortunate encounter with a shark hereabouts, sea lion bulls can be quite aggressive and they have been known to inflict serious injuries on careless swimmers, although Brian suspected that they probably regretted it after the event and resolved never to do it again unless it was to somebody who really deserved it – like, for example, that local guy who'd condoned the killing of sharks.)

But back to that magical experience. Because it was genuinely magical and it was made even more magical towards its end when the Nature-seekers were joined by two enormous green sea turtles, which underwater were as unconcerned with the Nature-seekers as those sea lions had been on the beach. All this, thought Brian, as he dragged himself back into the panga, would be a hard act to follow. But, as he would discover, it would be followed – by a whole series of magic acts, some of which would be even more thrilling…

That, however, was for later. Right now, there was a boat to catch – before it set off for their next destination – and a daunting luncheon to eat, a meal that Brian would soon realise was in competition with the on-board evening meal to win the 'main meal of the day' award. It would prove to be a close-run race.

Anyway, that next destination was South Plaza, a tiny island off the east coast of Santa Cruz (and therefore almost directly north of Santa Fe), which is paired with an equally small island, cunningly named North Plaza. Both these islands are uplifted slabs of sea floor rather than volcanic remains, and they are separated by a channel that is less than one kilometre wide. When the *Beluga* arrived in this channel, Brian was struck not so much by the islands' beauty as by their bareness. To him, they still looked like uplifted slabs of sea floor – which somebody had tried to embellish with the minimum of vegetation. When he then got *onto* South Plaza, he didn't really change this first impression.

It was a dry landing – onto a small man-made quay. So no problems there. And, here, what presented itself to the Nature-seekers was a very flat island, no more than a kilometre long, and tilting up gently over a distance of just one hundred metres until it ended at what were apparently vertiginous cliffs. Oh, and its surface was studded with what Brian had taken to be patches of dying moss but which were, in fact, mats of something called sea purslane, interspersed, here and there, with more of those *opuntia* cacti seen back on Santa Fe – only not quite as tall. And that was it. Whatever managed to live on this giant paving slab in the Pacific Ocean had either a very small and very unadventurous appetite or a very empty belly. Or, for just a few, as Brian and his companions were about to find out, a very innovative way of overcoming the poorest of poor *tables d'hôte*.

Yes, it appears that back in 1997, high water temperatures caused by El Niño wreaked havoc on the seaweed beds around the Galápagos, and about half of all the archipelago's marine iguanas starved to death. However, amongst the survivors were a number who either sought food on land or, better still, came to an arrangement with a few land iguanas who themselves had very little to eat – like those living on that virtually empty plate known as South Plaza. And the nature of this arrangement was the insemination by a number of male marine iguanas of a number of (much larger) female land iguanas to produce a small population of marine/land iguana hybrids!

Marine iguanas have sharp claws with which they can grip rocks underwater and so eat the seaweed. Land iguanas do not. This prevents them climbing those tall cacti to feed on their flesh, and instead they have to wait for food to drop to the ground. However… the hybrids have the claws and are therefore able to exploit the cacti much more easily *and* still eat seaweed underwater. Essentially they can survive in both a sea and a land environment, or, put another way, they can supplement the paltry food supply on South Plaza by feeding on stuff that grows all around it. Not exactly a full à *la carte* solution, but it must be a darn sight better than just that crap *table d'hôte*.

Darwin, in his first lecture on South Plaza, had explained this fascinating phenomenon, and had gone on to point out that the marine/land hybrids were viable but that they were sterile, and consequently extremely rare. There are probably no more than a handful of them (none of which were seen). However, what he did not touch on was how a normally diffident and unassertive male marine iguana would have plucked up the courage to date a much bigger female land iguana – and what he would have chosen for his chat-up line. Brian couldn't imagine. And then he had it – of course. It would be: 'What's a nice girl like you doing in a Plaza like this?' Or, there again, maybe iguanas aren't into chat-up lines at all, or if they are, they'd probably do a lot better than that. Even with a mouthful of seaweed.

Well, having digested this remarkable revelation of cross-species behaviour, Brian then had to swallow another, this one concerning the habits of a… swallow-tailed gull. There was one sitting on a nearby cactus, a rather handsome creature rendered in black and white, with a scarlet ring around its eye – and with an amazing lifestyle, in that it is the only nocturnal gull in the world! Yes, quite incredibly, this chap on the cactus would be off at dusk to fish fifteen to thirty kilometres from land – in the dark. And whilst it is known that it is quite partial to small fish and squid, it's not really clear how it manages this night-time feat. It may be through exploiting the bioluminescence of its prey or it may have special visual and sonar facilities – and in this context that red ring around its eye might help. But even so… who the hell would choose to spend its nights in the middle of an ocean, hovering around and having to find a meal in the gloom? Brian certainly wouldn't. No more than he'd have chosen to live on South Plaza.

It really was pretty threadbare in terms of vegetation. It did, however, close up, have a certain stark beauty, albeit, thought Brian, stark beauty probably very soon loses its appeal, particularly if one is starving. Yes, despite those noble and novel efforts of the local iguanas, this really was a place for just seabirds and sea lions. And when Darwin's party had walked those one hundred metres from where they'd landed up to those hidden seacliffs, that's just what they found. For here, flying around were various boobies (no sniggering, please), some red-billed tropicbirds and a couple of brown pelicans. Oh, and on the edge of the cliffs were old, spent bulls who, just like most of the Nature-seeker husbands, were living out their days free from the stress of competitive mating and everything that that sort of stuff entailed. Instead they could just lounge around, even if they had to climb up some ruddy great cliffs to do this – which Brian thought beggared belief but, according to Darwin, was exactly what they did. Such are the unfathomables of the natural world.

Well, a little less unfathomable was the path which, in a loop, took the Nature-seekers back down the slope of the South Plaza slab and to that man-made quay where they'd first disembarked. Here they were collected by the pangas and returned to the *Beluga*, there to be served with more food for their evening meal than has been seen on *Plaza Sur* for the last ten years. And then, after what had proved to be a wildlife-packed day for them all,

Brian took Sandra back to their cabin to provide his wife with what he hoped would be the perfect full stop to this pretty-well perfect day. Yes, he thought it was about time to lift her eyes from the circumscribed horizons of places such as Santa Fe and South Plaza and invite her to scan the more expansive horizons of the whole of South America – by his imparting some more 'interesting facts' about another of its component countries. And the country he had chosen for tonight was Suriname.

Now, he was pretty sure that she knew where Suriname was – at the top right-hand corner of South America, sandwiched between Guyana and French Guiana – but he doubted that she knew too much about its incumbent president, a gentleman (in the loosest possible terms) by the name of Dési Bouterse. So he would now 'fill in that gap'.

'Sandra,' he started, as soon as she'd got into bed, 'shall I tell you about the guy who runs Suriname?'

Sandra looked across at her husband who was in his own bed, and she was clearly about to say 'no'. But she just wasn't quick enough and Brian carried on.

'You see, Suriname, as well as being the smallest country in South America, is also the only one to have as a leader a guy for whom Europol has issued an arrest warrant...'

'What!'

'Yes, this guy... errh, Dési Bouterse, is not what you'd call whiter than white. Back in the 1980s he was the sort of *de facto* leader of Suriname when the country was run by the military, and in 2010 he became its elected president. But the point is that back in the eighties, he was a pretty naughty boy and was very probably responsible for any number of his fellow Surinamese not making it to old age. And then he got involved in drug trafficking. In fact, in 1999, he was convicted *in absentia* in the Netherlands – which, of course, used to own Suriname – and sentenced to eleven years in prison. Hence that Europol arrest warrant…'

'Not an ideal CV for a president,' observed a now mildly engaged Sandra.

'No. But it clearly impressed his son, who ended up being sentenced to eight years for international drugs and arms trafficking – and furthermore, it's maybe not the worst CV you could have if you're called upon to run what is modern-day Suriname…'

'Meaning?' enquired Sandra.

'Meaning that Suriname is now an established and growing transhipment point for South American drugs destined for Europe, and it's also renowned for its degeneration into corruption ever since it got its independence from Holland back in 1975.'

'Ah…'

'Yes, ah. In fact, Suriname is an ideal candidate for recolonisation…'

'Oh God.'

'No, it is. I mean, loads of the locals cleared off to Holland because it became so bad after independence, and it's still in a complete bugger's muddle – and a bloody menace to the rest of the world. You know, through its drug trading stuff. Whereas next door, in French Guiana – which is officially still part of France – the locals enjoy the highest GDP per capita in the whole of South America. And I'm sure the downtrodden plebs of Suriname are quite well aware of that…'

'Yes, Brian, but we've had all this out before. You cannot go round proposing recolonisations. You'll get into all sorts of trouble.'

'Yeah,' conceded Brian. 'But not because my new "altruistic colonisation" idea wouldn't work, but just because it's not PC – even when you've got a clear-cut case like Suriname, where everybody would probably welcome it with open arms. Other, of course, than the guys at the top, the same guys who are exploiting its dysfunctional independence for their own personal and selfish ends…'

'Well, I hope you got a sympathetic response from Ban Ki-moon. I mean, I am assuming you've brought this wonderful idea to his attention…'

Brian looked at his wife and grunted. He'd just received the final full stop to his perfect full stop to the day, and he knew it. He would now leave Sandra to go to sleep and turn his mind to other things before he did the same, things like that remarkable cross-species arrangement between marine and land iguanas. It was just so remarkable – and so disconcerting. Hell, he thought, what would happen if any of those nocturnal swallow-tailed gulls ever got it together with our own opportunistic herring gulls? Blimey, you wouldn't be safe eating your Mr Whippy even after dark…

*O*vernight, the captain took the *Beluga* due east. He was heading for San Cristóbal, the most easterly of the Galápagos islands. It was a journey that started out with the normal pronounced rolling and the normal intrusive engine noise, and it probably continued with these unavoidable accompaniments until it ended. But Brian would not have known this – because he slept like a log. Yes, it seemed he was taking no time at all to acclimatise to the inescapable features of the *Beluga*'s ocean locomotion, and Sandra, he would discover, was having similar success. She was not, however, having such a dream-filled night – and, unlike her husband, she certainly wasn't dreaming about bioluminescent ice cream…

It was those thoughts in Brian's head before he'd dropped off. They'd continued into his unconsciousness and had manifested themselves as a vivid image of a gloomy Skegness beach, on which Charles Darwin was studying a luminescent 99 ice cream, while all around him were silent hovering herring gulls, all of them wearing elaborate, Elton-John-type, red-coloured specs. But then it got worse. Because both Mr Darwin and the beach disappeared, and in their place was a newscaster on a TV channel called 'Cross-species News', announcing with glee that Frankie Boyle had inseminated an amoeba, apparently with the intention of producing an offspring that as well as thinking it was funny would also think it could think, neither of which it would ever be able to do – obviously. So just as well then that it would be so sterile that it was an absolute certainty that the F. Boyle bloodline would be permanently snuffed out.

It must have been a residue of this dream-state thought that caused Brian to be in such a good mood when he woke, a mood that was in no way dented either by the appearance of a not quite perfectly blue sky or by the promise of horseflies…

It was true. Darwin, the previous evening, had imparted the not very welcome news that the site of their first expedition on San Cristóbal was a hotspot for horseflies. This was a sheltered beach beneath an old volcanic cone called Cerro Brujo, and whilst it apparently had a huge expanse of fine white sand that was reminiscent of powdered sugar, it also had a complement of large biting insects that was reminiscent of the contents of Brian's worst nightmares (Frankie Boyle excepted).

Nevertheless, Darwin assured his flock that the horseflies were worth it. And so were the sandflies! And this was because at the back of the beach was a lagoon that was home to both great egrets and great blue herons, and off the beach was some easy but worthwhile snorkelling. And anyway, in 1835, while Captain Fitzroy was climbing that Cerro Brujo cone, one of his muckers, a guy who went on to appear in a Brian dream about see-in-the-dark ice creams, took his first walk here. Yes, this was where Charles Darwin had made his inaugural venture into the Galápagos ecology. So how could Brian and his friends not follow in his footsteps, even if it might mean the odd bite for all concerned? And even if it might mean a slightly more challenging wet landing?

Yes, there was quite a swell near the beach, and disembarking from a panga was more a test than it had been at Santa Fe. Particularly as there was an audience, and this audience was not made up of a Galápagos hawk and a gang of Galápagos sea lions but of a clutch of Galápagos visitors, a score or more of swimsuited tourists who, like the Nature-seekers, were risking insect bites – and not really adding to the peace and the serenity of this beautiful spot. In fact, this place, in Brian's mind, was far too popular to be anything but an also-ran in the highlights of his Galápagos adventure. There were four boats anchored off the beach, and all of them had brought to this 'remote spot' more than enough people to make it feel anything but remote.

Oh dear. People were having the effrontery to spoil Brian's experience of the Galápagos archipelago – by sharing it with him. This would not do. Didn't they know he was very sensitive to crowds – or to more than a handful of people, come to that? Especially if those people were being so inconsiderate as to be sitting on a supposedly pristine beach on an otherwise isolated stretch of a Galápagos island.

Well, he got over it – sort of. But he quickly decided – and agreed with Sandra – that a walk along the beach and a look at the lagoon might be abandoned in favour of an early return to the water. Not above it in a panga, but below it with a snorkel. This would have the advantage of avoiding all those beach-type perils, including sand in any available interstice or orifice, sunburn, stubbed toes – and, of course, the mouthparts of all those unthoughtful biting insects (to say nothing of the company of all those inconsiderate strangers).

It was done. Directly after their witnessing a forty-something Darwin doing a standing backflip on the beach (!), Brian and Sandra were afloat in the shallows of the Pacific Ocean, and within a very short time they had been joined by the majority of the other Nature-seekers. It seemed that they too had been overcome by a distaste for the company of either unknown humans or unseen biting insects, and, like Brian and Sandra, were eager to see what the sea had in store.

Well, a short summary of what it had in store might be 'not much'. There were some fish around – particularly where one was required to risk a calf or an elbow coming into contact with undersea rocks – but there weren't many fish. Furthermore, the sea was very murky, and this murkiness was not helped by the continued arrival of other inflatables containing more of those people to whom Brian would never be introduced. Even, he thought, if their inflatable ran him down, a possibility that eventually graduated to a probability – if only in Brian's mind – as ever more vessels appeared carrying clients from what must have now been an armada of boats off the coast.

It was quite strange really. Brian had never studied hyperbole – because he'd never had to. It just came to him naturally. So, even though there was only a trickle of people being ferried to the beach, he could make it sound as though it was a rerun of D-Day, in exactly the same way that he could paint a picture of a veritable cloud of horseflies when he had seen only one – and not one of the Nature-seekers had been bitten. But perception *and* perspective were everything. And from his perspective he could perceive only a disappointing visit – to this stunning white beach – and he was very pleased to find himself back on the *Beluga* and on his way to its next destination. This was the one and only town on San Cristóbal – and the capital of the whole Galápagos province, a place burdened with the somewhat challenging name of Puerto Baquerizo Moreno.

Had the Ecuadorian president, Alfredo Baquerizo Moreno (1859-1951) been called instead Alfredo Fuerto, this settlement of 7,000 would have found itself not with a tongue-twister (that encourages even the locals to refer to it as simply 'Cristóbal') but instead with a name that just rolls off the tongue. But there you go. You can't rewrite history, just as you can't stop the *Beluga* rolling when it's underway and you're trying to eat lunch. You can, however, leave the lunch table quite promptly and join a quartet of other Nature-seekers on the flying bridge, there to take in the coast of San Cristóbal as it passed by on the left – and to look out for the appearance of Puerto etc.

This quartet was made up of the two married couples: Josh and Madeline, and Horace and Sally. They were all of a similar age (about ten years younger than Brian and Sandra) and they were all eminently 'civilised'. That is to say, they were all the sort of people with whom, on a small boat, one would willingly spend two weeks of one's life, and they were already proving themselves to be stimulating companions.

Josh was a retired businessman – and a little enigmatic. So Brian never discovered what his business had been, and was left to try to imagine what it could possibly have involved. He eventually concluded that it was nothing 'normal' – like dealing in clothes or the manufacture of car parts – but something intensely arcane and desperately dull, like the procurement of flanges and gaskets for commercial hydraulic compressors, or something not in the least bit arcane and dull, like the fitting-out of strip joints. Anyway, he was a really pleasant guy who had a tendency to talk in short, considered 'spurts' and a tendency to be able to spot and identify even the littlest of little brown jobs. He also had a lovely wife: Madeline.

Madeline was the antithesis of a loud and opinionated woman – and of an obese woman. She was quiet, thoughtful, attentive, very kind – and quite slim. In fact, if the world was full of Madelines, we would need only half the food we grow, half the land we use – for everything – and, more importantly, it would be a far better place. There certainly wouldn't be any conflict and there wouldn't be much noise. Brian thought Josh was a very lucky person – or at least very good at choosing a partner.

Horace was fortunate as well. For not only did he have a temperate nature, a sharp mind and a good sense of humour, but he also had an extremely pretty wife: Sally. She, apparently, had helped him in his self-made business, an enterprise that provided commercial lighting anywhere around the world – and the sort of stimulation that made Horace appear younger than he was. He would prove to be an ideal companion on this trip – and a dab hand at underwater photography. Not the David Attenborough took-six-months-to-film-it type, but the bloody-good-for-a-hand-held-camera-whilst-snorkelling variety. And he could often even remember what he'd 'snapped'.

Anyway, as well as helping her husband with his business, Sally had also been a nurse, and this showed in her nature. She was another Madeline – albeit shorter and... well, just slightly more 'pleasingly shapely'. However, unlike Madeline, she was sometimes (justifiably) forthright and she rivalled her husband in the sense-of-humour stakes.

So, all in all, not a bad set of chaps with whom to be sharing a flying bridge – and, of course, the anticipation of arriving in Puerto Baquerizo Moreno, an anticipation, it might be said, that rose to a climax when PBM appeared in the distance – and only shrivelled entirely when they'd seen it close-to.

Initially, as the *Beluga* turned towards the town to find a mooring within a whole flotilla of boats, Puerto Baquerizo Moreno didn't look at all bad. It looked like a somewhat laid-back fishing port (which it was) nestling rather comfortably at the back of a turquoise-blue bay and set against the greenery of the island beyond it. Its status as a capital and as an administrative centre was very well hidden (as was the nearby San Cristóbal Airport that links it to mainland Ecuador). In fact, even when the Nature-seekers were within just yards of it, it looked just as it should. There were some well-used piers and some obvious evidence of fishing – but there were also a refreshing number of sea lions around. Brian had been told about these creatures and how the locals have even provided them with a small beach in the town for their preferential use. But he had not expected to see them in such close proximity to the 'business part' of town, or draped about in such numbers. They were on the back of boats in the bay, on buoys in the bay and on the steps of the pier where the Nature-seekers eventually disembarked (by using an alternative ramp).

Anyway, here on the town's 'esplanade' it was still all OK, even if some of the shops and 'cafés' beyond the piers didn't look exactly chic. But then the Nature-seekers were loaded onto a bus, and the bus set off – to take them to the object of their excursion: a lake – and the real nature of Puerto Baquerizo Moreno was revealed.

It wasn't pretty. Indeed, it was a bloody mess. Here, thought Brian, the thesaurus entry for 'scruffy' could enjoy an extended workout, and the workout would have to include 'tacky', 'unkempt', 'shabby' and 'run-down'. It might even have to extend its session by borrowing some other descriptions, descriptions such as 'unfinished' (as in 'never-to-be-finished'), 'derelict', '(possibly) abandoned', 'shambolic' and 'litter-strewn'. It was as though the 7,000 people who had made this town their home had no sense of aesthetics and certainly no sense of pride. And if that sounded like a deeply unjustified, middle-class assessment of the inevitable results of poverty, then so be it. Because, in the first place it was true, and in the second place poverty and a disregard for one's environment are not joined at the hip. Brian had previously seen really poor people living on the banks of the Brahmaputra, whose humble villages were both spotless and neat. He'd seen others who were equally impoverished, carving out a living in the depths of Papua New Guinea, whose own villages were not only clean and tidy but were also filled with vernacular works of art in the form of their wonderful houses. But this place... well, what were they up to?

This is a town on an island in the world-famous Galápagos archipelago. It is occupied by people who, through their fishing activities and latterly their involvement in the tourist trade, are not desperately poor. So why do they need to make such a blot on the unique landscape and why do they feel they need to live in what looked to Brian like the meanest of urban squalor?

Now, it has to be said that Brian did have a bit of a thing about the way so many people in this world, through their activities or through their disdain for their immediate environment, seemed intent on promoting ugliness in all its forms. It was as though they wanted to make this the indelible mark of mankind: a level of despoilment and degradation visited on their own little patch that no other living animal could even contemplate let alone achieve. But to pursue this disgusting practice in somewhere as precious as the Galápagos seemed not just malicious but also highly immoral. And it didn't stop on the outskirts of town either. For here, along the road into the interior, was more scruffiness, more despoilment – and more litter by the minute – as demonstrated by the pillion passenger on a moped who clearly thought that the roadside ditch was a suitable receptacle for her now-empty pop bottle. As she cast it into the ditch in full sight of the busload of Nature-seekers, Brian felt really despondent and not very proud to be human.

Jesus! This lake thing had better be good, or he might go into a terminal decline.

Well, he would soon find out, because the bus was now in the process of being parked, and within minutes the Nature-seekers would be… climbing a sodding great flight of steps!

Oh dear. Brian hadn't been paying enough attention during that briefing back on the boat. Because only now did he remember that Darwin was bringing them to this lake, not because it was a regular lake, but because it was a lake in an old caldera. And, of course, as old calderas tend to be 'up' somewhere, they often entail a climb. And in this case, not just a 'short boardwalk' (as maliciously described in a guidebook aboard the *Beluga*), but a set of wooden steps rising quite steeply into the distance and no doubt stopping somewhere near the bottom tier of heaven. And if not at the bottom tier of heaven then at the lip of the caldera that held *Laguna El Junco,* the fabled body of water that once held out the promise of lifting Brian's mood.

Well, for now he'd just settle on something that could lift his frame up that stairway to heaven, and he wouldn't mind if the rain held off as well. Yes, it was now not just a little cloudy but a lot cloudy and those clouds looked as though they meant business. Nevertheless, the ascent was commenced – by Darwin and by all his willing and not so willing disciples, and Brian's reservations were soon confirmed. This stairway had far too many rises in it and it also had the nature of an escalator – going down – in that the top of the stairway appeared to be getting further away. Indeed, Brian found he had to stop on a number of occasions on the way up (and so did his wife). And all this did was give him a view of the surrounding *farmed* countryside (complete with cows and wind turbines) and a confirmation, as if he needed it, that San Cristóbal was pretty well screwed up and had as much in common with a pristine environment as did downtown New York. So… that terminal decline might still be achieved.

However, finally he was at the rim of the caldera, and there was the lake. And thirty seconds later, just as Darwin was explaining that what was left of the natural vegetation here was under threat from introduced blackberry, common guava and other invasive species, there was not the lake. Because a curtain of mist had now joined the Nature-seekers on their elevated observation point and the lake had become completely obscured – never to make an appearance again.

Darwin did suggest a (quite long) walk around the lake, but let slip that the path they would need to take was a little dodgy in stretches – especially in the mist and more especially when it rained. So that offer was enthusiastically eschewed and the Nature-seekers embarked on a further engagement with that long stairway, this time in a downwards direction (obviously) and whilst being rained on (obviously). It would now take only a lightning bolt to hit Brian, and he would have had the most perfect expedition imaginable – not.

Ah well, you can't win 'em all – was the nature of Sandra's consoling words. And at least Brian hadn't been bitten by anything, and the bus, even though driven at a reckless speed, managed to return him and his fellow travellers to Puerto Eyesora without any loss of life. So, it really could have been worse. Although not by very much...

Needless to say, both Brian and Sandra were pretty relieved to be back on the *Beluga* and with the prospect of no more steps to deal with but just the demands of an oversized meal – and that would be a doddle. In fact, Brian might even have an opportunity to work on his and Sandra's designation on this trip, and maybe push for that 'cool but not that cool' appellation. Although, there again, given their dismal showing on the ascent of those steps, maybe they'd already defaulted to just 'willing but wimpish'. Or, with Brian's (over)reaction to the squalor of Puerto Baquerizo etc, maybe even to 'the miserable misanthropes'. Never mind. There was still a chance to work at it over dinner. Or there would have been if the table had not included two new guests.

There were eight people at the table in all, including Brian and Sandra and the increasingly subdued Bill and Andrea. Then there were Evan and Mandy. These Nature-seekers were another middle-aged couple from the south of England who had already proved themselves to be both jolly and bright. Evan had spent his life in IT, and was now spending as much time as he could taking photos. Mandy, his appreciably smaller and more attractive wife, was spending her time being both congenial and considerate. In fact, she had already been very kind and very responsive to Sandra. And then, making up the final pair at the dinner table, were Shane and Shelly...

Earlier in the day, this pair had landed at San Cristóbal Airport, having travelled from their home in San Francisco. From there they had been ferried to the *Beluga* and had installed themselves in its one remaining unused cabin (there were eight cabins and only fourteen Nature-seekers). And they would now be accompanying their British shipmates for the remainder of the Galápagos trip. This late insertion into an 'established' group of foreigners must have been a little daunting for them, and probably almost as daunting as it was for their new table companions as the table talk advanced. And that is 'advance' in the sense of Bill and Andrea and Evan and Mandy becoming mere observers as Brian found himself 'chairing' a presentation by Shane, a presentation that was principally about Shane and one that removed any possibility that Brian could work on his preferred designation. In fact, it was during this meal that he decided to abandon this futile pursuit completely and just let the ship's passengers decide for themselves. Even though they'd all have their work cut out in evaluating the Shane and Shelly Act, and especially Shane.

He was not unpleasant – at all – but he did appear to be keen to mark out his 'intellectual and identity' territory as quickly and as forcefully as he could. The intellectual elements of the territory were reinforced by his discussing his business, which had, until recently, been the changing of people's lives with the aid of a three-day course – and... well, with some sort of 'new way of thinking'. (This proved rather hard work for him, in that he had overlooked the fact that he was addressing a tableful of Brits, and none of them had left their innate scepticism, cynicism – and their suspicion of life-changing techniques – back in their cabin.) The identity bit didn't go too smoothly either, especially when Shane made the observation that all new initiatives in the world now originated in California – with a straight face and in all seriousness. It was probably at that point that Brian began to suspect that Shane's and Shelly's joining of the *Beluga* would probably be like two new choristers joining an existing choir, and it soon becoming apparent that whilst they did not sing out of key, they would always insist on singing in a different key to that chosen by the rest of the choir.

They certainly didn't seem to be in tune when the dinner finished and the Nature-seekers were assembled in the bar, in order to inaugurate the time-honoured custom of 'listing'. This cherished practice had been somewhat delayed, in that it should really have kicked off on their first evening aboard. But that was now about to be put to rights – by a three-day catch-up listing. And what this would entail would be Darwin laboriously going through a preprinted list of Galápagos birds and animals, agreeing with the assembled naturalists what birds and animals had been seen – so they could then tick them off on their own copy of the list. This was common Nature-seeker practice – and just a little bit nerdy. Furthermore, because this was the Galápagos and there were only a limited number of birds and animals, it was nerdier than ever – because the list went on beyond birds and animals to include insects, shrubs, flowers – and fish!

This extension of the list to include what had been seen underwater by the snorkelers – in this case, over the preceding two days – turned a laborious exercise into a ludicrous exercise. Because Darwin was obliged to use his computer to project onto a screen endless pictures of colourful fish in a rather tiresome attempt to establish which of these fish might have been clocked by his team. No wonder that the two Americans would continue to insist on singing in a different key – and, in due course, absent themselves from these peculiar post-dinner listing sessions entirely. No wonder too that, at the end of this particular three-day, drawn-out session, Brian was more than happy to be back in his cabin – and preparing to deliver his next interesting address on a South American nation. And having, the previous evening, dealt with the continent's smallest and possibly naughtiest nation, tonight it would be the turn of its most dysfunctional nation: Venezuela.

Brian and Sandra had both been there – when it had yet to descend that socialist slope into the mire of complete hopelessness and dislocation. But that wasn't about to stop Brian lecturing his wife on 'a few interesting facts' concerning this moribund nation. And, as would become his standard practice, he started as soon as they were both tucked up in bed.

'Well,' he began, 'tonight I thought I'd enlighten you on Venezuela – and on the whole country, not just its president.'

'Whoopee!' rejoined a resigned but stalwart Sandra. 'I can hardly wait.'

Brian ignored the tenor of this response and launched into his address.

'Right. Well, as you know, Venezuela is in the shit – big time. In 2015 it succeeded in achieving the world's highest inflation rate – at over 100%. And it now suffers from really acute shortages of milk, coffee, rice, oil, butter, all sorts of medicines, toilet paper, breast implants – apparently – and probably even white truffles and beluga (no relation) caviar. On top of this it has become one of the most corrupt countries on the planet and it has really excelled itself by coming ninety-ninth out of ninety-nine in the world's "Rule of Law Index". In fact, it is now one of the most dangerous places on Earth, with a murder rate that has led to a body count over the past decade that mimics that in the Iraq War – even though it is nominally at peace. Then there's its significant involvement in the drugs trade, its operation of one of the most violent prison systems imaginable – with hundreds of prisoners killed and maimed each year – and its removal of *The Simpsons* from children's TV channels as being 'entirely inappropriate for children'.

'What!'

'I just wanted to check that you were still paying attention.'

Sandra harrumphed and Brian carried on.

'OK. But why, may one ask, has this country arrived at such a sorry situation, particularly when it is known that it has the largest oil reserves in the Western hemisphere and the eighth largest natural gas reserves in the world…?'

'I have a horrible feeling you're going to tell me,' interjected Sandra.

'I am,' responded her husband. 'And it's all very simple. Because back in 1988, a certain former career officer by the name of Hugo Chavez launched a revolution and introduced a new constitution, the aim of which was to "boost the economy with increased spending, reduce economic inequality and poverty, ensure an equitable distribution of wealth, and generally engineer a heaven on Earth…"'

'You mean like Mr Corbyn wants to do?'

'Yes. But in the case of Mr Chavez, he was able to do it – with all those oil revenues he had – right up until he'd squandered so much money on social engineering – and corruption – but had failed to spend anything like the amount that was required to maintain oil production, that it all started to go wrong. And that was even before the oil prices had fallen off a cliff and before the charismatic Chavez had been succeeded by the current lummox, the all too hopeless I-have-no-idea-what-I'm-doing-but-I'm-not-going-any-time-soon Mr Madura, a gentleman who, all on his own, has redefined what it really means to bring a nation to its knees.'

'Well, that was all very interesting, Brian. And apart from anything else, I did need cheering up. I mean, Brian, first that mope about the state of Puerto whatever it's called, and now this dissertation on the wretchedness of Venezuela. Crikey, haven't you got anything encouraging to say? Haven't you found anything about Venezuela that is in any way positive?'

Brian hesitated, and then he responded.

'Well, now you mention it, Venezuela has amassed more Miss Universes and more Miss Worlds than any other country...'

At which point, Sandra appeared to subside into a weary despair and Brian concluded that his wife had probably had more than enough of Venezuela for today – in just the same way that all sane Venezuelans must have had more than enough of deluded socialist idiots for the whole of their lifetime. Unless maybe they can cross one of these idiots with an irreproachable, intelligent paragon of virtue who has a distaste for populist fantasies and a grasp of basic economics. Or better still, forget the cross-breeding, just junk the current idiot, and bring in the paragon. Or so Brian thought...

5.

Ron looked down and surveyed the scene. To his right was the 'big island', and to his left, almost directly beneath him, was the much smaller 'small island'. And between these two islands were three of those moving things, those things he often took a ride on, either when he was pooped or when he wanted to get somewhere else but just couldn't be arsed to get there under his own steam. Only these particular things weren't moving at the moment. All three of them were completely stationary – and therefore any one of them would serve very well as an early-morning perch. In fact, that one there would, that small one he recognised as one he'd used before – and that had all those sticky-out bits at the top. Yes, that one would be ideal. So, having made his choice, he put his flight mode into 'swoop' and within seconds he was approaching his chosen sticky-out bit, one of those right at the top of the 'thing' and with splashes of poop on it. That told him that it had been used before and that it would have no trouble whatsoever in supporting his weight. And he was right. As his feet made contact and he folded his wings, his perch felt secure and he knew he'd made a good choice. Then, as if to confirm this, out of the blue arrived Ken, who immediately plopped himself onto another of those same sticky-out things just feet from his own – and nodded in his direction. Great! A super, safe spot for a bit of a rest and now with some company as well. Heck, what could possibly be better – and what more could he want?

Well, strangely enough, these final two thoughts were exactly Brian's thoughts at that very same time. He had woken after another night on the move – which he had slept through – to discover that the captain had brought them to another slice of heaven. Outside the back window of his cabin he could see the tip of a headland and out of the side window, a rather low-profile 'islet', and both headland and islet were framed by the statutory turquoise-blue sea, with a… sky-blue sky above. Oh, and then, as if to make this further corner of heaven just that little bit more heavenish, swooping down from the sky was one of those magnificent frigatebirds (as opposed to one of those *great* frigatebirds) and then, almost immediately, another. They must, thought Brian, have chosen the *Beluga* as a morning roost. Just as they'd chosen it on a couple of occasions over the last three days to use as a taxi. And good for them. He'd have done just the same himself – had he been born into this world as a magnificent frigatebird, an idea which had more than a passing appeal for Brian, as he knew he was never likely to be described as even marginally magnificent in his present nondescript form.

Anyway, he was delighted to be where he was – which was in a boat moored off a place called Gardner Bay. And it was called Gardner Bay because that flatish islet just a few hundred metres away was called Gardner Island, and he couldn't believe that this was just a coincidence. However, to have any sort of bay, one, of course, needs a preferably reasonably sized island of which the bay is a part, and that island, in this case, was Española. This is the most southerly of the Galápagos islands, and lying, as it does, to the south of San Cristóbal, it is also one of the most easterly in the archipelago and therefore one of its oldest. In fact, it is thought to be an uplifted submarine lava flow, with its surface tilting from high vertical cliffs on its southern coastline to its (close-by) low and sheltered north coast, where there is a fine, two-kilometre-long sandy beach. Indeed, so fine, that it had attracted two further boats this morning. But at least they were small boats and their presence didn't even make a dent in Brian's paradisical assessment of the *Beluga*'s current situation. No more than the assembled company at the breakfast table could put much of a dent into yet another pile of food...

It was all Pedro's work, the diminutive chef who was either paid by the weight of food he served or who thought that the Nature-seekers were all intolerably thin. That said, the food wasn't just generous in its quantity but also commendable in its quality – as well as being so varied that even breakfasts were entirely unpredictable. They might all include toast and cereals and coffee and tea, but it was anybody's guess as to what the fruit juice would be made of – or whether Pedro would serve up fried eggs, pancakes with honey, scrambled eggs, something meaty like sausages and bacon – or a bewildering combination of all these offerings – with some cold cuts thrown in as well. And he produced these mountainous breakfasts and the Andes-sized main meals of the day in the tiniest galley imaginable, a diminutive cupboard of a room that boasted hardly any flat surfaces at all. Where the hell he prepared and then served all this food was even more of a mystery than how he cooked it. And it wasn't just for the Nature-seekers but also for the *Beluga*'s crew. Quite clearly, as Darwin had observed when he'd introduced the crew on their first day aboard, Pedro was the most important crew member of all – and nobody, including the rest of the crew, could possibly have disagreed.

There were five other crew members, and of these, it was a guy called Abel who had most dealings with the *Beluga*'s guests. He was a young chap and he was the boat's steward, which meant that he looked after the cabins (and had a whole repertoire of decorative folded-towel designs) and he transported the vast quantities of food from the galley to the tables. He was the only member of the crew who spoke any noticeable amount of English. José didn't – but he didn't really need to. Because José was the captain and, as already indicated, he did most of his work at night when everybody else was asleep or trying to sleep, and he presumably then slept during the day in his miniscule cabin. Roberto, the engineer, was similarly invisible for most of the time, and Brian could only think that he was continuously busy, oiling and greasing whatever it was that needed to be continuously oiled and greased. Or maybe he was seasick all the time. Gilbert and Jonathon weren't, because these two sailors were the guys who as well as keeping the boat looking shipshape – as opposed to boatshape, which it managed all on its own – ferried the Nature-seekers from boat to shore and back again in the *Beluga*'s two pangas. They were both quite beefy and had obviously been on a Pedro-fed diet for quite some time, albeit not long enough to have become panga-threateningly obese.

Brian was musing on obesity as he rose from the table. It really had been another large – and irresistible – spread. But then he mused on something else, just as Darwin was embarking on another briefing, this one concerning the danger that lurked on that nearby fine sandy beach. And this was the danger posed by a large, not to say enormous, centipede. Specifically, it was the Galápagos centipede, *Scolopendra galapagensis,* which can grow up to thirty centimetres long and which comes equipped with an impressive pair of fangs with which it poisons its prey. It apparently makes a terrible pet and it can't even be housetrained.

Anyway, the subject of Brian's latest musing was not this animal *per se* but where it lived – on that long sandy beach. Because, what he'd thought was that it was now about time that he and Sandra became a little non-conformist in their behaviour. And the form that this non-conformity would take would be their staying on board the *Beluga* while all their companions were ferried to Española to take a walk along the beach. Not exactly the sort of non-conformist conduct that would get one burnt at the stake, but merely the sort that recognised that the *Beluga* was parked in an extraordinarily nice spot – with views of both the beach and Gardner Island – and that the idea of taking in these views from the comfort of the *Beluga* was highly attractive. On this already hot morning, it was certainly more attractive than the prospect of an unshaded promenade along a beach in search of a possibly belligerent centipede, and what's more it would allow Brian to play at being Roman Abramovich for a couple of hours...

Well, not really. Lazing on the *Beluga* with just one's wife hardly replicated the Abramovich boat experience. In the first place, even his smallest superyacht would dwarf the pretty *Beluga*, and in the second place, Brian suspected the views from the *SS Abramovich* were rarely of islands in the middle of the Pacific and much more frequently of just lots of other superyachts tied up in some horrifically swanky Mediterranean marina. What's more, there were probably always more flunkies around than there've been managers of Chelsea. There had to be – if every oligarchic need was to be met – right down to the timely capture of distressing flatulence, which Brian understood was now often done for Russian oligarchs with the help of a trained '*pétomanager*' and a medium-sized Fabergé egg.

Nevertheless, Brian was still glad that he had made the choice to stay aboard – and that Sandra had agreed to stay with him. He didn't, of course, get the Abramovich experience or anything like it – which was probably a very good thing. And neither, incidentally, did Sandra, which was no more than an inevitability because quite obviously, to be a Russian oligarch, one has to be a man. But... they were both able to relish their situation in such a wonderful setting, and they even had a fantastic view of those two magnificent frigatebirds. Both non-oligarchs had stationed themselves on a lounger on the sundeck, and there, just a few feet from them, were these two... magnificent birds. They were perching on the derricks from which the pangas were hung when not in use, and they were entirely unconcerned with their human observers. So Brian and Sandra were both able to study at their leisure these large (hundred-centimetre-long) black birds, each with its long hooked-at-the-end beak, and each with the look of a true man o' war of the skies. For that's what these guys are: formidable pirates who, with a wingspan of up to 245 centimetres and the largest wingspan-to-weight ratio of any species of bird, are able to manoeuvre superbly on the wing, and by doing so, harass most other seabirds and thereby rob them of their food. Brian understood that this process could involve grabbing their quarry by the tail as a way of making them regurgitate their catch – which they would then scoop up in mid-flight – but he had not yet witnessed this himself. Perhaps he would very soon.

However, before then, there was some snorkelling to attend to. Yes, their companions had returned from the beach, having successfully encountered the aforementioned centipede, and there was now the offer of a snorkelling expedition off Gardner Island.

Brian signed up immediately. The snorkelling, Darwin promised, would be different from that which they'd already done, because the sides of Gardner Island just kept on going down where they met the sea, and therefore the snorkelling would be in very deep water. It was. And the surface of the water was quite 'restless'. But all this just added to the experience – along with a host of new fish and some vaguely familiar fish, many of which would be only half-remembered by the time this evening's listing session arrived. But that really didn't matter. What did matter was relishing the delights of an undersea world, witnessed by only a lucky few and by hardly any Russian oligarchs at all. Oh, and an extended snorkel in quite choppy water also provides one with an appetite and the self-belief that one can tackle a Pedro lunch.

Brian acquitted himself quite well at the table and as well as consuming his fair share of comestibles he was even able to digest some background information on the one pair of Nature-seekers who have so far not been mentioned. This was John and Thelma, and John and Thelma were an exceptional pair in that they were both 'measurably older' than any of the other Nature-seekers. In fact, they were both in sight of their eightieth birthday – but one would never have guessed it. John was a retired executive, and whilst a little 'old school', he was still a quite stocky, healthy-looking guy with boundless energy and an overload of enthusiasm. He had already participated in all the snorkelling sessions and, as would become apparent over the next few days, he would participate in absolutely everything. Thelma was similarly 'up for everything'. She might have acquired the face of a good-looking dowager, but in her acid-yellow top and with her two walking sticks she would tackle anything – very successfully. She also retained a youthful outlook on life, lacked any pretensions – and she was slightly wicked. She had, for example, been removed from a Concorde aeroplane earlier in her life because she had imbibed a little too freely of the complimentary champagne.

Which, apart from reinforcing her reprobate credentials in Brian's mind, also made him rather jealous. Heck, not only had she flown on Concorde, but she had been ejected from Concorde as well – because of drink! And how many people can claim that?

Anyway, after the meal and after a short voyage along the north coast of Española, Brian and Sandra found themselves sharing a panga with John and Thelma (and four others) as this little craft made its way to their next visitor site, a place called Suárez Point. This is indeed a 'point' on the extreme north-west tip of Española, and it comes equipped not only with a handy little jetty, but also with a complement of blue-footed boobies, an army of Sally Lightfoot crabs and a host of spectacular marine iguanas.

Well, the jetty needs no further amplification – other than it provided the Nature-seekers with an easy dry landing. But those three varieties of Galápagos inhabitants certainly warrant some further discussion, and where better to start than with what is one of the iconic birds of the Galápagos: the blue-footed booby.

This is a fairly large bird that is related to gannets and, like gannets, has a teardrop-shaped body, a formidable conical bill and a plunge-diving feeding strategy. However, unlike gannets, it has a rather unflattering name – stemming from the Spanish '*bobo*', meaning 'clown' or 'fool' – and ascribed to it by early Spanish sailors because of its supposedly clumsy behaviour on land and its failure to realise that early Spanish sailors were, by and large, not into ornithology in a big way, but instead into hitting over the head any bird or animal that didn't run away – and then eating it. It also has very blue feet – as in unmistakable bright, light-blue feet that make it look... well, just a little bit funny. Nevertheless, its blue feet are important. Because they play a key role in courtship rituals – and therefore breeding – with the male booby kicking things off, so to speak, by displaying his feet to attract a mate. In fact, he dances – on his blue feet – and if he gets it right, the object of his choreographic cavorting will come and join him and, with him, dance the 'booby two-step'. If all goes well, the dancing will then involve a bit of mutual 'sky-pointing' – face to face – and it will culminate in a bit of blue-footed copulation (not forgetting some associated male whistling and female honking – as one might expect).

So, here we have a remarkable bird that might be a little comical and a little clumsy on land, but one that is, without doubt, utterly charming – and in its ability to plunge dive, quite extraordinary. For this bird is able to dive in synchrony with others of its type – onto a school of fish – and is also able to exploit the inshore waters of the Galápagos by having the facility to use its airborne-torpedo skills in water that is only half a metre deep. So, not very comical if you're an unsuspecting sardine. Oh, and not very comical if you're a blue-footed booby chick and one of your bigger siblings has just read up on the practice of 'facultative siblicide'.

Yes, that charming blue-footed booby sitting next to the jetty and almost smiling into Evan's camera may have started off his booby life by murdering his brother or his sister. This is because blue-footed boobies lay two or three eggs five days apart – leading to 'asynchronous hatching' – and if there are then food shortages in the nest, due usually to environmental conditions, chick number one will kill its siblings by pecking them to death or by expelling them from the nest. And mum and dad won't say a word. They are just passive spectators to this grisly behaviour – or maybe they just remember their own experience as chicks and are made incapable of intervening through guilt. And anyway, 'facultative siblicide' isn't anywhere near as bad as 'obligate siblicide'. Because in this latter practice, a sibling almost always ends up being done away with, whereas in the former, siblicide may not occur at all – if the environmental conditions are more favourable. So, that's good, isn't it? And some of us will still even be able to append that word 'compassion' to whoever they believe created our world. And, after all, sometimes – but not always – life is tough – particularly if you happen to be a number two or a number three blue-footed booby chick...

Mind, things probably aren't a great deal better for Sally Lightfoot crabs. These chaps, which were scrambling everywhere around the jetty – and which scramble everywhere along the western coast of the Americas as well as along the shorelines of all the islands in the Galápagos – are a 'food source', and that's not something one would ever want to be. Nevertheless, these ubiquitous representatives of *Grapsus grapsus* are not the easiest things to catch. When young, they are black or dark brown and therefore not that easy to spot as they move over the dark lava rocks in search of some tasty algae. And even when they become adults and inexplicably adopt a flamboyant red, yellow and purple coloration that can be seen a mile off, they are exceedingly difficult to catch. As observed by none other than John Steinbeck, they have an extremely fast reaction time, and by scampering on their tiptoes – in that 'lightfooted' manner – they appear to be able to run off in any direction they choose.

So it could be worse for them, and it would be worse for them if we found them edible – which we don't – and we apparently use them only for bait. If we can catch them, that is. Possibly when they are distracted by their practice of 'cleaning symbiosis' – in the form of their taking ticks from marine iguanas. Which is an ideal way to leave Sally Lightfoot crabs and to pass on to make a few erudite comments about Española's very special marine iguanas.

Yes, marine iguanas in the Galápagos occur as seven different subspecies or races, and those on Española are easily the most colourful. The younger ones are mostly a regular blackish colour, but the older, larger representatives of these *Amblyrhynchus cristatus venustissimus* types, when the mating season arrives, abandon any attempt to pronounce their scientific name and instead undergo a dramatic colour change. They develop noticeably pink flanks, and their legs, tail and dorsal crest all begin to lose their charcoal-to-midnight tint in favour of a lighter hue. Yes, incredibly, these corporeal extremities turn into the same bright and light blue as is worn on the feet of their blue-footed booby neighbours. The result is an animal that looks as though it has been drawn by one of the animators from Walt Disney's first *Fantasia* film, although how they would have been cast in this first film is far from clear. After all, not one of the pink and blue marine iguanas draped over the rocks of Suárez Point was actually moving, and creating a dance routine to reflect their demeanour would have been an almost insurmountable challenge. Española's marine iguanas might be dramatically colourful, but like all marine iguanas, they are essentially inert for most of their lives and generally about as *peppy* as a pound of potatoes. In fact, even though it must have been the mating season, it looked to Brian as though most of this lot couldn't even manage a bonk let alone a bop. And furthermore, a lot of the smaller ones risked being denied any sort of activity at all – by their being trodden on…

Darwin was now leading his Nature-seekers inland, and it became very apparent very quickly that some of the younger iguanas had a preference for the shade of shrubs. And as these shrubs lined the path and the shade they provided tended to make these dark iguanas very difficult to spot, they ran a real risk of being squashed underfoot. Because the last thing they would do would be to move away from the visitors to their island. It's not what they did. And it's not what the boobies did either.

Yes, the Nature-seekers had moved away from iguana land and were now walking – carefully – through a mixed blue-footed and Nazca booby colony, and the adults and chicks of both sorts of boobies were largely indifferent to the presence of these visitors. They barely took any notice. Even when Shelly tripped down an incline (due to a failure to heed the advice to wear something other than flip-flops) and let out an almighty scream, the birds were left entirely unmoved. So Brian and his colleagues were all able to take in some exceptionally close views of lots of bundles of white feathers – and their rather smarter parents – and Brian was able to anguish over the breeding habits of these new Nazca boobies. Because the colour-restrained Nazca boobies, as well as conducting their plunge-dive feeding further out to sea than their blue-footed relatives, have also opted to go that little bit further in their approach to parent-condoned siblicide. No mere facultative siblicide for them, but instead the full-bloodied, red-blooded obligate siblicide. Which, as will no doubt be remembered, means that most of the charming giant white powder puffs sitting and panting on the guano rings that constitute their nests will have been responsible for pushing their younger siblings to their less than humane death – probably at the hands of one or two mockingbirds. Even though mockingbirds don't have any hands...

Anyway, that's just life – and death – on Española, which is probably why Brian felt marginally relieved when his gang had passed through the colony and when Darwin had assembled them to observe the workings of a refreshingly siblicide-free blowhole. It was situated just below the south coast's high cliffs – and it blew as advertised, although not spectacularly enough to stop Brian musing on what part of his body he would choose to turn bright blue if he could partially mimic those torpid iguanas. In the end he didn't choose the obvious part – even though this might have been quite good fun and it might also have been potentially startlingly arousing. No, he settled instead on his right hand, on the basis that with a bright blue right hand and a not so bright pink left hand, he would no longer be prone to confusing his left and his right – which he had been for as long as he could remember. So, pragmatism won out over the theatrical – again – right up until it was suddenly interrupted by a bit of excitement.

Española, apart from being home to marine iguanas, boobies, crabs – and some especially pretty lava lizards – is also home to waved albatrosses. Indeed, Española hosts approximately 12,000 pairs of these birds – which is the overwhelming majority of the world's population of these wonderful creatures (there are a few more that nest on a place called Isla de la Plata, near the Ecuadorian mainland). However, from a visiting Nature-seeker perspective, the fact that Española was the base for what is essentially the only endemic albatross in the Galápagos was of passing interest only, because their breeding cycle meant that the last waved albatross would have left this island almost two months before, and the albatross colony would be empty. So when what must have been the very last (and a very late) pair of these birds made an appearance in the sky above them, Darwin's charges were both very surprised and very excited. Their leader assured them that this was a quite unprecedented sight at this time of year, but a most welcome one, in that it had enabled them to witness what was almost certainly the final albatross flight from this island until all those thousands of albatrosses returned here to breed once again.

So, not a bad end to a fascinating visit, and, what's more, nobody had trodden on an iguana – or on a sea lion. (There was one of these larger creatures occupying the jetty when it was required for use by the *Beluga*'s panga-taxis, and care had to be taken to avoid a sea lion encounter that could potentially involve teeth and a loss of blood – and not the sea lion's blood.) Then it was only a matter of preparing to tackle another Pedro-produced feast, surviving an extended listing session after the meal and then hoping for an uneventful voyage overnight back to the island of Santa Cruz. Oh, and before that voyage got underway, there was also the small matter of Brian's presentation on his next South American country. Tonight he'd chosen Chile.

He started by informing Sandra that for this country he was going to ignore politics and presidents and instead talk about *pudús*. This did not appear to bring any relief to Sandra but just a sense of confusion. She looked not only slightly irritated now but also somewhat perplexed. However, 'perplexed' would soon be replaced by 'bored' when Brian proceeded to explain what a pudú was. It was, he announced, the world's smallest species of deer – at just thirteen to seventeen inches tall and thirty-three inches long – and it lived in the thickets and dense forests of the southern Andes of both Chile and Argentina. (So not even an animal unique to his chosen country!) Anyway, he went on to point out that it should never be confused with a puku or a kudu (which, as Sandra already knew, were two species of antelope that lived on a different continent), and he was just about to pronounce on the pudú's endangered status – of course – when Sandra asked him whether a lecture on the smallest deer in the world was really the best thing he could assemble in respect of Chile. Wasn't there something marginally more interesting and possibly less 'worthy'? Well yes, there was. Which is why Brian changed tack, away from pudús, and instead began to instruct Sandra on the subject of the *Casa de Vidrio*.

'You see,' he started, 'there was this sort of "artwork" called the *Casa de Vidrio*, which, as its name suggests, was a glass house. And it was set up in Chile's capital, Santiago, in 2000, to enable the citizens of that city to observe all the goings-on of a young actress who had agreed to live in it for two weeks. And I mean all her goings-on, all the revealing and intimate bits included...'

'Why?' interrupted a suddenly animated Sandra.

'To lay bare, so to speak, the blatant double standards in Chile and, in particular, to protest against the city's enthusiastic embrace of *café con piernas.*'

'You've lost me.'

'Chile has a traditionally conservative culture. I mean, divorce there was illegal until recently. Films were heavily censored. And even polling places were segregated by gender. Nevertheless, Santiago had spawned lots of these *café con piernas* – which literally means 'coffee with legs' – and what these places were... well, they were places where the all-female serving staff were "dressed to arouse". I mean the waitresses wore miniskirts and heels, and in some of the establishments they "graduated" to bikinis and lingerie and they even had raised catwalks and mirrors and things, to... well, to "optimise" the view for the patrons.'

'Are you making this up, Brian? Or are you just remembering a dream?'

'No. It's true! And it's all to do with why they set up that glass house back in 2000.'

'Really. And did it work? Did that actress getting her kit off have any effect? Or did it just give all those Santiago voyeurs another cheap thrill?'

'Well, I don't really know. But I think these coffee shops still exist…'

'Mmm,' murmured Sandra, 'perhaps you should have stuck to… what were they called…?'

'Pudend… I mean… pudús,' spluttered Brian.

Sandra rolled her eyes, and then she brought tonight's exposition to a conclusion.

'Jesus. You know, you men are all the same. One-track minds. And we know where that track leads to, don't we? And it's not to any sunlit uplands, but to somewhere that's quite literally the reverse – as so plainly revealed by that little slip of the tongue then. I only hope, Brian, that if I'm going to be subjected to any more lectures over the coming days – which I'm sure I am – that they manage to stay well clear of both the track and its destination and that they include no references whatsoever to naked actresses or to lingerie. Have I made myself clear?'

Sandra had – by the wobble in her voice towards the end of her admonishment. She had just wanted to shut Brian up for the night, not to scold him – really. And Brian knew that. Just as he knew that people in glass houses should never throw stones – and they are ill advised to take their clothes off as well. Especially when it's *chilly*…

6.

or Brian, the voyage overnight was not entirely uneventful. It was a fairly long voyage – all the way back to Santa Cruz – and inevitably it was accompanied by the boat's normal engine noises and by its normal rolling sensation, both of which Brian had learned to ignore. However, not so on this occasion. For some reason he found himself awake around midnight and he then remained awake for the next two hours.

However, this wasn't a problem. In the first place, he soon realised that the dull throbbing of the boat's engine and the vessel's acute side-to-side motion could both be relished. There was something almost womb-like in the sensation they created. But there was more. Because the ambient sound and the regular oscillations, taken together, had the effect of triggering in his brain the repeated refrains of what was one of his favourite recordings of all time. Yes, as he lay on his back in his tiny cabin, rocking gently from side to side, Brian was able to hear Joan Baez singing Bob Dylan's 'A Hard Rain's a-Gonna Fall', and so well, that it was as though she was in there in the cabin with him. It was a really memorable experience, and it was only when Joan's voice was beginning to become hoarse through its overuse that Brian, in an attempt to relieve her, turned his attention from music to a consideration of some of the world's most intractable problems. He kicked off with overpopulation, which proved as insoluble a problem as ever, before then moving on through resource depletion and the alarming spread of beards until he eventually arrived at phones. Well, not phones as such, but their almost constant use by the youth of the world, where 'youth' meant anybody who had been acquainted with the symptoms of puberty but not yet with wrinkles or sags. But, anyway, the reason he'd arrived at this destination was the thought that these youthful sorts, if they found themselves in an awake-in-the-night situation on a small boat in the middle of the Pacific, and couldn't get a signal for their phone, would certainly not be engaged with Joan Baez, or with their intellect and trying to solve world problems, but instead would be in a state of panic.

Heck, what would they do? Brian gave it some serious thought – without knowing too much about the intricacies of smartphones – and concluded that they might possibly choose to review the thousand or so selfies they'd taken on the trip so far, or they might even try to take a few more, or they might find a couple of mindless computer games to play. This, of course, would go some way to settling their burgeoning sense of panic, in that the simple act of just holding their device would give them a measure of comfort. But the fact remained that they could not use it to talk to anybody, not to any one of all those other people who, like themselves, cannot now exist without the constant exchange of chatter that a modern phone allows. Quite what all these people chatted about, Brian hadn't a clue – and he didn't want a clue. If he did have a clue, he suspected he would probably be even more despondent about the future of the human race than he was right now. And he could well do without another load of despondency.

There again, there was his other theory – concerning the constant use of phones for so-called communication – and if he revisited this on this wakeful night he would become *unmanageably* despondent. Because this theory concerned the identity of whoever it was at the other end of the phone…

You see, Brian found it literally incredible that so many people could have so many 'friends' to talk to, and even if they did have an inordinate number of 'friends', then they all led such generally uneventful lives, they could not possibly find anything like enough to talk about – to fill in all those thousands of hours of calls they made every year. So… what he'd formulated in his mind was some sort of 'Cyber Controller', a sort of virtual organiser/oracle who was constantly available for all smartphone users and whose job it was to tell them how to go about their lives. That's why, when you see a modern young mum in the street, one hand on the handle of a pushchair and one hand pressing a phone to her ear, she looks so distracted. Because what is happening is that she is receiving information on how to negotiate that nearby zebra crossing, or maybe on how to find her way home – or possibly she is being advised as to whether she should buy some milk for her baby rather than another bottle of Coke. She has somehow lost her ability to make her way through life on her own and, like all the other lost souls of her generation, has capitulated to the phone and become a willing automaton of the digital age.

Brian would have been the first to admit that his theory did have a few holes in it, and it wasn't by any means clear as to who might be playing the omnipotent Controller – or how he answered all those millions of calls all at the same time. But that, for Brian, was a mere detail, and the empirical evidence was just too strong to dismiss out of hand. How else, he thought, could one explain so much use of a handheld phone – and through this sustained use, the emergence of more and more people who have problems with attention spans, with verbal communication, with normal manners and with… errh, just thinking? And then there was the onset of panic on any occasion when the Cyber Controller could not be reached and instructions not received – on issues such as how to deal with being awake in the middle of the night on a small boat travelling between two islands in the Galápagos archipelago.

Well, he was still thinking about smartphones when he finally dropped off to sleep. And when he awoke again, at about six-thirty in the morning, he was no longer thinking about anything to do with the overthrow of intellect by invasive innovation, but instead about the programme for today. Because today would be all about what the Galápagos is so renowned for: its celebrated and almost incomparable giant tortoises.

It started after another assault course of a breakfast and after an inspection of the contents of Academy

Bay. This was where the captain had parked his boat, and he'd parked it here because Academy Bay, on the south coast of Santa Cruz, is the effective parking lot for Puerto Ayora. And Puerto Ayora, as well as being the most populous town in the Galápagos, is also the home of the Charles Darwin Foundation, an institution which is not unconnected with the wellbeing of giant tortoises and which, consequently, was the Nature-seekers' first destination for today.

Well, there were a lot of contents of Academy Bay. It was just full of boats, and some of these boats were frighteningly large. They made the *Beluga* look like a toy and, in Brian's mind, they made the prospect of a visit to Puerto Ayora look like… well, less than a joy. With all these assembled visitors, it was clearly not going to be a quiet and peaceful place, and if its 12,000 inhabitants displayed the same habits as their counterparts in the disgusting Puerto Baquerizo Moreno, back on San Cristóbal, it could be a lot worse than just not quiet and peaceful.

However, that was to prejudge, and Brian decided he should take a more optimistic view of their intended destination and wait until they were ashore to make any proper assessment of this second *puerto*. This was just as well. Because when his panga made it to Puerto Ayora's rather substantial jetty, it *was* busy – and definitely not peaceful – but it was almost pretty. And down below the jetty, in surprisingly clear water, were some reef sharks and even a couple of turtles. Maybe Puerto Ayora would be a lot better than he thought.

Well, yes it was – at least on its seafront. Not quite St Tropez, but where Darwin had corralled his flock for the first briefing of the day, there was some civic tree planting and some decorative paving work and a backdrop of fairly decent-looking cafés and shops. Indeed, this almost-orderly manifestation of Puerto Ayora's commercialism extended all the way along Avenida Charles Darwin, the route taken by the Nature-seekers to get them to the site of the Charles Darwin Foundation. Nevertheless, one could have successfully argued that its 'resort' nature made it almost indistinguishable from somewhere like Tenby (on a sunny day) and one could also have become genuinely concerned that such an overtly holiday-sort-of-place existed in such a uniquely precious environment as the Galápagos. Which is exactly what Brian did. Shit, if he couldn't get them for despoilment and disfigurement (just yet), then he could still have a go at them for incongruity and maybe insensitivity as well.

What the residents of Puerto Ayora could not be held accountable for, however, was the heat. In the absence of a cliff-top breeze or an open-ocean gale, it was excruciatingly hot. So hot, indeed, that the Nature-seeker ensemble needed very little coaxing to stop at an open-air fish stall on Avenida Charles Darwin, a stall which wasn't particularly smart, but one which did offer more than a little shade. It also offered a remarkable close-up view of some Galápagos wildlife. This is because its blue concrete counters were just yards from the sea, and with these counters being covered in fish and with the prospect of the odd fish-bit appearing on the floor beneath and around them, two normally sea-based representatives of this wildlife were almost always in attendance. They were on this day. Directly under the counters or loitering right next to the fishmongers were a few hopeful sea lions, and a little further away and closer to the water were half a dozen pelicans, their huge beaks closed but their eyes wide open, no doubt keeping a constant lookout for that next tasty bite. These were brown pelicans, very large birds with improbably large pouches (capable of holding up to thirteen litres of water – and hopefully a meal) – and with some improbably close relatives: the frigatebirds. Yes, these clumsy-on-land comics are actually accomplished plunge divers, and they may well have developed their enormous pouches as a defence against the piracy habits of their frigatebird cousins – albeit no such defence was required here. No, all they needed in this waterside fish emporium was a soupçon of good fortune – in the shape of the next bit of fish trimming falling right at their feet.

It all made for a fascinating pause for the Nature-seekers, and despite some commendable blocking tactics adopted by Shane, it provided all those with cameras – and particularly Evan – with some memorable shots of both pelicans and sea lions – and a much needed rest before the unshaded-marathon part of the walk got underway.

By golly, it was hot. And by golly, there was hardly any shade to speak of, and as Darwin's group left the retail stretch of the *avenida* and embarked on the approach road to the Foundation, there was no shade whatsoever. Moreover, when they entered the grounds of the Charles Darwin Foundation, there wasn't much of... well, anything at all...

That might sound a little harsh. But given Brian's

state of almost total saturation, having endured that walk through the oven that was Avenida Charles Darwin, it was almost understandable, particularly when one takes into account that the Foundation exists to protect and support Galápagos wildlife – and its tortoises in particular – and it is not there to provide a five-star 'visitor experience'. One can, of course, observe a number of giant tortoises, all looking about as active as Brian felt, and one can listen to (young) Darwin's dissertations on these beasts and on what the Foundation is doing to breed more of them and so help in the protection of their various species. But frankly, that can get you only so far, and one cannot help noticing the absence of anything inherently interesting amongst the jumble of buildings that make up the site, just as one cannot help noticing the intense heat and, even worse, the presence of other visitors in the shape of some not-so-quiet Americans. They were organised into two groups, and both groups included a disproportionate number of US citizens who had clearly graduated from the High Volume Voice Projection and Short-distance Shouting Institute. Brian could barely believe it. He had, after all, met plenty of softly spoken Americans in his time. But the majority of these guys… well, he wondered whether there was some sort of competition going on – for the title of this month's loudest, most bulbous visitor to the Galápagos, with maybe the possibility of picking up the much-coveted annual title as well. (And yes, there was not much *leanness* in evidence either; just the sort of shapes that occur naturally in the biggest of the giant tortoises…)

Brian sometimes wondered why he'd been blessed

with such a sunny disposition. Maybe, he thought, it was to deal with hot, sticky, noisy, rather unrewarding situations such as this visit to the Charles Darwin Foundation. It was, after all, very clear that, on this occasion, his knowledge of the saintly work being undertaken by this saintly set-up would not be enough on its own, and no matter how successful they were in breeding more tortoises and reintroducing them into the wild, he'd still have found this visit rather uninspiring and... well, just a bit of a trial. So, it was a bloody good job that he was just such a naturally happy – and undemanding – sort of chap. That said, there was nothing he'd like to do more – now – than to demand a glass of cold beer and preferably somewhere shady to drink it.

It was just as well then that it was now time to leave the Charles Darwin Foundation and for the Nature-seekers to make their way back to the jetty and to their awaiting pangas. But not before a pit stop at one of the hostelries on Avenida Charles Darwin, where Brian and Sandra were able to drink a toast to that great scientist from the past and to all those who are now helping to keep his name alive in the Galápagos with all their sterling work – at that less than captivating institution down the road.

Anyway, the *Beluga* felt more inviting than ever when Brian and Sandra made it back there for lunch, and the shower felt pretty inviting too. So, suitably reinvigorated – and more than adequately fed – they, like all the other Nature-seekers, were more than ready for a return to Puerto Ayora – and for a bus ride to who-knew-where.

Well, they all knew where really, in that Darwin had

told them that they would be making an excursion to a farm in the centre of Santa Cruz – to see 'wild' giant tortoises. And that's not 'wild' as in incensed or 'wild' as in truly wild – but just 'wild' as in free to waddle around a ruddy great farm and to go more or less where they pleased. Which didn't sound like the genuine pristine Galápagos experience, but it was probably a darn sight better than being fried in a worthy institution whilst, at the same time, being assaulted by self-amplified Americans. Brian was certainly prepared to be impressed. Just as he was prepared to be less than impressed with the sprawl that was Puerto Ayora…

In short, it was worse than Puerto Baquerizo Moreno, the town on San Cristóbal about which he had been so scathing. As soon as the bus left that almost pretty seafront of the town, that same lack of care and that same lack of anything to do with pride or with a sense of responsibility for the environment came into view. It was garbageville, the standard mix of substandard and no-standards buildings, initially cheek by jowl but then petering out into an untidy landscape of 'structures', some lived in, some once lived in and some looking unlikely ever to be finished let alone ever lived in. And this general air of scruffiness and almost wanton neglect persisted even into the countryside. Because, as on San Cristóbal, the locals on Santa Cruz have made inroads into the interior – to farm, to scratch a living – and to degrade the local environment to the point that it looks tired and abused. Hell, Brian's naturally sunny disposition was really being put to the test now, and he could barely wait to be off this bus and instead lost in the depths of that tortoise haven which he and his friends had been promised.

Eventually, they did arrive there, and there *were* tortoises around; quite a few of them actually, either sharing fields with cattle on the way in to the 'haven' or dotted around the cattle-free grounds that surrounded the hacienda. That is to say, the barn-like café that had been constructed by the farm's owners to accommodate the drinking, feeding and relieving requirements of their tortoise-demanding guests.

This barn-like structure also housed a huge empty tortoise shell, the bony home of a long-gone monster of a tortoise, which could now be used for the purpose of instruction or, if preferred, for the purpose of tortoise impersonation. Darwin, of course, first of all used it for instruction. But he then switched into impersonation/entertainment/partial-instruction mode by crawling into the shell and then lifting himself up on all fours and so creating the vision of a not quite normal giant tortoise, but one with an awful etiolated-limbs condition together with an oversized head. Not to be outdone, Josh followed Darwin into the shell (after Darwin had withdrawn – obviously). And then Shane wriggled his way in. It was at this stage that Brian thought it was all becoming a little like an initiation ceremony for some sort of Masonic splinter group, and he decided (immediately) that he would remain outside the shell – and uninitiated. He did, after all, have an appointment with some other shells, and these shells contained very much living giant tortoises – all with regular-sized limbs and normal-sized heads.

They were, as already reported, dotted around the vicinity of the barn, and as the Nature-seekers wandered between them, Brian began to test his knowledge of these remarkable creatures. Because, unlikely as it might sound, he had not spent all his time at the Charles Darwin Foundation hiding from the sun and from the racket of loud Americans, but he had also taken in some of his guide's enlightenment on the subject of these giant reptiles. He knew, for example, that the tortoises here were representatives of a total population of Galápagos tortoises of something like 20,000 individuals – and that this total population was made up of eleven separate extant species and that these eleven species could be split into two distinct groups. The first group comprised the saddleback tortoises, which were those that live on sparsely vegetated islands and have therefore evolved the sort of (saddle-like) shell that allows them to reach up to whatever vegetation exists. The second group comprised the dome-shaped tortoises, which live on the larger (higher) islands where they have always had access to plenty of suitable food at ground level and have therefore not needed to take the saddleback route of evolution. Santa Cruz falls into this latter category of islands, and consequently the giant tortoises on this farm were of the dome type (and specifically examples of *Geochelone nigrita*), and, as such, they could grow up to weigh as much as 250 kilograms and have a carapace that measured up to 1.5 metres.

Some of the guys here were that sort of size, and could only be described as genuinely splendid – if just a little bit... inanimate. Yes, as Brian was already well aware, he was never going to witness a giant tortoise sprinting through the bush, leaping from a rock or, indeed, swinging with ease through the trees. With their enormous weight, their conformation and their ponderous nature, that just wasn't their bag. Instead they either just shuffled about or didn't shuffle at all, in the sense that they became essentially inert. And only when they were having tortoise sex – which can apparently take several hours (i.e. not at all like us) and involve loud snoring and grunting noises from the male (i.e. exactly like us) – was there a bit of even half-lively movement.

So, for Brian at least, despite their genuine splendidness – and their rarity as a creature – they did have a bit of a problem in holding his attention for more than a few minutes. In fact, it did occur to him that no matter how giant they were, tortoises did have a bit of an image problem when compared to some of our more obviously animate animals, and therefore it was maybe time for a bit of inventive copywriting on their behalf – right now and in respect of the particular domed giants here. So he had a go, and in due course, he managed to compile: 'an animal that is generally extremely stable (other than when [literally] upset), an animal that is easy to feed, an animal that is a doddle to groom, an animal that is generally very undemanding, an animal that is safe with children – and that will probably outlive them – and an animal that is very quiet or actually quite interesting to watch on those rare occasions when it isn't'.

Well, it probably wouldn't have sold many, thought Brian, but his copywriting was a lot less harmful than ignoring Darwin's instructions not to stand right next to the tortoises (and so cause them stress), which is exactly what one person was doing, a person who had an American accent, an American wife and a cabin back on board the *Beluga*. Really! And after we gave them their independence as well. Brian was not impressed. Although he was with the lava tunnel…

As Brian had learnt, lava tunnels are cylindrical-shaped caves formed when a low-viscosity lava flow develops a hard crust, and the crust then thickens to form a roof over a still-flowing stream of lava – which eventually flows all the way out and leaves a void beneath the crust. Some of these tunnels can be just inches in diameter. The one on this farm, through which the Nature-seekers gingerly made their way, varied between ten feet and twenty feet in diameter, and would, thought Brian, have accommodated all 3,000 specimens of Santa Cruz's *Geochelone nigtita* tortoises. At which point he also thought that this probably meant that despite that sterling bit of copywriting, he was completely tortoised out and would now like to be back on the *Beluga*. Eventually he was, having first endured the ride back to Puerto Ayora and then a further encounter with its dreadful squalor. It hadn't got any better while he'd been away, just as Pedro's portion sizes hadn't got any smaller…

Yes, it was soon eating time again, and that meant time to deal with another generous helping of calories – and, for the other Nature-seekers at Brian's table, time to deal with a handful of his random opinions. They seemed to cope quite well with his assertion that the problem of excessive net migration into the UK would soon be solved – by more and more of its indigenous population deciding that, as it was no longer their country, they should simply choose to emigrate and so make the net migration figure a sizable negative. They even managed, with a bit of coaxing, to accept that he had a point when he insisted that torture is still rife in the UK – in the form of keeping hundreds of thousands of very old people alive, when all they really want is a painless and dignified death. But then, when he tried to maintain that extra-judicial killings had a certain merit – because, as their name implied, they must involve an 'extra bit of justice administration' – they just wouldn't buy it. Neither would Sandra, who made this known to Brian in no uncertain terms – and suggested that he should now offer no further opinions and that he should even remain silent during the post-dinner listing session. This he did, only imposing any of his views again when he was back in his cabin, when it was then time to impose them on Sandra. And these would be his views on Argentina…

'Sandra,' he started imaginatively, 'I think it's time that I filled in a few blanks in your knowledge of Argentina…'

Sandra gave Brian a look, which in their current nautical situation could only be described as 'mutinous'. However, she failed to follow through with anything like a real act of mutiny or even with any words, and Captain Bligh was away once again.

'You see, not many people know this, but Argentina, at the beginning of the twentieth century, was a very wealthy place. By 1908, with all its beef and wheat exports, its per capita income was the seventh highest in the world – after… errh us, the US, Australia, New Zealand, Switzerland and… errh, Belgium. In fact, that made its income per capita 70% higher than that of Italy, 90% higher than that of Spain, and a whopping 180% higher than that of Japan…'

'Brian,' interrupted Sandra, 'there isn't going to be a test on all this stuff in the morning, is there? Because I…'

'No,' reinterrupted Brian. 'I'm just trying to point out that Argentina, just one hundred years ago, was in the Premier League. Whereas now, as we all know, it couldn't even make it in a temperance league…'

'But why would it want…?'

'I mean that since about the 1930s, despite all its natural resources and all its national potential, it has gone so far backwards that it has ended up as just an upper-middle-income country – at best. It's had a history of Peronism, state terrorism, repeated economic crises, bouts of hyperinflation, flights of capital, and some of the biggest debt defaults on the planet. And that's going some, particularly when you've had such a flying start.'

'But why?' asked a not entirely engaged Sandra.

'Search me. Maybe it's the… you know, the hand of God. I mean, for some reason, he dealt them a shit hand as regards their economy and their culture, and then he *gave* them a hand so that they could beat England back in 1986…'

'Soccer balls!'

'Well, I don't know. But I do know why they've so abused the Falklands…'

'You mean with their rather persistent claim?'

'Ah well, it hasn't been persistent *historically*. I mean, as far back as 1860, Argentina indicated that it had no problem with our ownership of the Falklands, and even its own maps of that period didn't reflect those islands as being Argentine. OK, it had made the odd complaint about our presence, but it wasn't until 1941 – when things had begun to fall apart economically – that it raised the issue of Falklands' sovereignty in its own congress. And, of course, ever since then it's been making an absolute meal of it – and an absolute mess of it when it tried to take them by force. And it's all such a load of bollocks…'

Here Brian paused in order to adopt his 'most affronted' expression, and then he continued.

'I mean, in the first place, the UK claimed and settled the Falklands before Argentina even existed, and before we did, there was no indigenous or settled population there. The islands were empty of people. Anyway, since then, they have been continuously and peacefully occupied by us rather than by them – other than for the two months when they illegally grabbed them – and so much upset Mrs Thatcher. And when you then remember that self-determination is supposedly a universal right, enshrined in the UN Charter, it is extremely difficult to see how Argentina should not just be given the bum's rush and told to sod off – and stay off. Quite simply, even the poorest paid lawyer will tell you that the sort of continuous, firm possession as exemplified by 'us' in the Falklands, especially if it's been undisputed by force (for more than 150 years), is easily sufficient to create an indisputable sovereign title. And that lawyer might even tell you, without wanting an additional fee, that the only real reason that successive regimes in Argentina have insisted that the Falklands should be theirs is that they have had a repeated need to distract their supporters from the dire economic plight of their country. And, for no additional fee, I'll tell you that this need is unlikely ever to go away – unless, of course, the hand of God intervenes once again, and Argentina starts to sort itself out. But I wouldn't hold your breath…'

At this stage of the dissertation, Brian stood down his affronted expression and adopted another. It was one of sudden recollection. And then he spoke.

'Oh, and if you want any more proof that Argentinians really do need to sort themselves out, then I can provide this in the form of a fact. And this fact is that Argentina has the highest number of psychiatrists per capita in the world. Even more per capita than in the States!'

Well, he was now wearing his 'game, set and match' expression – and Sandra was wearing a look of fatigue laced with hope, hope that her husband had concluded his didactic assault for the night. And it was OK. He had. In fact, he was already looking forward to another overnight trip in the company of Joan Baez – and another tussle with some of the world's more intractable problems. Like, for example, how to convince all those doubters in the world that, despite their tearing and nipping tendencies, tortoises don't have any teeth…

7.

In the event, Joan Baez failed to make an appearance and the problem of educating the world in the non-dental nature of tortoises was left unresolved. Instead, Brian slept like a baby as Captain José piloted the *Beluga* towards an island called Santiago.

This island is situated to the north-west of Santa Cruz, and whilst not quite as large as Santa Cruz, it is, unlike Santa Cruz, happily uninhabited. Furthermore, despite the severe problems cause by introduced species such as goats, pigs and rats, it does sustain its own complement of wildlife, and this complement even includes an endemic species of giant tortoise (which is apparently no more animate than those observed back on Santa Cruz). Anyway, its tortoises were not on Darwin's advertised itinerary for the day, as the Nature-seekers' experience of this island would be very much restricted to its non-tortoise-inhabited shoreline, and starting with its rocky coast near a small offshore island called 'Chinese Hat'.

It was no secret that 'Sombrero Chino' was so named because as well as being more or less round, it also has a profile that is apparently reminiscent of... a Chinese hat, as in the sort of headwear formerly seen on Chinese labourers and the like – although on this new sunny morning, through the window of Brian's cabin, the island's profile put him more in mind of some enormous fossilised flying saucer. There again, thought Brian, the term 'flying saucer' was probably not available when it was time to give this small island a name, whereas Chinese *coolies* – as they were then referred to – and their headwear, would probably be known worldwide. Well, that was all very well, but Brian did wonder whether, in retrospect, it had been the right name to choose. After all, China is currently busy hoovering up all the little islands it can get its hands on, such as those far-from-its-shores Spratly Islands in the South China Sea (on which other, rather closer countries may well have a better claim). So, with a name like 'Chinese Hat', isn't there a real possibility, thought Brian, that one day China will just turn up, assert its ownership (over its own hat) and start building an airstrip and then a military base just like it's done on so many of those Spratly Islands? And as Ecuador is already one of China's client countries, would this current legal owner of Chinese Hat and the rest of the Galápagos archipelago do anything about it? Well, these and other questions were the sort that constantly plagued Brian's life – and could sometimes make him late for breakfast if not forcefully reminded to get a move on by his wife. She, incidentally, when Brian verbalised his anxieties concerning Chinese expansionism into the Galápagos, informed him that she thought he was talking through his hat...

Anyway, the reminder worked, and Brian made it to breakfast, and after this he made it onto a panga, and both pangas then set off for Flying Saucer Island. It wasn't far from where the *Beluga* was anchored, but it took some time to get there. And this was because Darwin wanted his charges to observe whatever wildlife was about – either under the water or on the rocky coast of Santiago. This wasn't difficult. The water was crystal clear – and revealed a number of fish and a number of rays – and the coastline was bereft of cover and provided the Nature-seekers with their second view of a Galápagos hawk and their first ever view of a Galápagos penguin!

Now, the vast majority of the world's penguins are found in either the southern continents or in sub-Antarctic waters. Only these Galápagos penguins live permanently in the tropics. And the reason that they are here is that their ancestors probably followed the cold Humboldt Current north, until they happened upon the Galápagos archipelago with its bountiful supply of food, and decided there and then not to make the long return trip to the frozen south. Of course, this wasn't to say that they didn't have to adapt – and they have adapted. For example, these small upright birds have now evolved the 'flimsiest' plumage (shortest feathers) of any penguin, and this allows them to tolerate water temperatures far above those in the southern oceans. Furthermore, they no longer nest on bare ground in order to use the warmth of the sun in the incubation of their eggs, but instead they employ deep, shady crevices in which their eggs will be protected from the *intensity* of the sun.

So, once these sorts of adjustments had been made, being a Galápagos penguin must have been like being a penguin on permanent holiday – on a bunch of islands on the equator. Only, of course, it wasn't quite that simple. The reality is that these little chaps are very exposed to the effects of an El Niño in their relatively newly adopted home, and it is reckoned that each time an El Niño occurs, their population crashes by anything up to 65 or even 75%. Which is why there were possibly more than 10,000 of these birds in the past, but now, there are no more than 2,000 – although they are pretty good breeders and, in theory, they will be well able to recover their numbers relatively quickly. The fact remains, however, that Galápagos penguins are very rare birds – as well as being the only penguins that are found in the northern hemisphere.

This last northern hemisphere fact was announced by Darwin as the Nature-seekers were making the most of their first view of this delightful flightless bird. At which point Brian could not resist challenging this assertion by reminding Darwin that there was another population of penguins exclusively endemic to the northern hemisphere and residing in London. Darwin looked perplexed to say the least, and Brian was then obliged to prompt his memory by recounting how this population had first come about – in the seventeenth century and during the reign of Charles II. That was when, he explained, the posh penguin, Tarquin, having got the better of the passive penguin, Mannequin, and then the mute penguin, Harlequin, made his move on the orange-selling penguin, Nellguin – and the rest was history.

Well, Darwin, quite understandably, asked Rick, who was sitting beside him, whether Brian had possibly hit his head or whether he was simply inebriated. Rick, to his credit, said it was neither, but just a sad manifestation of poor English humour being aired in an inappropriate situation and at an inappropriate time, and that if they all ignored it, it would probably go away and they could all return to the proper business of this morning's expedition. Which is what all those in the panga proceeded to do, and the panga was soon heading off for a wet landing on *Chapeau Chinois Island* and Nellguin penguins were never mentioned again.

What were mentioned, when the wet landing had been completed, were lava gulls. These were not fanciful birds, fashioned from lava and dreamt up by Darwin in response to Brian's Nellguin penguins, but real sooty-grey birds – which are even rarer than Galápagos penguins. As Darwin explained in some detail on the oven sands of the landing beach, there are thought to be no more than 400 pairs of these gulls in the world, and they all live in the Galápagos archipelago. The good news was that they appear fairly resilient in the face of the human colonisation of their habitat, and as natural scavengers they have even adapted well to human settlements, where they are often seen perched around harbours or lurking next to fishing boats. Indeed, the attraction of easy pickings in places such as Puerto Ayora was probably why Brian failed to catch sight of any of them during his walk on this island. Or, there again, it could have been because they blend in perfectly with the lava on which they often stand – and Chinese Hat, in close up, was just one ruddy great heap of lava. Spotting a lava gull against a vista of lava rubble would, Brian thought, be just about as difficult as turning Chinese

Hat into 'Chinese Airstrip and Military Base Number Forty-Three', albeit rather more welcome.

Well, the walk on Chinese Hat, which ran along the coast from the beach, did have its points of interest – such as mini lava tunnels, 'lava on lava', the odd sea lion pup and the odd marine iguana – but it was a fairly barren environment, and Brian did find his interest wandering – right up until it was firmly apprehended by the topic of iguana penises…

Inexplicably, Brian had remained entirely ignorant of this intriguing aspect of iguana anatomy for the whole of his life, and it was only now, when Darwin had embarked on an impromptu lecture on the *intromittent organ* of a nearby marine iguana, that this ignorance would be breached. And to start with, it was breached by Brian learning what an intromittent organ was, which was, of course, the 'copulatory organ' of a male animal, otherwise known as a penis – or, if one is talking about an iguana, as a *hemipenis*. And that is what Brian was finding so fascinating – and so revealing about the iguana intromittent organ: that these creatures have two of them! Well, before Darwin was able to elaborate on why any animal might need or want two penises, Brian's mind was already racing. Was it just a case of carrying a spare – in readiness for that very rare occasion on which the first one didn't work? Or maybe it's like the way they went about bombing in the Second World War: send out a pathfinder and, when the target has been located, let in the second guy to deliver the payload. Or, there again, maybe it's just as simple as being set up and ready to deal with either a left-handed or a right-handed screw (thread)…

Well, he was well wide of the mark. And the truth was both a little more bizarre and indeed a little more gripping – literally. Because what he learnt was that all lizards and snakes have these hemipenes, and that in the case of lizards they are hidden away below the tail, ready to be *evaginated* (i.e. turned inside out) whenever the need arises. And when the need and the hemipenes do arise, not only does the love potion get conveyed down an external groove in whichever hemipenis is used, but the hemipenis will have first been secured into the right place by the spikes or hooks that it has at its end! Furthermore, it will not only be the right place but also the right partner, because these spikes and hooks will not be in random positions but instead they will be arranged in rosettes, so that a 'reproductive isolation' is achieved through a 'lock and key' mechanism. And in plain English that means that different, species-specific arrangements of barbs and grappling hooks mean that individuals of one species can only ever mate with individuals of that same species – and hybridisation is prevented.

Brian was captivated by these revelations, and had he been less captivated he might have asked Darwin to clear up one or two of the queries these revelations raised. For example, how did those marine iguanas overcome the lock and key mechanism in their mating with land iguanas back on South Plaza? Or, of more interest to Brian, how did the male iguanas go about choosing which hemipenis to use – or did they have a choice? And inevitably, did the lady iguanas get anything out of sex other than a very sore feeling where they didn't want it and maybe even a desperate need for some tweezers after the sex act was concluded?

Then there were Darwin's closing remarks about the 'copulatory equipment' of tortoises and turtles, which apparently comes in the singular, so to speak, but also comes in prodigious proportions. Indeed, it has been reported that many owners of these retiring reptiles have been absolutely flabbergasted by the size of their pet's equipment – and rather unnerved by its appearance. It seems that it looks less like a regular penis and more like a bagful of their internal organs or, in some cases, like an out-of-control, grow-it-yourself, purple Triffid. So God knows what the donger of a Galápagos giant tortoise looks like – or whether the lady giant tortoises, if they had a choice, might just vote for a hemipenis instead – just as long as it didn't come with skewers and crampons attached.

Brian found himself standing by himself – pondering – as Darwin and the rest of the Nature-seekers moved off along the trail. And even when he caught them up and tried to take in the ambience of Chinese Hat, he was still distracted by an awful lot of pondering. In the first place there were still all those unanswered questions. And in the second place there was the fact that his own species clearly didn't know how lucky it was – to have such uncomplicated and such 'proportionate' equipment – and the females of his species didn't know how exceptionally lucky they were in having to cope with what could only be called very smooth operators – who, even in the absence of any tread, couldn't resort to a spare…

Anyway, the walk on Chinese Hat eventually came to an end, and it was time to return to the *Beluga*, and then, before lunch, time to go for a snorkel, this time off that rocky Santiago coast. This proved unexceptional but quite interesting, and much of the interest was provided in the form of the presence of pipefish. These chaps look a little like stretched-out seahorses. They have the same seahorse sort of snout and their bodies are long, thin and snakelike. Brian looked them up in a reference book when he got back on board, and was not surprised to find that they have neither penises nor hemipenes, but that instead they go about the procreation bit by the female pipefish first transferring her eggs through an ovipositor into a brood pouch on the male. After this they both rise through the water and he bends into an S shape, fertilises the eggs and then sinks back down through the water column. Oh, and he, like his seahorse relatives, then assumes most of the parenting duties. Which all sounds a lot less fun than the mechanics of human procreation but possibly a lot less painful than those of iguana procreation.

Fortunately, lunch finally provided a successful full stop to Brian's thoughts on impregnation techniques and their required apparatus, and instead he considered how well he was being fed – and how poor Shelly was in the arena of submarine spatial awareness. This was not, of course, a critique of her ability to be spatially aware of thumping great submarines, which Brian suspected was no worse and no better than the rest of the group. But it was an objective assessment of her ability, while snorkelling with the rest of this group, not to barge into them with increasing regularity. And avoiding them was really easy. All one had to do, while swimming along gently, was to look around at the fish and other marine life, and also to look around at one's fellow snorkelers to establish where they were. That way, one avoided them. But not so Shelly. She seemed to find it impossible not to crash into them from behind or to barge into them amidships. And then not even to offer any sort of apology, but instead just to carry on as though no collision had occurred, seemingly intent only on singling out her next crash-for-splash victim. Well, it wasn't the worst thing in the world, but it was rather irritating – and Brian doubted she'd ever make it as a lady pipefish. He did, however, think she'd make it ashore. Because, over lunch, the *Beluga* had been sailing up the east coast of Santiago, and it was now anchored off a place called Sullivan Bay. And on the mainland behind Sullivan Bay was an apparently unmissable sight that none of the Nature-seekers and neither of the Americans would possibly want to miss. Even though it was inanimate and non-procreative…

Others were keen not to miss it as well. There were three other boats anchored here – between the beach of Sullivan Bay and a truly dramatic-looking islet called Bartolomé – and they all, no doubt, had aboard them, people who were keen to get ashore. Accordingly, Darwin soon had his team members installed into the *Beluga*'s two pangas, and the pangas made for the shore – and for the promised inanimate (ground-level) spectacle.

Within minutes, the whole team was there – and standing on the spectacle. Because what they had all come to see was a large black lava flow, created by a volcanic eruption in 1889, and one that looked to all intents and purposes as though it had been created only yesterday – and by a team of a thousand talented artists. It was, after all, not just black and shiny but it was also presented in a mosaic of swirly, ridged or 'ropey' formations that were truly amazing. The official name for this sort of 'ropey' lava is *pahoehoe,* a Hawaiian term derived from the Hawaiian for 'paddle' (probably because of the swirly shapes and not because it was very good for making paddles with). Anyway, it was well worth the trip to shore, and it represented for Brian and, he suspected, for the rest of the group, the most impressive display of lava that they had ever seen – or had ever walked on.

It even had a few extra features. To start with, there were a number of deep and potentially dangerous crevices within the lava, ready and waiting to catch the unwary. Then there were a couple of 'moulds', formed, Darwin told them, from when the lava flow had overwhelmed what were apparently some examples of a shrub called *Maytenus octogona* – and which, thereafter, thought Brian, had been reduced to what might be called some examples of *This-Maytenus-is-a-complete-gonna.* And then there were a few specimens of something called *Brachycereus nesioticus*, or, more simply, lava cactus, a pioneer plant that is able to establish itself on barren lava flows – and to cause Brian to have yet another puerile thought, this one not about any more 'gonna' nonsense, but about… procreative equipment again. And this was because of their appearance – which is of a cluster of upright spiky phalluses that could possibly turn the head of even the most frigid of iguanas. Incidentally, Brian made the mistake of relaying this last thought to Sandra, whose reaction was to check whether her husband had been protecting his head against the sun and then to suggest to him that he should waste no time at all in getting his head under water.

This last piece of advice wasn't, of course, as vituperative as it might sound, and merely recognised that the Nature-seekers and their American companions were back on the beach and, as promised, there would now be an opportunity for some off-the-beach snorkelling. Brian therefore took Sandra's advice, and his head was soon under water, along with quite a few other heads (off those other boats), and this abundance of heads didn't make for the best snorkelling possible. Nevertheless, he did clock a few more fish, and when he returned to the beach, he was treated to the sight of the forty-something Darwin once again performing his favourite party piece: his amazing standing backflip – which, just a couple of hours later, would almost be his undoing...

This was when the group had just sat down to their dinner back on the *Beluga*, whereupon the door leading out of the dining room slid open and Darwin appeared – looking anything but his normal 'Darwin cool'. In fact, he looked incredibly pale – and, as became apparent, he had every reason to. This was because, as well as doing backflips on the beach, Darwin also did them off the very top of the *Beluga* and into the sea – by first climbing onto the awning that covered the boat's top deck. Indeed, he had performed one of these gymnastic impossibilities only minutes before his appearance – not to impress anybody, as no one was around, but just as the quickest way to secure a much needed refreshing swim. Unfortunately, as he explained to the diners in a slightly shaky voice, on this occasion he had secured not a refreshing swim but instead a sudden, very intimate encounter with a shark. In fact, he had nearly landed on it. And this wasn't a harmless reef shark or even a fairly harmless hammerhead shark, but a 'big shark'. Darwin couldn't be more specific than this as he had spent very little time studying it, but just the shortest time he could getting himself away from it and out of the water – and then checking that he still had a full set of limbs. Later on, he would volunteer that it could have been a great white or an oceanic whitetip, neither of which species is renowned for its affection for man. But right now, all he could confirm was that it was very large – and that it was the first such shark he had ever encountered at the end of his backflip-into-the-water routine. Oh, and that he had already decided that on this particular evening he would not be bothering with another swim.

Well, this rather unexpected incident was going to be a hard act to follow. But Brian thought he would give it a try, by, over dinner, offering his table companions a little of his home-grown wisdom – and despite Sandra's vain attempts to distract him. And she did want to distract him, because he had embarked on that aspect of his home-grown wisdom that concerned 'cultural appropriation'. Now, this is supposedly all about people finding offence in other people 'appropriating' elements of their own culture, especially if those doing the 'appropriating' are members of what had once been a dominant culture and the elements 'appropriated' are those of a culture that has been dominated in the past. All this Brian explained to his table companions in some detail, and then he went on to describe a couple of examples of this egregious behaviour, choosing the incendiary act of English university students wearing Mexican sombreros handed out as a promotion for an English Mexican restaurant and the thoughtless adoption of yoga by a Canadian exponent of this discipline in order to improve the fitness of a bunch of disabled students at a Canadian university.

He then went on to admit that it might, indeed, be offensive to some people if the elements of their culture that were appropriated were dealt with disrespectfully or disparagingly – but that he not been able to find any real examples of such behaviour. Furthermore, all the examples he had been able to find pointed not to a genuine theft of cultural identity or to the piracy of intellectual property rights – but instead to a load of precious PC types getting their knickers in a twist. And what's more, he suggested, wasn't 'cultural imposition' a great deal worse than even the idea of cultural appropriation, when the imposition was made by one set of people on another (indigenous) set of people who wanted nothing at all to do with the culture that was being imposed?

Having received a few tentative nods of heads from around the table, Brian then pressed on to his principal point – which was how to put a stop to all this nonsense at a stroke. And this was that he and all his countrymen (and countrywomen) should start to kick up a bloody great fuss about the cultural appropriation of their very own language. Hell, the English language is ours. And it is at the core of our identity. So how can it be right that half the world has pinched it for their own use – without even a thank you let alone any sort of royalty arrangement? Enough is enough, claimed Brian, and there should now be a team of lawyers put to work, to bring a case through the international courts requiring 'foreigners' either to desist from using our language without our permission – or to pay handsomely for the privilege. The result would be one of two things. Either we would become the richest country on the planet – without a great deal of effort – or, more likely, the whole concept of cultural appropriation would be revealed for what it is: another example of offence being taken against stuff that was never designed to cause offence, by people who should basically just grow up and sort themselves out – and go out and buy themselves a sombrero.

Well, Brian's fellow table guests weren't nodding their heads anymore, but nobody actually challenged his proposals, and before they could Sandra interjected by observing that it was very sad that black music of the sixties and seventies in the form of soul music had degenerated into its present-day manifestation as 'rap', and wouldn't it be great if, instead of all this tuneless stuff, another Marvin Gaye or another Smokey Robinson came along? Bingo! Cultural appropriation was forgotten, and the meal ended with a series of contributions from around the table concerning the merits of different soul artistes and the part some of them had played in the contributors' 'romantic awakenings' nearly half a century before. Then it was time for a listing session, after which came cabin

M/Y Beluga – looking very pretty

M/Y Beluga – looking inside

A land iguana in a hurry

A blue-footed booby – caught blue footed

'I'm feeling a bit off colour.'

The fishmonger's not so little helpers

A dubious giant tortoise

A real giant tortoise

Really ropey lava

Blimey!

Panga time

Returning 'home' time

Sea lions seat lying

A greater crater

Marine iguana central

Getting ahead, lizard style

time for all – and lecture time for two. And tonight's lecture would be on the subject of Guyana, if, that is, Sandra would allow it…

His wife's reluctance to be Brian's captive audience – yet again – made itself known as soon as he announced that it was Guyana's turn. And it made itself known in the form of the following declaration. 'Brian,' she said, 'we have both been to Guyana and we both know quite a lot about it. So how can there possibly be anything else worth knowing about it that merits your taking up more of my time?'

Brian was taken aback, but soon regrouped – behind the shelter of an affronted and slightly hurt expression.

'Well,' he replied, 'if you think you know absolutely everything about a whole nation state just because you've been there…'

'Oh, get on with it,' interrupted Sandra. 'I should have known better…'

And he did get on with it, kicking off with a few 'national facts'.

'OK. Guyana is the only English-speaking country in South America. It has a population of just 750,000, 90% of whom live on the coast. It has one of the largest unspoilt rainforests in South America, covering more than 80% of its land area…'

'… and it plays international cricket as part of the West Indies cricket team,' finished Sandra. 'Oh, and St George's Anglican Cathedral in its capital, Georgetown, is one of the tallest wooden structures in the world and the second tallest wooden house of worship in the world after the Todaiji Temple in Japan.'

'How do you remember that?' squeaked Brian.

'I told you. We both know more or less everything there is to know about Guyana, only my memory is better than yours when it comes to details like the name of a temple in Japan. So why, Brian, are you bothering?'

Well, the count was coming up to nine, but Brian managed to get to his feet just in time, and countered Sandra's powerful blows with a punch of his own.

'I bet you don't know everything about the El Dorado Rum Distillery…'

'You mean that distillery we passed on the way into Georgetown?'

'Yes.'

'Well, what is there to know? It distils rum. End of story.'

'Ah, not quite. Because you see, it still operates… stills that were first used in the eighteenth and nineteenth centuries. And what's more, it has what's called a wooden Coffey still – named after its inventor, an Irish guy by the name of Aeneas Coffey – which is similar if not identical to the original Coffey still, and is the last fully working example of its kind in the world!'

Sandra gave Brian one of her most withering looks, and then made the following observation. 'Brian,' she said, 'you know something? I don't really care. And I don't even really like rum. So why did you not take heed of what I said to start with? As lovely as Guyana might be, it does have a limit to its "facts of interest" – and we both seem to have a fairly good knowledge of them all. And I mean, if you're having to scrape the bottom of a rum barrel in an attempt to find any more, then I think that only goes to prove my point. And in conclusion, I think you should now say not another word on the subject of Guyana and give us both a literal and much needed rest. End of message.'

Well, Brian had little choice but to accept this advice to retire, and the evening was therefore concluded forthwith. But not before Brian, who still had in mind that lecture on Chinese Hat, had the very last word.

'Sandra,' he said, 'do you realise Guyana sort of rhymes with iguana?'

If she did, she didn't confirm it, and Brian wasn't unduly surprised...

8.

The Earth bulges at the equator. That is to say that its diameter at this girdle around the planet is some twenty-seven miles greater than it is at the poles. Furthermore, the equator is 24,901 miles long. But despite this sizable hump and the equator's enormous dimensions, Brian failed to notice it – completely. As José, the captain, took the *Beluga* north-east from Santiago to the Nature-seekers' next destination – and across the Earth's equator – Brian simply slept like a baby and was entirely unaware of its existence. So too, one might imagine, were all those on board other than José himself. Only he would have known it was there, and then only because he had a GPS readout to tell him. At sea, not only is there no sensation of crossing a line, but neither is there any evidence of this line – in the form of a post, say. And no, Brian's washbasin was not emptying at the time and, even had he been there rather than asleep, there would have been no direction of swirl to observe. Furthermore, it has to be admitted that even if there had been water disappearing down the plughole, this supposed manifestation of the *Coriolis effect* would almost certainly have been overwhelmed by many other factors, including the obvious motion of the boat, and would have provided no real evidence of when the southern hemisphere was being abandoned in favour of the northern hemisphere. So all in all, sleeping through the equatorial transit was probably a good decision by all the Nature-seekers. And for Brian, it meant that when he woke up – to a new day and in a new location – he felt rested, unbothered by his missing the equator – and excited. In fact, very excited, because the *Beluga*'s new location was Genovesa!

Genovesa is a very small island, having a surface area of just five square miles. It lies in a remote situation to the north-east of the other Galápagos islands, and it was formed, as they all were, from volcanic activity. However, in Genovesa's case, the volcano responsible for its formation was a 'shield volcano', meaning that it was built up over time to form a volcanic cone with broad gentle slopes, so that when one side of its caldera eventually collapsed, its submerged crater became an enormous enclosed bay. Indeed, this *Bahia Darwin* is a full 2.5 kilometres wide, and gives the island the shape of a chunky horseshoe when observed from above. When observed from the deck of the *Beluga*, moored in the bay, this horseshoe shape can easily be appreciated, if, that is, one is not entirely distracted by the beauty on show. It really is a superb spectacle, and Brian, for one, soon decided that José had brought them all to another even more upmarket chamber of heaven.

Breakfast was consumed eagerly as, the previous evening, Darwin, as well as unintentionally networking with dangerous sharks, had made it clear to the Nature-seekers that Genovesa was a hotspot for birds. There were apparently lots of them around and there were some that would not have been observed at close range before. So everybody was keen to board the pangas as soon as possible and to head off to a small sandy beach at the northern, sheltered side of the bay, there to take in the promised delights.

Well, a wet landing later and they were all there – and there were even more delights than promised.

At the very edge of the beach were some unconcerned sea lions, and next to a large and tastefully placed rock towards the end of the beach were a couple of Galápagos fur seals. Now, to start with, the Galápagos fur seal, like the Galápagos sea lion, is confusingly not a true seal. It is technically a 'fur sea lion'. Furthermore, although it is smaller than the Galápagos sea lion, and it has a shorter snout and larger eyes... well, from the illustrations in the books on board the *Beluga*, it didn't look that different, at least as far as Brian was concerned. Accordingly, he had consigned it to the 'don't bother with' category along with Darwin's finches, and was working on the assumption that all the brown, flippered sausages he saw were sea lions, not least because, due to their habits, the fur seals are much less frequently seen by visitors – than are the sea lions.

Nevertheless, these fur seal chaps had been pointed out by Darwin, and Brian had to admit to himself that he could see that they were different – just. But on a dark night or after a few pops... well, he wasn't so sure. And underwater at speed... no way. Unless of course he saw them one hundred metres down, fishing for squid, which is apparently something they do that sea lions don't. But there again, if he was one hundred metres down, he would be in no condition to observe anything, and telling apart fur seals – which aren't really seals – from sea lions would not be at the top of his 'to do' list.

Believe it or not, all these thoughts went through Brian's head as he squinted in the direction of the Galápagos fur seals before they disappeared into the sea, which was when his attention was then caught by the first of the promised birds. These were some red-footed boobies, and they were flying close overhead. Brian already knew that they were the smallest of the three Galápagos boobies (i.e. smaller than the blue-footed and the Nazca boobies), but only now that he was on Genovesa did he realise that he would be visiting what was the largest red-footed 'boobery' in the world. Yes, these guys prefer the outer islands in the archipelago, close to deep oceanic water, which constitutes their preferred feeding grounds. Indeed this is why, although the most numerous of the three local boobies, they are not often seen. However, they can be seen – in great numbers – in their colonies, and their biggest colony/boobery, with up to 140,000 nesting pairs, was here on Genovesa. In fact, part of it was no more than twenty metres from where Brian was still standing – in some mangroves beyond the beach.

He was soon closer to these mangroves, with all the other Nature-seekers, and it was Española all over again: boobies and booby chicks just feet from where one stood, and all of them quite unconcerned at the presence of a load of perspiring humans. True, these guys had prehensile (red, webbed) feet, which enabled them to grip branches and to build their nests off the ground – within the mangroves – but it was still that same display of charming innocent indifference, which had already become one of the hallmarks of the Galápagos experience. Brian was enchanted yet again and, at the same time, doubly delighted. Delighted in the first place to learn that by laying only one egg, red-footed boobies, unlike their blue-footed and Nazca counterparts, do not indulge in either facultative or obligate siblicide. And delighted in the second place that both the parents and the chicks, sitting within the vegetation, made such easy subjects for his camera. Just like the great frigatebirds did in the colony next door...

The Nature-seeker group had now moved on no more than thirty metres, and the mangroves were no longer decorated with boobies but with what could be described as the boobies' neighbours from hell, those huge marauding pirate birds who, given half a chance, will steal what the poor old boobies have caught from the sea – and who can never be trusted to babysit. Although, there again, these whopping great birds are rather splendid, and the males, in their impressive 'zoot suits', are not only splendid but simply outrageous.

Remember, Brian had seen these birds at close quarters already – sitting on the *Beluga*. However those birds had been just resting. They hadn't been trying to 'impress the totty', which is exactly what a dozen or so of the males were doing on Genovesa, and within only yards of where the Nature-seekers had now gathered. It was a display that none of the Nature-seekers would ever forget.

You see, the frigatebird, as a 'courting aid', has an enormous posing pouch. This isn't, of course, anything like a *Homo sapiens*-type posing pouch. In fact it has nothing whatsoever to do with that tacky genitals container, which is sometimes worn by males of our species in the misguided belief that it will encourage the attention of women (which it almost invariably does not). No. Instead it is a pouch below the male frigatebird's beak, with which he poses in a quite often successful attempt to gain the attention of women – as in frigatebird females. And, when employed, it is very large and it is very red. Yes, when a male frigatebird's fancy turns to breeding, he first chooses a suitable nesting area and then slowly, over twenty minutes, he pumps air into his startlingly red throat pouch until it looks like a scarlet, marginally over-inflated, oven-ready turkey – or maybe just like a big, scarlet, oval-shaped balloon. But whatever it looks like, if a lady frigatebird flies in, he attempts to titillate her with it while, at the same time, indulging in a bit of head-shaking and a bit of 'shrill trilling' (possibly not the easiest thing to do if one has a big pouch of air beneath one's chin). Anyway, all this enthusiasm may not be unconnected with the fact that there will probably be other male birds vying for the female's attention by posing with their own inflated pouches, and only if he manages to out-pose them will he have any chance of winning his girl. In the frigatebird world, size (of pouch) does matter – along with colour, animation, high-pitched noise – but definitely not subtlety or reticence. Oh, and sheen is important as well. Magnificent frigatebirds have black plumage with a purplish sheen; great frigatebirds have black plumage with a greenish sheen. And in this particular colony, purple would have been a turn-off – as it was a *great* frigatebird colony.

It was quite a sight: a group of ardent males, all with inflated scarlet pouches, all head-shaking and trilling for all they were worth – and, in this case, for just one lady frigatebird who looked conclusively unimpressed. Indeed, it looked as though she was trying to decide whether Jilly Cooper should be best known for her writing or for that rather attractive gap in her front teeth. No way was she contemplating a bit of 'ow's yer father with some balloon-festooned suiter, no matter how inflated his balloon and no matter how much he shook his head or trilled his trill. And anyway, there was no privacy here. I mean, look at all those gawkers over there. Anyone would think they'd never seen a posing pouch before…

Ah yes, Brian was now imposing his own anthropomorphic thoughts on the proceedings, which must have meant that it was time to move on – after first bagging a whole load of remarkable photos of these remarkable birds. And he did move on, and in doing so he was able to study a beautiful Galápagos dove at close quarters, observe some charming little fish in a shallow lagoon, catch a glimpse of a stingray as it dashed about in another lagoon, and discover quite a few small marine iguanas, none of which had even a single evaginated hemipenis on display…

And then it was time to reboard the pangas. The Nature-seekers had used up their allotted time, and there were now more visitors arriving from another boat (and, compared to the Nature-seekers' own practised routine, making a complete balls-up of their wet landing). In fact, based on their dismal performance, Brian suspected that they probably wouldn't have known what an evaginated hemipenis was even if one hit them in the face. And then he thought he should abandon all thoughts of reproductive organs for the rest of the day and instead begin to anticipate the next expedition. Because the next expedition would be undertaken with the aid of a snorkel.

Yes, as soon as the Nature-seekers were back aboard the *Beluga*, eight of their number, including Brian, were back on the pangas and heading off for the mouth of the bay, where some more deep-sea snorkelling would be undertaken. This sounded like a great idea – right up until the pangas made their way to the crater wall at the western edge of that mouth and the sea became... well, rather restless. The pangas' engines were being put to the test, and so too were the pangas' occupants – by frequent showers of spray as the inflatables made it through the waves, and by the prospect of snorkelling in such obviously rough water.

However, their misgivings were entirely misplaced. Because as soon as they were in the water, the roughness of the sea became only a minor concern, and they had other things to distract them. For example, there were some new fish to observe, a few sea lions to enjoy, and quite some way down but directly below them, were a couple of hammerhead sharks!

Brian had seen these chaps before – on the telly. But he had never seen them in the flesh, so to speak, and he had certainly never found himself swimming with them before. Indeed, if anybody had told him that by snorkelling in the Galápagos, he would have found himself in this position, he would not have engaged in any snorkelling. Hell, these sharks were at least ten feet long, and Brian knew that by having their eyes on the extremities of their hammer-shaped heads, they could see above and below them at all times. Which meant that as they swam below him they could see he was there. Furthermore, they are not vegetarians and they do eat things like other sharks, and it is not unknown for them to attack humans, especially if there is blood in the water. Nevertheless, Brian immediately realised that, like his fellow snorkelers, he was not in the least bit afraid but just thrilled beyond belief. This was because he was privileged enough to be sharing for just a little while the not too intimate company of these magnificent creatures, and he also knew that negotiating the M25 in the rush hour was a lot more dangerous than swimming with even a whole shoal of hammerhead sharks.

Yes, hammerhead sharks are only *potentially* dangerous to humans, and far, far less dangerous than we are to them. These particular hammerheads off Genovesa were a couple of 'scalloped hammerheads' (*Sphyrna lewini*), and this species (along with most other hammerhead sharks) is one of the most commonly caught sharks for 'finning'. And 'finning' is the rather innocuous term for catching sharks, cutting their fin off, and then throwing them back into the sea to die a miserable death. This revolting practice (as sanctioned by the president of Ecuador, remember) is all in aid of providing multitudes of Chinese diners with a rare delicacy, and a delicacy that will soon become much rarer still. Populations of scalloped hammerheads in parts of the Atlantic Ocean have already reduced by 95% in the past fifty years, and it won't take too many more dishes of shark-fin soup to see these wonderful creatures killed off completely. Yes, all for the sake of a load of vulgar, ill-mannered, noisy diners in that black hole we call China, we will soon have brought about the extinction of a marine work of art. Better, thought Brian, that it was the load of diners who were exterminated, and preferably by their being introduced to their *plat du jour* while their *plat du jour* was still alive. That is to say, by being thrown into a shoal of sharks who are still swimming in the sea and who have already had an appetiser in the form of a bucketful of blood. And yes, he really did believe that.

For now though, he was just able to relish his experience, and to decide that swimming with sharks wasn't anything like as scary as he'd thought. Well, at least it wasn't just as long as one wasn't an aficionado of shark-fin soup and one also eschewed the possession of ivory trinkets and the use of tiger parts. And amen to that.

Needless to say, lunch was devoured with relish, and it included only potato soup. After which, it was time for the third expedition of the day, this time to the mouth of the bay on the east – and to 'Prince Philip's Steps'. These 'steps' were named after our very own Prince Philip, after he visited this outpost of the Galápagos archipelago on the *RY Britannia* back in 1965, and the first thing Brian noticed about them was that they weren't really steps at all. They were more akin to a rising jumble of flattish rocks, and had been given that title of Prince Philip's *Steps*, only because somebody had put in place a rather inadequate handrail. He then thought that if Prince Philip ever returned here, this well-known visitor site might thereafter have to be renamed Prince Philip's *Stannah Stairlift*. Hell, it proved a bit of a struggle for even the young, sprightly Brian...

Nevertheless, he made it in the end and he then found himself with his fellow Nature-seekers on a trail that took him past more nesting Nazca boobies and more perching red-footed boobies and towards the outer edge of the caldera crater, above which were hundreds of birds. Some of these were boobies, some were storm petrels (of which more later) and some were frigatebirds, doing what frigatebirds are renowned for. Yes, at last Brian and his friends were able to observe their airborne piracy in action. Because here were more than a few frigatebirds using their formidable beaks to grab boobies by their tail and then dangle them until they regurgitated their food, after which, with a remarkable ability to manoeuver at speed, they would catch the food and make off with it. Brian felt very sorry for the dispossessed boobies, but he could not help feeling a deep admiration for the skill of the 'brigands'. They really were accomplished and spectacular raiders.

They also had no cause to descend Prince Philip's Steps, an operation for the Nature-seekers that was fraught with more danger than their ascending them. However, ultimately all made it down without mishap, and all were soon back on board the *Beluga* and, if they were anything like Brian and Sandra, they were savouring the delights of a cool shower after what had been an exceptionally hot hike. They may even, like Brian and Sandra, have been experiencing some challenging motion in the shower, because within minutes of their returning to the boat, José had it under power and was taking it at speed away from Genovesa and back to Santa Cruz. This course of action had been adopted to enable him to moor off the north coast of Santa Cruz before nightfall, and so enable the Nature-seekers to enjoy a stationary and therefore hopefully restful night. Furthermore, because Santa Cruz lies to the south of Genovesa – in the southern hemisphere – the forthcoming voyage would take the *Beluga* over the equator again. Only this time it would still be light and all the Nature-seekers would probably still be awake!

They were. So that when there was just a quarter of an hour to go before the equator was crossed, they were all available for an assembly on the bridge, and for what turned into a delightful little party, hosted by the captain himself. Specially cooked bread was provided – along with some rather strange egg-fortified cocktails – and when the GPS latitude indicator inched down to 0.00.000 a little cheer went up on the bridge and a little more eggy cocktail went down a number of throats. But thankfully, at least in Brian's mind, King Neptune and his court failed to put in an appearance. And later on Brian was able to enjoy an egg-free alcoholic drink.

He was also able to enjoy another stupendous evening meal, despite this one having been prepared by Pedro while the *Beluga* was moving at (high) speed. No one could work out how he did it. Or at least no one on Brian and Sandra's table could. This evening they were sharing it with John and Thelma, Evan and Mandy – and Shane and Shelly. Which meant that after touching on the impossibility of preparing food on a rolling boat and discussing at length how it would be difficult to imagine spending a finer day in a finer wildlife environment, it fell to Brian to save the day – again. And in this instance, saving the day was all about his shielding his table companions from what could sometimes be the unsettling views of… well, Shane. Or maybe that should be his sometimes *discordant* views. But however one described them, Brian thought it his duty to either provide some possibly discordant views of his own, or better still, some suggestions that were designed to draw contributions from around the table and so enable the sharing of the shielding duties with his fellow Brits.

If it is not understood what is meant by this tactic, then it might just become clear when it is explained that Brian first of all proposed a couple of 'useful inventions' that had yet to be invented but that, when they were, would prove to be a boon to mankind. Number one was a device to let you know when 'Thought for the Day' on the *Today* programme had finished, so that you could turn your radio back on. Number two was a device to tell you how far through the week you'd got before you'd reached your weekly units allowance, but a device that would work only if your allowed alcoholic intake was 'achieved' in the last or the penultimate day of the week. As Brian went on to explain, being informed that you had utilised all your allowed units at any point in the first five days of the week could be quite alarming and much more injurious to your health than over-imbibing. Then, having provided these two examples (and having educated Shane and Shelly as to the nature of 'Thought for the Day' and the *Today* programme), he then invited his fellow diners to suggest 'useful inventions' of their own.

Initially, they were reluctant to do this. But, with a little more encouragement, Thelma suggested that the world would be a much better place if somebody invented a discrete hand-held device that could disable both the music in shops and the music in pubs. This suggestion was met with almost riotous approval by the Brits at the table and by a confused silence on the part of Shane and Shelly. It was then followed by a suggestion by Mandy that there was also scope for a similar machine that could eliminate the infuriating background music that one currently had to endure on more than 90% of all televisual offerings. This suggestion elicited identical approval and confused responses as had the one before.

Then it was Evan's turn, and what he suggested was that somebody should invent a device that would disable the coverage of any aspect of the election of an American president until just one week before the election itself. This met with the universal approval of the table, including that of Shelly and Shane. In fact, it even encouraged Shane to propose a new invention himself, this one a programmable robotic barber that would provide a reliable and consistent haircut to all its clients every time it was employed. Brian was really impressed with that one, and he said so. He was equally taken by John's suggestion of a device to remove calories from pork pies and Evan's idea for self-cleaning gutters. However, he was only lukewarm about Shelly's idea for a Lazy Susan turntable to fit an oblong table, and he thought Sandra's idea for a gadget that would allow people to live-pause their lives was just totally silly, albeit highly attractive. In fact, even more attractive if it had a rewind capacity as well...

Anyway, Brian's distraction efforts had done their job, even if the inventions proposed had possibly revealed an interest, on the part of those at the table, in the more superficial aspects of life at the expense of the serious and the important. Nobody, for example, had proposed a gadget to solve overpopulation and nobody had put forward the idea of a device to prevent shark fins ending up in soup. However, such is the nature of over-dinner games, and at least, for once, Shane had joined in rather than piled in with his views. And that wasn't a bad thing. In fact, it was only a pity that after the post-dinner listing session, when Brian and Sandra were back in their cabin, Brian hadn't learnt a lesson from Shane but instead piled in himself – with his next instalment of his treatise on the countries of South America. Tonight it would be Uruguay's turn, and in the absence of a device to switch off annoying husbands, Sandra would be obliged to endure it.

It kicked off with a question.

'Sandra,' asked Brian, who was sitting up in bed, 'do you know we were instrumental in the creation of Uruguay?'

Sandra, who was also in bed but lying down, looked fleetingly nonplussed but responded quite promptly. 'I don't recall doing that at all,' she said, 'but if that's what you say...'

'I mean Britain,' growled Brian, 'not us. As you damn well know...'

'Well no, I didn't know actually. I had no idea Britain was...'

'Don't be silly,' interrupted Brian. 'You're just being perverse.'

'Well, better than being perversely persistent...'

Brian huffed and then he restarted his address as if the exchange with Sandra hadn't ever happened.

'Yes. Well, Uruguay was created in 1828 through the Treaty of Montevideo, and this was a product of British mediation that led to Brazil and Argentina recognising Uruguay as an independent state...'

'Very magnanimous of us...'

'... and in this way we managed to contain both Brazil and Argentina as well as consolidating our commercial interests in the region...'

'Ah.'

'Yes. Ah. However, it all worked out very well. Not too many people know this, but Uruguay, with a population of just 3.3 million, crammed into the second smallest country on the continent – after Suriname – is often regarded as 'the Switzerland of South America'. I mean, it's ranked first in South America for democracy, for peace, for lack of corruption and for press freedom. On top of that, it is prosperous; it has a thriving middle class and it can claim to be one of the most liberal countries in the whole world. It has legalised the production, sale and consumption of cannabis; it has made same-sex marriages and abortion legal, and overall it is demonstrably one of the most socially developed countries in Latin America, scoring much better than many others on stuff like tolerance, personal rights and "inclusion" issues.'

'Why?' interjected Sandra.

'Well, assuming it's just a coincidence that nearly 90% of the population is predominantly of European stock...'

'Brian!'

'... it may be something to do with what is said to be the country's healthy distrust of... well, let's call them charismatic or messianic leaders. You know, the sort we've seen in recent years in Venezuela, Bolivia and Ecuador – and in Argentina for what seems like forever. They don't do epic politics, apparently, just boring democracy – and it seems to work. I mean, on top of all the stuff I've already mentioned, they are a magnet for foreign investment and they are even self-sufficient in terms of renewable energy.'

'I'm convinced,' announced Sandra. 'They really do major in the boring.'

'I didn't mean...'

'I know what you meant,' interrupted Sandra. 'But isn't there anything rather more interesting about Uruguay than its laudable approach to press freedom?'

Brian had to think for a minute, and then his eyes lit up and he responded to his wife's pointed question.

'Well, actually, Uruguay has the longest national anthem in the world. It lasts five minutes when it's played in full. Only, because it's so long, normally just one verse and the chorus is sung...'

'Give me strength.'

'Oh, and of course Uruguay is the only country whose name in English has the same letter three times in its first five letters…'

Sandra didn't say a word. Brian wasn't entirely sure why, but he eventually decided that it was probably as a result of a number of things, not least the demands of the day and the excitement of crossing the equator. After all, he was beginning to feel a little poleaxed himself, so it was understandable that she had little to say and that she was now… well, apparently asleep.

One minute later, Brian was as well.

9.

It had taken Brian no time at all to acclimatise to a stationary boat, but falling to sleep immediately didn't mean that he would have a completely undisturbed night. That would have involved his dreams closing down along with the *Beluga*'s engines. Only they didn't. Instead they went into overdrive and provided Brian with a busy and 'fun-packed' night, so ensuring that, on this occasion, he was denied the sort of undisturbed sleep that he so much preferred. And worse still, the main feature in his seemingly endless cavalcade of dreams was one in which he managed to splice together not only sharks and the equator but also the Chinese.

He did this quite often. He took one event or one observation from the last twenty-four hours, and then he braided this with another recent event and maybe with one or two more of his recent thoughts, and he ended up with a sometimes quite elaborate dream that was both preposterous and entirely credible. Or at least entirely credible in that special world we create in our sleep, a world that is never bound by anything as mundane as reason, logic, sanity or sense. Well, in this particular instance, he took 'the equator', then he took 'finning' and finally he added the Chinese, and from these three elements he concocted not so much a dream but more a nightmare, a nightmare of the worst kind imaginable.

Essentially, it involved the current Chinese administration discovering a Ming Dynasty document that, in the administration's eyes at least, gave them sovereignty over the whole of the equator where it ran through international waters. This enabled them to lay claim to it in the same way that they have already laid claim to the Spratly Islands in the face of international opinion and international law. However, they had in mind using their new property not to build airstrips and military bases (as even in the mad world of dreams, that would be a bit of a stretch) but instead to use it to introduce some much needed efficiency into the mutilation of sharks. Yes, forget the artisan approach to collecting shark fins for their essential culinary requirements, and replace its inefficient, ad-hoc methods with some large-scale, systematic techniques that would ensure that Chinese soup bowls were full to the brim of shark-fin soup right up until every last shark had been killed.

What they did was set up a base on Chinese Hat – with the full agreement of the president of Ecuador – and from here they established a huge fleet of giant trawlers. These craft were fitted with giant shark-impervious nets, and the plan was that they would steam backwards and forwards along the equator in order to catch every last shark in the world and then cut off its fin. And nobody else would be let near their circular killing ground. This equator-defined abattoir was, after all, their own sovereign territory and anyway, nobody else in the world had such disgusting, shark-exterminating eating habits and therefore nobody thought it worth risking a confrontation by introducing their own trawlers into the bloodbath.

It all made for a very vivid dream/nightmare, and Brian even remembered what this exercise in accelerating the extinction of sharks was called. It was called 'The Great Trawl of China'. And in Brian's dream, there were so many trawlers engaged in catching every last shark, that the whole enterprise was visible from space. Although, there again, it did all begin to get a little hazy when the trawlers started to net not just sharks but also elephants, rhinos, tigers and even pangolins. But such is the world of dreams. And such is the world we are now obliged to share with that modern-day, despicable, reprehensible and unremittingly brutal China...

Well, as might be imagined, Brian, when awoken at five-thirty, was not entirely rested. But tough. As Sandra reminded him immediately, the day was due to start with a panga ride before breakfast – starting at six o'clock – and he therefore needed to ignore any morning fatigue and get his skates on. He also, she suggested, should get some DEET on. Darwin, in briefing them about their early morning panga excursion, had gone to quite some lengths to explain how Black Turtle Cove, a network of mangrove-fringed lagoons on the north coast of Santa Cruz, was a favourite hunting ground for mosquitoes. Even if one just sat in a panga, and didn't even set foot on land (which one couldn't do anyway), one was quite likely to get bitten. And probably not just once.

So, suitably invigorated with an almost cold shower and suitably smeared with repellent, Brian boarded one of the pangas with Sandra, and this and the other panga began to make their way to mozzieland and what promised to be an interesting start to the day.

He was not disappointed. The interest kicked in within just a couple of minutes after leaving the boat, when it became apparent to all those on board the diminutive pangas, that Gilbert and Jonathon, their drivers, were going to have to negotiate what looked like some serious breakers to get to their destination. Brian didn't really understand how these things worked, but between a moderately choppy sea and the significantly calmer waters of Black Turtle Cove, there was a line of very active water. And that is very active as in extremely active and on a scale that dwarfed the ridiculously small dimensions of the inflatables. How the panga drivers were going to cope, Brian had no idea. But that they would cope, he was sure. Just as he was sure that if the pangas did overturn, it wouldn't necessarily be curtains for all. With their lifejackets on, one or two of the Nature-seekers were bound to make it. Even if they missed out on the cove.

Well, as it transpired, both panga drivers were able to read the turbulent water in a way that Brian could read... well, a shopping list prepared by Sandra. And just as he invariably came home from Waitrose with all that was required – when Sandra was otherwise employed – so Gilbert and Jonathon were able to pilot their craft safely through the maelstrom – when the maelstrom allowed. That is to say, by timing their approach superbly, they were able to make a dash through the boundary between choppy and calm without even splashing any of those on board. Brian was very relieved indeed and now just concerned about those mosquitoes.

Initially, none materialised, so he made do with becoming concerned about the seating in the panga. These inflatables are the standard oval shape, and their sterns are occupied by an outboard motor and a panga driver, allowing the eight Nature-seekers on each vessel – with the addition of Darwin on one – to occupy their two sides. What this means is that on each side of each panga, four lifejacket-encumbered passengers sit on its inflated edge, facing… four other lifejacket-encumbered passengers. This does not make for an ideal arrangement for wildlife watching, especially when most of the wildlife to be watched is beneath the surface of the water. This concern on Brian's part was soon reinforced when the first of this morning's turtles was observed. Or should that be when the first of this morning's turtles was spotted by Darwin (who was standing up in his panga) and then comprehensively not observed by any of the Nature-seekers? This was because their view was obscured by a facing Nature-seeker or, in turning around and trying to look over their shoulder, they either looked in the wrong direction or became distracted by the need to stop themselves from falling overboard.

Clearly, in this predicament, two things were needed. The first was the need for Brian not to be so negative about what was no more than an inevitable aspect of undersea wildlife observation from a panga. And the second was the need for some enhanced accuracy in the calling regime, allied to some nifty but careful upper-body twisting in order to catch sight of whatever had been called before it had swum out of sight.

Result! Within only a few minutes, Brian and most of his companions had managed to observe a couple of Galápagos green turtles as they had swum towards and then under the panga – and slowly enough to allow all those on board who had adopted the necessary twisting technique to enjoy a really good view. And nobody had fallen in the water.

Brian considered the consequences of such a fall, principally because he wasn't confident that he could avoid such a fall indefinitely. (His balance hadn't ever been perfect, and he was certainly not a natural when it came to twisting one's body on a not very stable rubber seat.) He decided that these consequences might include getting wet and getting away quite successfully from any mosquito threat – at least while one was submerged – but that there would be no real danger involved. The water in the lagoons of the cove was as calm as the proverbial millpond and it was no more than four feet deep. Furthermore, those turtles in the water were hardly a threat. They *were* big, but Brian knew they were almost entirely herbivorous and would react to a body falling into the water just as they had reacted to the Nature-seekers' bodies as they'd snorkelled. They would ignore it. That said, Brian had heard it reported that male green turtles can get so randy during the breeding period that they will try to mount anything, even a middle-aged Brit they might encounter in the water. At anything up to

1.3 metres long and weighing up to 150 kilograms, that could be a bit of a problem. Although, there again, not a very probable problem, and about as likely to happen as being propositioned by a ray…

Ah yes, there were rays here as well – beautiful 'leopard rays', or to give them their more usual name, 'spotted eagle rays'. Brian had never encountered these chaps before he'd come to the Galápagos, and not only had he now swum with them, but here he was being able to observe them in the shallows – very well and with only a modicum of twisting discomfort. They are, of course, quite fabulous. In shape, they are mostly just 'wings' with, to the rear of the wings, a long narrow tail armed with defensive spines. In size, they can grow up to two metres across, although the specimens here were no more than half this size. And in 'decoration'… well, the whole of their top side is black but dotted with white spots and their underside is white. As Brian would be the first to admit, this 'leopard livery', when added to the graceful 'flight' of these creatures as they move through the water, makes them one of the most beautiful sights in the whole of the natural world. And one worth some quite serious, heavy-duty-type twisting, and even the risk of a Brit overboard.

However, in the event, there were no nautical mishaps of any sort whatsoever, even on the way back to the *Beluga* through a now abated maelstrom. Nor were there any bites from mosquitoes! So all in all a very good start to the day, and one that would help sustain all the Nature-seekers as, after breakfast, they were set adrift from the *Beluga* and 'abandoned' to the delights of Santa Cruz.

Well, 'abandoned' might not be an entirely accurate

word to use here. Nor, for that matter, might be the word 'delights'. But in any event, the first thing to happen after the first meal of the day, was another panga ride for all the Nature-seekers, after which the *Beluga* set off without them for the south coast of Santa Cruz. It was all to do with reprovisioning, you see. The *Beluga* had been at sea for a week, which meant that a mountain of food had been consumed, along with rather a lot of what comes in bottles. And to re-equip Pedro's larder and to restock the bar, it was now necessary for the Nature-seekers' yacht to visit Puerto Ayora and pick up new supplies. However, given the limited attractions of Puerto Ayora, as already alluded to, it had been decided that while all this business was being attended to the Nature-seekers would be otherwise entertained, and this entertainment would take the form of a bus ride through Santa Cruz. This would take most of the day, as the bus would have to make its way from the very north of the island to its capital in the south, whilst at the same time taking in a number of 'points of interest'. But of course, before any of that could happen, the pangas had first to deliver their cargo of Nature-seekers to the shore, or more precisely to a landing stage that proved to be both surprisingly large and surprisingly busy.

Yes, during breakfast the *Beluga* had sailed just a little way east from Black Turtle Cove towards the channel that divides Baltra Island (of airport fame) from Santa Cruz to its south. This meant that the Nature-seekers' panga ride was only a short one – to where a small ferry service linking Baltra and Santa Cruz draws dozens of people who are either travelling to Baltra's airport or who have just arrived at the airport and are travelling away from it. Inevitably then, the ferry's landing stage/terminal on the Santa Cruz side of the channel was a bustling sort of place, albeit not a particularly interesting one. In fact, the only thing that Brian would be able to remember about it after the event was that it had a popular tuck shop but only a little in the way of any sense of organisation. Indeed, for quite a few minutes there appeared to be some doubt as to whether there would actually be a bus to carry the Nature-seekers south. But then it did appear: a workmanlike rather than 'executive'-style charabanc, and the Nature-seekers were soon all aboard it.

Brian immediately adopted his inquisitive mode, and first of all he applied it to the 'bus park'. As he suspected, it wasn't so much a regular bus park – or car park – but more an expanse of bare earth adorned with a few battered containers. 'Infrastructure' had yet to put in an appearance. It was much the same as the bus started off and joined the road leading south, a stretch of almost tarmacked highway, edged by one or two cars and quite a few lorries. These latter vehicles, Brian deduced, were here not because of the ferry but because of the business being conducted in the channel that the ferry crossed. And this business was the unloading of containers from sea-going ships onto the decks of a pair of tenders, and these tenders then taking their cargo to the shore. It seemed that there was no other way to get this sort of bulky stuff into the Galápagos, just as it seemed to Brian that sooner or later some of that currently absent 'infrastructure' would inevitably arrive. It would 'make sense' to build a proper deep-water port – maybe just along from the ferry terminal – after which it would 'make even more sense' to put in some handling and warehousing facilities along with a proper lorry park and maybe a proper bus park and car park too. Then, before you knew it, more development and more people would follow in the wake of this 'infrastructure', and this threatened archipelago would become threatened even more.

Now, it cannot be denied that Brian had an unsurpassed ability to interpret any given situation or any given circumstances in the most negative way imaginable. In fact, if, on this morning, the Desolate and Disconsolate Society had been seeking the gloomiest, most negative, most pessimistic person who happened to be within fifty kilometres of the equator – anywhere in the world – then Brian would have been their man. That said, he was probably right… Put street lighting in your village, and in ten years' time your village is twice the size. Put a mains sewer in, and it'll be three times the size. And so it is with 'essential infrastructure'. And that would still be true if Brian was a world champion optimist. It's just the way things are. Or at least that's the way things are in Brian's little world…

Never mind. The bus was now on the open road, and his inquisitive mode could now switch to 'road conditions' and 'scenery'. Well, his curiosity was soon satisfied. The road was straight and tarmacked here and there, and the scenery was… well, nondescript. It was just an expanse of scrub, stretching off into the distance. Which, of course, was good! It meant that agriculture hadn't reached the north of Santa Cruz – yet

– and probably most of that scrub was native vegetation, providing a home to native species. Crikey, Brian was almost on the point of being cheerful. And furthermore, Darwin, at the front of the bus, had just announced that they were now very close to their first 'point of interest', and this meant that some cheerfulness might really be secured – within minutes. After all, Brian had never before encountered a pair of giant sinkholes!

Now, sinkholes are those voids that every now and again open up in somebody's back garden or under a road. They can be caused by the collapse of old mine workings or, more often, by a variety of natural processes involving some sort of subterranean erosion. However, most of these sinkholes are quite modest in size and would have difficulty in swallowing much more than a family-sized car together with maybe a small herbaceous border and a rotary drier. The Los Gemelos sinkholes are not like this. They are in another league. In fact, they are in a super-league, with one of them measuring more than 150 metres across, the other more than one hundred metres across, and both of them being more than fifty metres deep. And they are this size because once upon a time they were empty underground magma chambers, and when their roofs collapsed – due to tectonic plate movement and/or erosion – these giant craters were the end result.

The Nature-seekers were now off the bus and observing the smaller of these two sinkholes. It was no more than a few yards from the road and its scale really was stupendous. Indeed, it was so large, thought Brian, that even taking account of the vegetation that carpeted its floor and its sides, it could have housed the whole of Jack Whitehall's ego. And that meant it was a bloody great big hole. That said, that's all it was: a bloody great big hole, and frankly it held a limited amount of interest for any of the Nature-seekers. Of more interest was the vegetation that surrounded the hole and in particular one endemic species for which this whole area was renowned. This species was *Scalesia penunculata* or 'Tree Scalesia', one of the fifteen *Scalesia* species endemic to the Galápagos, and the tallest of these species, growing to a height of fifteen metres or more. And what makes this plant especially interesting is that, despite its size, it is a member of the daisy family and, with a dome of branches above its unbranched trunk, it looks a little like a (giant) calabrese flower head. In fact, it is often referred to as the broccoli tree, albeit one will never find it served with peas and potatoes and the Sunday roast. Obviously.

All the Nature-seekers were able to inspect these remarkable plants as they followed a trail around the edge of the sinkhole and then more of them after they had crossed the road, and picked up the trail around the second sinkhole. Yes, the road builders of Santa Cruz had chosen to build the primary road on the island, and the only road that leads to the north, between two whopping great cavities, and cavities that might one day become just one even more whopping cavity – with the remains of a road at its bottom! Anyway, this second larger sinkhole, mused Brian, was so vast that it could probably have accommodated not only the egos of Tony Blair and Gordon Brown combined but also their collected mistakes and misjudgements. It was that humungous.

Full marks to Darwin then for spotting within its extensive cloak of vegetation, a rare woodpecker finch, one of those impossible-to-tell-apart finches, but one which could actually be distinguished from its cousin finches by its habit of acting as a woodpecker (there being no 'real' woodpeckers in the archipelago). Bonus points to Darwin as well for injecting a bit of genuine interest into what would otherwise have been... well, just a rather hot hike around two rather big holes.

These were Brian's thoughts anyway, and he didn't think he was being unduly churlish in his assessment. If these two holes, he thought, had been in Cheshire or Lancashire, say, then they would definitely have been a must-see for the whole family. They would have been given a name – like the 'Devil's Footprints' or maybe 'Old Nick's Nostrils' – and they would have spawned a visitor centre, an extensive car park, a clutch of reasonably priced cafés, a couple of pubs and a whole range of shops, selling everything from hole-themed T-shirts to hole-themed fudge and hole-themed furry toys – and of course they would have needed a whole army of Health and Safety 'experts' to prevent the entire population of Britain plunging to its death... But the fact remained that, just like these holes on Santa Cruz, there would be nothing inherently interesting in these British holes, no matter how big they might be. In fact, Santa Cruz's two big-uns were only interesting at all because of their surrounding flora and the possibility of sighting a rare example of the island's fauna, and... possibly the remote possibility of witnessing these two big-uns becoming one very big-un, and the road between them becoming just a cherished memory. There again, the prospect of waiting around for another tectonic plate movement was not that attractive. Better to do what the Nature-seekers were about to do, which was to quit the sinkholes and head off for their next 'point of interest' – which was an 'eco distillery'!

It took some time to get there and it involved their bus passing into the distinctly scruffy agricultural south of Santa Cruz, first observed by the Nature-seekers on their visit to the 'tortoise farm' just three days earlier. And when they got to the eco distillery Brian was obliged to revise what actually constituted 'scruffy'. Yes, this 'distillery' comprised a tatty open-sided shed, a slightly less tatty 'bandstand' sort of building, an ancient press, a small concrete lavatory block, and, beyond this lavatory block, a small galvanised tank.

The Nature-seekers disembarked the bus, and in due course, after he'd been woken up or had found his trousers, the chief distiller appeared, and then a couple of his distracted operatives joined him. One of them then fed lengths of sugar cane into the antediluvian press – while it was being turned by the other – to illustrate how the cane juice, essential for the distilling process, was produced. Following this the head honcho led the Nature-seekers past the lavatory block to show them where this juice was then taken. It was, of course, poured into that galvanised tank, and there it sat fermenting until it took on the appearance of what could have been a blend of brown Windsor soup and congealed cappuccino.

Brian was not impressed. He was even less impressed when the Nature-seekers were shown a further galvanised tank beyond the first which, with some piping, was meant to be the distillery's essential distillation plant, but which looked more like its essentially obsolete plant. Indeed Brian was beginning to suspect that this eco distillery had gone completely eco and had abandoned its distillation activities entirely, to minimise its impact on the environment to zero. But then two trays arrived, and on these trays were lots of small glasses and a pair of rather interesting bottles, and Brian was about to be proved wrong yet again.

One bottle contained neat aqua vitae; the other contained this same spirit but flavoured with anis. Both were delicious – at eleven o'clock in the morning. So too was the fortified cane juice and the spirit-fortified coffee served on the 'bandstand'. So that when it was time to leave this scruffiest of eco distilleries, Brian was convinced that all distillers are a boon to mankind and that late-morning snifters not only have the capacity to improve one's personal wellbeing but also the potential to promote world peace and to bring to an end all poverty and suffering around the globe. And he hadn't even drunk that much more than anybody else…

Lunch proved something of an anti-climax. It was on another tortoise-accessorised farm, although this one had no lava tunnels but just a large and busy restaurant. In Brian's mind, the food was OK, but only OK. And it was now also thunderingly hot. So he was very relieved indeed when it was announced that the bus would now be taking him and his fellow Nature-seekers back to the *Beluga*, or at least back to Puerto Ayora. There they would be offered some time to explore – or locate –

Puerto Ayora's subtle charms, but instead they would make a unanimous decision to be ferried back to their boat. It seemed that all of them had decided that they had already sampled quite enough of Santa Cruz and had no desire to add its badly groomed capital to its list of 'points of questionable interest'. No, all they wanted to do was what Brian wanted to do, which was to get back on board their floating haven, and in due course check its reprovisioning by visiting its bar.

Well, a due course later, and the checking had been completed, after which it became apparent that Pedro, in preparing the Nature-seekers' dinner, had attempted to utilise the entire reprovisioning of his larder. The meal was enormous. In fact, it was so large that at Brian and Sandra's table, it left hardly any room at all for any mealtime conversation. Horace did make a vain attempt to initiate some sort of discussion, and he did this by inviting all those around the table to consider all sorts of 'useless people'. And the useless people he had in mind were all those who inhabit the pages of glossy magazines, and fashion magazines and Sunday magazines in particular, and who can offer the world nothing other than a very good reason never to buy these magazines or even to open their pages. They included, of course, models, 'famous people', not so famous people, celebrity-tagged nonentities and a whole range of lobotomy jobs, the majority of whom have intellects even less substantial than their fashionably insubstantial frames. Well, what Horace had in mind was how to employ these people in something that was even marginally useful. However, all he established, with a small contribution from Delia, was a new name for them and a new collective noun for a whole group of them. Yes, for the eight Nature-seekers seated around the table, a gathering of these two-dimensional, good-for-nothing stick insects would henceforth be known as a 'vacuum of imbecilebrities'. But it would remain a mystery as to what use they could ever be put other than possibly their deployment as self-stacking sandbags to alleviate the impact of floods.

Incidentally, after the event, Brian would deny any responsibility for that sandbag suggestion. Just as he would deny snoozing through the evening's listings and only waking up properly when it was time to deliver his evening lecture. Yes, he was now back with Sandra in their room, and he had just announced that this evening it would be the turn of Colombia. Sandra responded to this announcement with a yawn, and without even waiting for the yawn to end, Brian was into his spiel.

'Mention Colombia,' he started, 'and most people think of drugs and if they think of anything else, then it's guerrillas. You know, that FARC lot, that band of bastards who've been terrorising the country for years.'

'Have you finished?' queried Sandra.

'Have I finished?!' screeched Brian. 'No, I have not. That was just my introduction.'

'Oh.'

'Right. Well, I see you seem to be a bit… errh, moody tonight. So I'll keep it short.'

'Good.'

'Yes. Well,' stumbled Brian, 'it just so happens that according to something called the "World's Happiness Index", Colombia is the happiest country in the world.

Furthermore, its national rollerskating team has won the World Roller Speed Skating Championship nine times in the past twelve years. They're a rollerskating powerhouse. And on a slightly different tack, shop mannequins in Colombia are made with enormous breasts – to reflect the country's preoccupation with surgically enhanced boobs...'

'Thank you,' interrupted Sandra. 'I appreciate your keeping it short...'

'But I haven't even...'

'No. But I have. Now go to sleep, Brian. And remember...'

'Remember what?'

'Remember to go to sleep. Now.'

And with that, the day was brought to an end, a day which had included turtles, rays, sinkholes, broccoli trees, two sorts of hooch, tortoises, lots of heat – and not enough of the *Beluga*. Yes, it had taken a day away from the boat and away from the sea to remind Brian just how much he was enjoying the nautical aspects of this expedition and how much better they were than most aspects of a populated Santa Cruz.

The good news was that tomorrow morning, the nautical would take over again, beginning with a visit to an island called Floreana. This is a small rugged island to the south of Santa Cruz, which, according to Darwin, had a number of attractions but no eco-hooch and definitely no imbecilebrities...

10.

*I*n Puerto Ayora, the *Beluga* had taken on not only victuals and booze but also a new captain. Clearly, a week of driving a boat around, mostly at night, and then having to sleep during the day in a cupboard-sized cabin had taken its toll, and José must have become desperate for a normal-sized bed in a normal-sized room – and a long rest. Anyway, in his place was a guy called Guillermo, and soon after setting off for Floreana, Brian had decided that Guillermo was a bit of a boy racer.

It had been the normal routine: let the passengers get to bed and, as soon as they had, start up the engine, weigh anchor and then set sail. However, for Guillermo that 'set sail' bit appeared to mean 'engage warp factor 9' – and then stay in warp factor 9 for the whole ruddy trip. It may, of course, have been just the state of the sea, but Brian thought not. And as he attempted to get to sleep in a boat that was constantly rolling from side to side more than it had ever rolled before, he was convinced that its excessive speed was a factor – albeit not necessarily… factor… 9. Obviously.

Well, he did get to sleep, and he stayed asleep for most of the night, save for those odd occasions when the sea and speed together attempted to throw him from his bed. At which points he would be bemused to see that Sandra, in her bed, was still emulating Rip Van Winkle and was quite clearly unaware of the boat's disruptive convulsions – before he then managed to fall back to sleep himself. Accordingly, despite the 'vitality' of the passage, Brian felt reasonably refreshed when he woke in the morning. And he certainly felt ready for Floreana.

Now, this island has been mentioned before – as the place that hosted the very first resident of the Galápagos archipelago, one Patrick Watkins, a marooned Irish sailor. It has also been mentioned that it then hosted the first official colony of prisoners and artisans and, in due course, it welcomed to its shores one Mr Charles Darwin of *On the Origin of Species* fame. However, what has not been mentioned previously is that Floreana lies at the southern extremity of the archipelago and that, whilst it is not very large, it does now house a small population of humans. Somehow, one hundred or so hardy individuals eke out a living in the island's one and only town, a place called Puerto Velasco Ibarra. And if these guys are ever in need of a day out, then they can always take the one and only road out of town up to Cerro Pajas, the top of the volcanic cone from which the island is formed. At 640 metres, it is understandably the island's highest point, and here, thought Brian, they must sometimes sit and contemplate what a very odd life they all live. Or maybe they just sit in Puerto Velasco Ibarra, and contemplate what might have happened fourteen billion years ago before the Big Bang. Who could tell? Brian certainly couldn't. No more than he could have predicted the subject of (the live) Darwin's first lecture as he and all the Nature-seekers arrived on a Floreana beach.

Yes. Ablutions and breakfast had all been dealt with, and the *Beluga*'s two pangas had delivered their cargo to a sandy beach near Punta Comorán (or Comorant Point) for a fairly straightforward wet landing. After which, Darwin was keen to apprise the Nature-seekers of some of the history of Floreana! This didn't include a reference to Patrick Watkins, but inevitably it included a reference to Charles Darwin, and to an event which happened sixteen years before Mr Darwin arrived, and which was rather less laudable than his purely scientific visitation. Because it seems that in 1819, a gentleman by the name of Thomas Chappel, who was the helmsman of a Nantucket whaling ship and a prize dickhead, set fire to the island as a prank. What was then Charles Island was a popular stopping-off point for whalers, who used it to collect fresh water and fresh supplies of plants and meat. And if they were prize dickheads they could set fire to the place. Better still, if it was the dry season, the fire would get out of control, and smoke would still be visible on the horizon even after a full day's sailing away from the island in search of a new crop of whales. So that when, many years later, a sailor who had been the cabin boy on Chappel's ship revisited the island, he found a 'black wasteland'. Vegetation had still to make a substantial comeback, and it is thought that certain of the species of both flora and fauna on the island never made a comeback at all. Which did make Brian think that in the very unlikely event that there is a hell, that Mr Chappel should now be inhabiting one of its more unpleasant neighbourhoods, having initially been assured that he will only ever be rehoused somewhere better when the whole of hell freezes over.

Well, the good news was that (most) things did eventually recover on Floreana, and it was now time for the Nature-seekers to observe this for themselves, and first of all by leaving the beach and then following a trail over an isthmus. Now, this isthmus formed a link between the landmass which was Floreana itself and the excrescence of Cormorant Point which was situated on its north coast. It also, incidentally, formed in Brian's mind a happy recollection of Terry Allen's wonderful 'X-Mas on the Isthmus', a song that includes any number of inspired lyrics, not least among them such gems as, 'Ah, there's something about X-Mas, That brings me to tears, Snowmen an' chestnuts, An' roastin' reindeers'.

However, that is to stray off the point. And the point is that the Nature-seekers, by taking the isthmus trail, had soon arrived at a lookout point that gave them a panoramic view of a large saltwater lagoon and a flock of flamingos. They were actually Caribbean flamingos – or *Phoenicopterus ruber,* a bird named after the remarkable phoenix, that mythical bird that consumed itself by fire only to rise again from the ashes. Well, no such incendiary displays apparent here, but just a group of 'living flames' feeding in the brackish water and possibly wondering whether there might be an easier way to feed than constantly bending down and straining tiny invertebrates from the water and the mud. Or maybe they were trying to remember how many of their kind lived on the whole of the Galápagos archipelago, to which the answer is fewer than 500 individuals. And the majority of these are on other islands. Floreana's complement may be as few as forty.

Darwin had provided this information, just as he was now providing a lead further along the trail that took the Nature-seekers to the other side of the isthmus and to another beach. This one was called White Sand Beach, for reasons which will not be explained, and it proved to be a highlight of the day. In the first place it was covered in turtle tracks, due to the fact that the sand dunes behind it are a popular nesting site for these creatures. And in the second place the surf was 'infested' with sharks. They were only modest-sized reef sharks, but they all appeared to have ingested an overdose of Ecstasy, and were all racing backwards and forwards through the shallow water as if their lives depended on it. Which, of course, they did. Because they were all chasing and catching fish. It certainly constituted an amazing display, and not surprisingly, Brian and all his fellow Nature-seekers soon became completely transfixed. And then it got better. There were turtles in the water as well and then some rays.

These were stingrays. They have the same flattened bodies as the spotted eagle rays, and the same long narrow tails. They can swim at quite a speed, but they spend much of their time hidden just under the sand, waiting for their prey. This can be a bit of a problem, because they have a very effective defensive sting at the base of their tail which, if inadvertently trodden on by a member of *Homo sapiens,* can inflict on that member a rather nasty wound. This fact was not unimportant, and this was because the Nature-seekers were to return to the beach on which they had first landed and from there they were to engage in some snorkelling, having first waded through some shallows that were known to be a hotspot for stingrays and hence for stingray stings.

Nobody bottled out. And nobody came to any grief. All that happened was that more fish and more turtles were encountered in the water, and certain of the snorkelers were so invigorated by their excursion that they willingly accepted the challenge of a snorkel around Corona del Diablo, or to give it its English name, the 'Devil's Crown'.

The Nature-seekers had returned to the *Beluga*, and it was now time to take the more foolhardy amongst them (including Brian) to what was an eroded volcano crater situated in the open ocean just to the north of Cormorant Point. It is very eroded. So that what can be observed is just a ring of jagged rocks poking out of the water, and as the foolhardy few approached it, a somewhat restless sea surrounding it. In fact, Darwin had let it be known that although this was reckoned to be one of the best snorkelling sites in the Galápagos – if not the best of all – it was ranked as 'moderate to difficult'. This was because of its open-sea position and the consequent strength of the currents that rushed through it and around it.

Well, maybe some of Brian's invigoration from his earlier snorkel was now wearing off, and with the size of the swell around the crown, there was every chance that it would wear off completely before he got in the water, with the result that he would feel like a first-rate plonker. There was only one thing to do. As soon as the panga had been parked and Darwin had given the go-ahead, Brian went over the side. Immediately he could appreciate the turbulence of the water, the depth and deep-blue colour of the water – and the presence beneath him of a not insubstantial hammerhead shark. For a few seconds at least, there was just Brian and this magnificent creature, and whilst for the creature those very few seconds might mean nothing, for Brian they would mean everything. They would constitute the single, most sharply defined, highest highpoint of this whole Galápagos adventure, and they might even go down as one of the most thrilling episodes of his entire life.

The shark swam off and by the time the other Nature-seekers were in the water it had gone. So Brian felt very privileged and a little concerned that the rest of this snorkel might prove to be something of an anti-climax. However, he need not have worried. The waters were full of turtles, rays and fish, and when the Nature-seekers' progress around the crown brought them to within the crater, there were more fish than ever. In fact, Brian became so captivated by the sights around him, which included a veritable carpet of fish, that he became distracted as well. Until such time, that is, as his forward progress through the water had completely lost its forward element. He was obviously swimming against a current that was easily equal to his own puny efforts and he was going nowhere, which is why everybody else was already climbing back on board the panga, something he would now do after he'd let the current take him to within its reach.

Pow! What an experience. And what an appetite generator. Brian felt he would have little trouble coping with Pedro's normal oversized offering. Indeed, much less trouble than Sandra would have in convincing him not to go on about hammerhead sharks for the whole of their lunch. After all, she reminded him, his table companions had just so much tolerance, and what's more, there were now other things to consider. Like, for example, what he would write on his postcard…

Yes, the next destination for the Nature-seekers would be Post Office Bay, a wet-landing site just down the coast from Cormorant Point, and famous for not much other than its… post box. This originated in the time of whalers and it is no more than a 'post barrel' on the top of a… 'post post'. In this, one is encouraged to leave a postcard (on which will be one's home address) – having first searched through all the postcards within the barrel in order to find any that have addresses located close to one's own. If one finds any of these, one is then bound to deliver them when one gets back to one's home country, and in the same way, the postcard one has left may be delivered by somebody else who then visits the barrel in the coming days, weeks or months. Oh, and it is customary to write a note or a greeting on the card as well as one's address.

Brian thought this all a bit silly. But rather than being churlish – again – he first composed a note and wrote this on his card. It read:

If you bring this postcard home
Pristine, torn or slightly creased
Then you'll earn a worthwhile drink
(If, by then, I'm not deceased)

Then, with Sandra and her card, he joined the other Nature-seekers for a short panga ride to the post office facility. Happily, the post barrel, which was just beyond the wet-landing beach, did not have, in attendance, the normal post office queue. Accordingly, the party of posters were soon able to sift through the contents of the barrel and locate a couple of cards that could be delivered back in Blighty and then leave their own cards for a similar process in the future.

Yes, Brian had been right. It was all a bit silly, but at the same time it was all very harmless. Even if the '200-year-old barrel' was only 200 years old in the same sense that Trigg's broom had been twenty years old. It and its post must have needed replacing every two or three years. Furthermore, the people who *posted* Brian and Sandra's postcards when they returned to England just two weeks later – rather than delivering them by hand – must have needed a clearer instruction as to how the whole process was supposed to work…

Talking of which, the truck on Floreana apparently wouldn't work at all. This was the one and only truck on the island that had been booked to take the Nature-seekers from Puerto Velasco Ibarra, which was just a little bit further along the coast, up to the heights of Cerro Pajas. This was the planned mid-afternoon excursion. However, word came through to the boat that the truck was currently unwell and wouldn't be mobile again until a spare part had been brought in from Santa Cruz or even from mainland Ecuador. And no way was it possible to walk to Cerro Pajas (at 640 metres).

That meant that the excursion was cancelled and it was

decided instead that Captain Guillermo would take the *Beluga* directly to their next day's destination, which was Puerto Villamil, the capital of the fourth inhabited island in the archipelago, otherwise known as Isabela Island. This would mean quite a long voyage west at Guillermo's normal super-fast speed. And this would mean an ocean transit where, in the interests of safety, one was advised to lie on one's bed. Standing up or walking around was something of a challenge and one that Brian thought he would eschew. Instead he would remain essentially horizontal on his berth – with his wife in her berth – and he would resort to some poetry. Well, in fact, following that encounter with the hammerhead shark, an encounter that had reminded him of his enormous contempt for all those bastards who cause the death of one hundred million sharks every year – and just for some fucking soup – he recalled some poetry that he himself had composed only a few years before. It was:

The shark is a creature of beauty.
He's as sleek and as lean as a cat.
And in water, as lithe as a leopard,
And in menace, as mean as a rat.

We kill him for kicks and for pleasure.
We kill him to 'harvest' his fin.
Which is why, when we meet him while swimming,
He'll be wearing a great, leering grin.

At last he has found his oppressor
In a place where he can't do him harm.

And the only decision he's faced with
Is to bite through a leg or an arm.

It can't be a pleasant sensation,
A deep, tearing wound to incur.
And to realise that after that mouthful,
You're not now the man that you were.

But really there's no need to worry,
Cos that mouthful will not be his last.
In a minute he's back for another,
And from there on it's downhill quite fast.

While you started with all your components
And with everything working quite well,
You're now just a soup in the ocean,
With bits washing round in the swell.

So when you next swim in the ocean,
Remember those sharks are there too,
And the soup of the day won't be shark's fin,
But it might be a soup made of you…

OK, so it was doggerel, not poetry. But who cares?
And who, other than those revolting fellows in the Far
East, could argue with its sentiments?

Brian was still mulling this over when the *Beluga*
began to slow down. After three and a half hours of all too
literal rock and roll, the movement of the boat betrayed
that its breakneck speed had been abandoned in favour
of a more sedate pace, and this might mean that it was

now nearing its destination. So Brian and Sandra decided to risk a walk in order to discover where they were, and the best place to walk to was the flying bridge. When they got there they discovered that Josh and Madeline had beaten them to it, and it was Josh who pointed out Puerto Villamil. It was off to the right, a mile or so along a rather featureless coastline, and it looked a modest sort of place. As the *Beluga* drew closer, its modest credentials were confirmed, although in common with the other two *puertos* visited in the Galápagos, it had moored about it a whole congregation of little boats. Soon the *Beluga* would be amongst them.

When it was, and on-board stability had been re-established, Brian and Sandra returned to their cabin to prepare for a relaxed evening of drinking, eating, talking and listing, and on this occasion some rather serious debate.

This far from flippant stuff started when, at the dining table, Brian overheard a remark Sandra was making to Mandy. It was to the effect that it was quite ironic that the word 'humanity' is the term one applies both to the quality of being humane, as in being compassionate, and to human beings collectively who, as a species, are generally far from compassionate and more often capable of being mean, selfish, intolerant and cruel. Well, with this trigger, and probably with mankind's treatment of sharks still reverberating in his mind, Brian took it upon himself to ask the seven others at the table what might be an appropriate measure of genuine compassionate humanity. And when he was sure that he had their perplexed attention, he sought to lessen their perplexity and to illustrate the nature of their allotted quest, by suggesting something that was one of the worst measures of true humanity, and this was 'piety'. This he argued had been proven to be associated with a lack of altruism and generosity and a tendency to be overly judgemental and non-empathetic. It was all something to do with what was termed 'moral licensing', which is the propensity to use something 'good', like being pious, to justify (often without being aware of it) something bad, like being really insensitive or being a complete and utter bastard. And he attempted to underline what he meant by drawing to the attention of his fellow diners the contemptible habits of all those religious zealots who currently infect our world and who regard being sickeningly pious as the very purpose of life.

This seemed to do the trick and Evan immediately made the observation that he'd always thought that the way we deal with people in their old age was appalling, and as a measure of humanity it sucked. He then went on to explain that he thought the desire to provide indefinite care to people who wanted nothing more than to sign off and disappear was more a measure of the self-indulgence of a pseudo-liberal society than it was a measure of humanity. Why, he asked, do we deny our fellow humans a painless and dignified death, when if it were a horse or a dog in their situation, it would be regarded as no more than a properly humane act to relieve them of their desperate and pointless suffering?

This contribution from Evan opened the floodgates, and first to gush through with her thoughts was Sally, and her own contribution to the debate concerned an emphasis of the dichotomy between humaneness as applied to other animals and humaneness/humanity applied to others of our kind. Because what she said was that it was clear that there was more humanity associated with administering a fast-acting drug to poor old Rover who had come to the end of his happy life than with a thousand aggressive interventions by doctors in the hope that a thousand 'remains of a human life' remained in their terrible condition for just a few miserable weeks more. There was a disconnect here, and if it did nothing else it illustrated how the desire to prolong life at all costs was, like piety, the worst possible measure of humanity.

This is when Horace joined the fray. He made the simple statement that maybe our treatment of other species in general was a much better measurement of our humanity than the way we treated our own kind. Possibly because our humanity towards our fellow man inevitably becomes clouded by stuff like ethics, culture, tradition and even guilt. Whereas, our humanity to all other animals is unadulterated by any such considerations and is therefore 'honest and pure'.

This is where Brian rejoined the debate he'd started, and what he did was to applaud Horace's contribution and then to 'widen' it. And he did this by suggesting that maybe the best measure of our humanity was how well we treated not just our pets but how we treated the entirety of life on Earth. Real humanity, he proposed, was treating every animal and indeed every plant in the same way as we would like to be treated ourselves. So, if we thought of ourselves as rhinos, we'd clearly prefer not to be killed for our horns. Just as if we thought of ourselves as the remnants of a population of endangered humming birds, we wouldn't want our last remaining habitat to be cleared – for the sake of yet another damaging plantation of coca. And whilst this all sounded maybe a little facile and maybe a little wishful-middle-class, it was true. There was, he suggested, that dichotomy between humanity and humanity's lack of humanity, because, as a species, we were not just stupid but selfish, and we were unable to understand that real humanity and real *compassion* mean being compassionate in our treatment of all life. Even that life we breed to consume and especially that life which, because of our numbers, now needs our assistance.

Well, it hadn't been an evening for a bundle of laughs, but there had been some stimulation on offer, and ultimately, around the table, a pretty well unanimous consensus. Yes, all eight diners had concluded that rather than using just our treatment of our own kind as a measure of our humanity, it would be far better – for us and for all life on Earth – if we calibrated our humanity by reference to the way we treated gorillas, tuna, otters, hornets – and pine trees and corals – and, of course, sharks…

Whether the measure should also include the treatment of a wife who wanted only to sleep had been left unresolved. Which was good news for Brian, because he was now back in his cabin with Sandra, and whilst she did look more than a little weary, he did have a presentation on Bolivia to deliver. And this he did by making the following announcement:

'Sandra. Bolivia is one of a number of landlocked states in the world that maintains a navy.'

Sandra looked at her husband, and in her expression there was no hint of humanity. Brian failed to notice this and carried on regardless – and on the theme of Bolivia's maritime ambitions.

'Yes, you see, following the War of the Pacific between 1879 and 1884, Chile annexed that part of Bolivia that had given it access to the Pacific Ocean, and it became landlocked. However, the country has never given up its claim on this corridor to the sea and certainly not its dream of once again having its own coastline. Which is why successive Bolivian governments have maintained a 'maritime consciousness' within the country, in the hope that a return to its maritime past will remain nothing less than a real and active "matter of honour".'

'But if they haven't got any sea…?' queried Sandra.

'Well, they do have some water. I mean, their not very large navy does patrol rivers – to prevent smuggling and drug trafficking – and they even maintain a naval presence on Lake Titicaca…'

'It's hardly like the real thing though, is it?'

'Ah. Well, in readiness for getting their Pacific coastline back, they also have a small but proper naval unit permanently deployed in Rosario – in Argentina.'

'Good grief!'

'Yes. Although I suspect it might not be much use if they came into conflict with… Argentina.'

'No.'

'Ah, and talking of which,' declared Brian, 'it was in a town just over the border from Argentina that Butch Cassidy and the Sundance Kid popped their clogs. It was in a place called San Vincente. And actually it wasn't

Butch Cassidy and the Sundance Kid; it was a couple of train robbers called Robert Leroy Parker and Harry Longabough. And they weren't killed in a shootout, but in the middle of the night – after a shootout. It's reckoned that one of them shot the other then killed himself – to avoid being captured. Which I have to say was a successful if a rather absurd solution to their problem...'

'You wouldn't recommend it to avoid being kept awake then?'

Brian regarded his wife and this time registered the expression on her face. It was time for him to shut up, time for him to recognise that his humanity required him to allow her to sleep. So he did. And instead of chattering on, he thought about that hammerhead shark off the Devil's Crown. Just as he would think about it again and again over the forthcoming months. Hell, how could he not?

11.

*B*rian awoke at exactly six in the morning. It was something he often did: re-entering the world of consciousness at a precise o'clock, whether it was five o'clock, six o'clock, seven o'clock or even eight o'clock. It was as though within that disorganised muddle of his mind he had a rare Swiss-made chronometer, a timepiece that could operate under the most testing of conditions and then stir him after he had achieved the required period of sleep – but only 'on the hour'. Minutes or even fractions of hours, his chronometer couldn't manage. Or maybe, to withstand the environment of his mind, that's just the way the Swiss had engineered it. But whatever… this waking on the hour was a fact. And if one did not subscribe to the involvement of the Swiss – which Brian certainly did not – it was also a mystery.

On this particular morning, Brian paused in his start to the day to consider this mystery. However, it remained as perplexing as how he, like most other people, somehow knew more or less how long they had been asleep, even though they had… been asleep at the time. Somehow the mind appeared to be able to retain a sense of the passage of time when it was either switched off entirely or aware only of the occurrence of dreams. Yes, waking at a precise time and knowing how long one had slept were both real mysteries. And having got no closer to solving either of these two mysteries, Brian began to contemplate some others...

Why, he thought, have academics, when interviewed on the radio or the telly, adopted the use of 'so' at the beginning of every response, if not at the beginning of every sentence? What was so wrong with 'well' or 'uhm'? Brian was at a loss to know, and it remained a mystery. Just like why anybody in the world took seriously anything Diane Abbott ever said. Then there was the identity of whoever is responsible for infantilising a whole generation of people through the use of all those stupid computer games – and what might be his or her motive? In Brian's opinion this was one of the greatest mysteries of all, and he would have given anybody else's right arm to solve it. I mean, here was somebody grooming millions of young innocents into becoming essentially vegetables, just morons who would be more than satisfied with no real-world life of their own and happy to play the sorts of puerile pastimes that their forebears had discarded by the age of nine. And who was it? Putin? Xi Jinping? Mark Zuckerberg? Blofeld? Or maybe even 'The Office of Tony Blair'? And the motive? World domination? Some sort of irresistible ideological imperative? Corporate greed? Or was it the only way that Tony Blair wouldn't go down in history as being the most arrogant, most misguided, most deluded and (by a short margin over Gordon Brown) the most loathsome British prime minister of all time?

Brian strongly suspected that he would never see this mystery resolved. Unless it became catastrophically apparent, probably at the point where the world had run out of functioning humans and the vast majority of its population were glued permanently to the screens of their ubiquitous smartphones. However, he had to concede that there was just as little likelihood that another mystery would be one day resolved, and this was why our armed forces haven't adopted a wheelie technology in place of their back-carried rucksacks. These rucksacks, Brian understood, could weigh anything up to ninety-five pounds, and surely, he thought, even for a strapping great marine, pulling ninety-five pounds on a set of wheels is far, far preferable to lugging it on one's back. And we're not talking about flimsy little wheels here that can cope only with the polished floor of an airport concourse, but big, heavy-duty wheels that could be made to cope with the very worst of terrains. Furthermore, these wheelie kitbags could be attached by a bracket to the back of a marine's belt, and that way he could still have both of his hands free and be ready for action. Yes, Brian was convinced; the case for military-type wheelie rucksacks was overwhelming. Which made their non-introduction into Her Majesty's armed forces a complete and utter mystery.

However, far from mysterious was the puncturing of his futile musings on all these unresolved puzzles by Sandra's suggestion that he got out of bed, having first of all (if he valued their relationship) paid her some attention. And so began the next day of their Galápagos adventure and their first day on the island of Isabela.

Now, it is worth at this point saying just a few words about this particular member of the Galápagos archipelago, and the first word should probably be 'large'. Yes, Isabela is by far the largest island in the Galápagos, and at nearly 1,800 square miles, it constitutes almost a half of the land area of the entire archipelago. It is also about four times larger than Santa Cruz, the second largest island in the group. Then there is its youth... Because, Isabela, sitting on the west of the Galápagos archipelago, is one of its youngest islands. It was formed just one million years ago – by the irresistible merger of six shield volcanoes. Furthermore, its youth is emphasised by the fact that five of these volcanoes are still active, making Isabela one of the most volcanically active places in the world. Indeed, one of these volcanoes, a giant called Sierra Negra, last erupted in 2005. And it was this volcano that Brian and his colleagues were scheduled to climb today – right up to its enormous crater!

Before partaking of breakfast, Sandra had asked her husband whether the itinerary for their trip had made clear that it would involve a close encounter with an active volcano, and Brian had not been able to assure her that it had. Whereafter he found it almost impossible to assure her that an ascent of said volcano was the most sensible of endeavours to embark on, particularly as the ascent would involve a hike of over two miles and a climb to an altitude of almost 3,700 feet. Nevertheless, a decision was taken to go for it, not least because all the other Nature-seekers were raring to go, and ducking out of this one would have been unforgivable. What's more, it would probably be a fantastic experience.

It started, as all their island expeditions did, in a panga. And the two pangas together first made a mini voyage around some offshore rocks, in order to observe some of Isabela's marine iguanas and some of its modest population of penguins. Then it was time to head to the mainland and into the waiting arms of its solitary port, the already mentioned Puerto Villamil. This place sits on the south coast of Isabela – towards the east end of this coast. And as (in Brian's mind) Isabela has the outline of a seahorse emerging from an egg – and facing left – that means that this modest port resides on the underside of the egg and a little towards its right. Where it resided on the scale of the ungroomed and the shabby remained to be seen.

Well, initially, all looked well. As Brian's panga approached a small wooden landing stage, there were just some small open boats to see, some of them with sea lions aboard, and beyond them some vegetation and some reasonable-looking buildings. But then the Nature-seekers boarded their 'bus' and it was soon 'Grotville' once again. As their transport made its way through the 'suburbs' of Puerto Villamil, it also made its way through yet another manifestation of the unkempt and the uncared for. It was a little like an unplanned holiday village, Brian thought; one built on a lava field, where the object had been to disfigure the landscape, and not only with the substandard quality of the buildings but also with an accumulation around them of every variety of detritus one could possibly assemble. And no. This wasn't just middle-class arrogance in play; it was the unavoidable truth that, in common with the inhabitants of Santa Cruz and San Cristóbal, the folk of Isabela didn't seem to give a damn. They didn't major in omnibus design either.

Ah yes. Brian was not content to be horribly mean-minded about Isabela's town planning. He also had it in for its transport system – as represented by its (one and only?) 'bus'.

You see, it wasn't actually a bus. It was a flatbed truck, onto which somebody had bolted six rows of metal chairs and then provided them with some cover in the shape of a metal canopy. So there was something a bit bus-like about it, and in many of the less fortunate parts of the world, it would pass muster as a regular bus without any sort of debate. However, the fact remained that it had more in common with the sort of open-sided transport one sees in theme parks, and it was not very comfortable. Particularly when Isabela's answer to Fangio engaged its afterburners and roared out of Puerto Villamil in the direction of Sierra Negra. In fact, Brian soon decided that he was experiencing not just an uncomfortable ride but also a ride that was unquestionably scary. No seat belts, no sides to the vehicle, no cushioning, probably no MOT, but instead just lots of speed and the sense that the driver was quite possibly self-taught and by no means necessarily stable.

Anyway, he managed to keep his vehicle on the road – just – and Brian attempted to distract himself by taking in the scenery. Initially this was quite a difficult task because the scenery lacked anything that might have been described as scenic. It was just indeterminate scrub and farmland, with the only points of interest provided by the occasional one-careless-owner-and-in-desperate-need-of-attention 'farmstead'. Oh, and there was an overcast sky as well, which did little to help but instead threatened some dampness to come.

Oh dear. But never mind, because the truck/bus was now climbing the enormous feature that was Sierra Negra, and farmland had almost given way to natural vegetation – and some quite impressive displays of erosion. Because skirting the tarmacked road, as it ascended the sierra, were deep water-created gullies, which not only represented a further potential hazard for the occupants of the bus but also a vivid illustration of how mankind's activities can so easily have an unintentional impact on the environment. Remove vegetation – by building a road or farming or forestry activities – and soon the soil that supported that vegetation is washed away. And in this instance Brian reckoned that there was a pretty good chance that the road would be washed away with it. He just hoped that this didn't happen until he and his friends had been delivered back to the *Beluga*.

It was just as he was wallowing in these murky depths of his world-class pessimism, that the driver brought his vehicle to a halt. Not through the use of brakes, but by disengaging his foot from the accelerator pedal and letting the slope of the road consume the truck's momentum. His brakes, Brian assumed, were held in reserve for emergencies. Or they might even be held in reserve back in a garage somewhere in Puerto Villamil. And that would only become apparent when the vehicle embarked on its homebound descent. But hey... all was OK now, and what's more, the driver had stopped his vehicle for a reason, and that reason was Darwin's catching a fleeting glimpse of a vermillion flycatcher.

This chap is a little treasure. Or at least the male is. Unlike the female, who has to make do with a palette of yellow, off-white and brown, he has brilliant vermilion undersides, a vermillion breast, throat and cap, and a black eye-band that runs to and joins his black back where this rises to the nape of his handsome black neck. He is therefore relatively easy to spot, with his brightness standing out as a marker against a background of green vegetation. That said, Darwin had only glimpsed him and had now lost him, even though he and all the Nature-seekers were off the truck and busy scouring the roadside vegetation with their assembled binocs. Then he was seen again. And then he came closer, and soon all Darwin's charges had observed him at length and he could join that 'list of birds seen' – with a special commendation for his beauty and his charm. He was really splendid, and he had provided all the Nature-seekers with a welcome pause in their ascent of the volcano and with a much needed stretch of their legs – given that after forty minutes of trucking, their legs would be very much put to the test.

The bus had left the flycatcher and now, after another ten minutes on the road, it was coasting to a halt in a small car park that was clearly its terminus. From now on it would be an ascent on foot. Or at least it would just as soon as the majority of the Nature-seekers had availed themselves of what, after that flycatcher, was yet another 'first' of this Galápagos adventure: a stand-alone public toilet. It wasn't grand, but neither was it connected to a tortoise farm or a tortoise-breeding centre. It was just sitting there on its own, and that made it a toilet to remember. And after a two-mile walk up the volcano and a two-mile walk back, quite possibly a toilet to revisit…

Anyway, that was for later. Right now, after the initial mass-relief session had been concluded, it was time for the walk, and that meant it was time to embark on a trek up a track. The track in question was broad and, to start with, quite muddy, after which it became somewhat upward and somewhat endless. In places it was eroded, in the same way that those road edges earlier on had been eroded, but it was still a fairly easy track to negotiate – if, that is, one discounted its upward incline. And quite frankly, this was rather difficult to discount. Brian, for one, was finding it very hard to ignore the fact that each step forward entailed lifting his entire body weight up by at least an inch. And if one stopped to re-engage with one's schoolboy knowledge of stuff like mass, energy, power and force, one would soon conclude that lifting one's own body weight again and again, even if in small incremental steps, was an exercise that could in no way be dismissed from one's mind. It represented a real physical effort, and unfortunately Brian had never in his life been an ardent cheerleader for even a modicum of physical exercise let alone a sustained physical effort.

Nevertheless, he could recognise when he was being a wuss – and when everybody else was not being a wuss, and just getting on with what was actually no more than a gently inclined stroll. Hell, it was already clear that the Nature-seekers were not scaling the outer walls of Sierra

Negra's caldera by using a vertical path, but instead by following what was a much more manageable route around the caldera. This meant that it was much longer than any vertical path – obviously – but also that it could offer those who used it the most modest of gradients, the sort of gradients that real Nature-seekers could take in their literal stride, and that Brian, if he had any sense, should just get on with and enjoy.

Well, in the event, he managed it. And so too did Sandra. There wasn't much to see beyond the coarse vegetation that bordered the track and there was virtually no wildlife around. But the act of just plodding up what did look very like an endless track became a joy in itself. And this joy was accentuated by being in the company of a group of like-minded souls who today had found themselves in the sort of splendid isolation that can only be offered by places such as an active volcano on a large and still largely uninhabited island in the Galápagos. One could also, of course, relish the privilege of such a walk – in the sense of how many other people in the world, at precisely this time, would somewhere be walking up an active volcano. Brian actually considered this as he trudged upwards, and concluded that an accurate number was impossible to arrive at, although it was probably a little bit higher than the number who belonged to Nicola Sturgeon's official fan club but quite a bit lower than those who had left it.

Anyway, after more than an hour of walking, Bill and Andrea had established a clear lead over the rest of the party. Which was why, without Darwin's guidance, they overshot the party's destination. This was a lookout point to the left of the track, which was obscured by some dense vegetation. Darwin felt obliged to call them back, lest they continued around the track that skirted the caldera and ended up lost or exhausted or both. When they had then rejoined the party and the party had made its way through the vegetation, it was not very long before a consensus had been arrived at. And this consensus was that the seemingly endless trek up the track had been more than worth it. This was because the view from the lookout point was not just stupendous, but it was almost literally stupefying.

The volcano's caldera, which had now come into view, was, like most calderas, essentially circular in shape and its floor was an expanse of just barren lava. However, that expanse of lava was absolutely immense, and it was absolutely immense because Sierra Negra's caldera has a diameter of no less than ten kilometres. That means you could probably have fitted most of Redditch into it, and other than losing their connections to Birmingham and having to cope with some unusually high temperatures, the citizens of Redditch could then have continued to go about their business as if nothing had happened. This wasn't, of course, a mental measure of the caldera's size that was made by other than Brian, but it might serve to illustrate just how enormous and just how spectacular this natural feature was – and how even more spectacular it must have been when it erupted.

Darwin had been at this lookout point when that last happened – in 2005 – and he attempted to explain to the Nature-seekers what he had seen and what he had felt. Because on that occasion the eruption was on the north side of the caldera – directly opposite from where they were now standing – and that eruption had caused lava to flow all around the eastern and southern edges of the caldera. This was still apparent, as was the colossal amount of lava that must have been on the move at the time. What was not apparent, however, but was now being made clear by Darwin, was the colossal amount of energy – and heat – that had accompanied the eruption. And he made this clear by informing his charges that it had been possible to observe the eruption from where they were now standing for only a few minutes, because the heat being spewed from the Earth, a full ten kilometres away, and the heat from the lava flow was just too intense to bear for any greater length of time.

Brian was impressed. Indeed all the Nature-seekers were impressed. Who would have not been? And who, if they were anything like Brian, would not have been made to feel really insignificant in the face of this enormous manifestation of 'natural indifference'? Yes, here was the result of the Earth doing what it does. By coughing up just a tiny fraction of its guts, it has had no trouble whatsoever in forming this absolutely gargantuan crater – as well, of course, as the whole island of Isabela – and at no time were we, the all-important masters of the universe, given even a passing thought. Yes, we are just incidental. We are just a transient, trivial tenant on this fabulous planet, and it sometimes takes a sight like the caldera of Sierra Negra to remind us of this fact. Which, Brian thought, was quite enough philosophy to last him for the rest of the day. And anyway, it really looked as though it could rain now. So wasn't it about time he and his comrades made it back down the track, ultimately to swap their trek for a truck and for some of them then to concern themselves about the existence of any brakes on that truck?

It was OK. The walk back down was as easy as pie – and the Nature-seekers weren't even rained on – and then the truck's driver adopted only a reckless speed on the way back to town and not one that was unquestionably suicidal. Furthermore, there was even a fleeting glimpse of another vermillion flycatcher on the way down. Although, as it was in exactly the same spot where the first had been seen on the way up, Brian thought it highly likely that it was the same bird. He also thought that Darwin and his fellow guides probably paid one of the locals to provide it with a supply of premium honey-roasted flies, bought from somewhere like Fortnum and Mason, and guaranteed to prevent this bird from ever leaving its patch, and therefore making it available for viewing by all those who might pass by on a truck. Oh, and the truck, when it got back to Puerto Villamil, *was* able to stop. Whether this was as a result of some sort of braking system or a side effect of some unknown natural phenomenon was never established. Brian leant in favour of the latter…

He also leant in favour of being idle in the afternoon. After lunch back on board the *Beluga*, he and Sandra could have joined a number of the Nature-seekers and returned to Puerto Villamil, there to visit another tortoise-breeding centre and to wander around some brackish lagoons. However, following his experience of heat, loud Americans – and tedium – at the tortoise-breeding centre on Santa Cruz, a further visit to another such institution held out only minimal appeal. As for the lagoons... well, now that he'd experienced Puerto Villamil, he was not especially eager to experience any of its 'attractions', no matter how much wildlife interest they might provide – and no matter how successful he was in suppressing his misgivings about the people of Villamil...

Yes, he had been doing some reading. And he had discovered that in 2007, some fishermen from Puerto Villamil had killed eight Galápagos tortoises, three of which had been over one hundred years old. Furthermore, not only did they kill them but they apparently cruelly tormented them first – and all for the worst of reasons. You see, these fishermen were engaged in an act of revenge. They were apparently pretty upset that the authorities were attempting to control their activities, even though their activities were illegal and constituted a fundamental threat to all marine life in the Galápagos National Park.

What they were doing was sweeping the floor of the ocean around Isabela, and dragging up starfish, lobsters – and sea cucumbers. Now, sea cucumbers have been described as the 'earthworms of the sea', because they do a similar job to earthworms on land. They consume and grind down materials into finer particles that bacteria can then break down as part of the 'nutrient cycle' of the sea, and where they are eliminated, the sea floor becomes hardened and can no longer be used by other bottom-dwelling creatures. Indeed, the environment is essentially fucked and it can take decades to recover. Unfortunately, sea cucumbers also feature (alongside shark fins, of course) as a must-have delicacy in the Far East, which is why the Isabela fishermen were quite happy to ravage a pristine marine environment in order to find them, and then kill tortoises as some sort of sick revenge when the national park guys sought to impose some much needed quotas on their catches.

Well, it will be no great surprise that any activities involving the nauseating eating habits of certain Chinese people and the decimation of a marine environment – and, indirectly, the brutal murder of some wonderful endangered animals – will not be well received by Brian. Furthermore, the fact that the decimation process has not been brought to an end will by no means help matters, and it could even be said that he has always had only the utmost contempt for anyone who has so little respect for the world around them. To fish – sensitively – is OK. To ravage – without any thought for the environment or for the future, no matter what are your needs – is odious beyond words. And you will find that sensitive little souls like Brian will want nothing to do with you and nothing to do with your scruffy little town. Instead, they will probably want no more than to stay on their sea-going craft and contemplate one or two more of life's endless and fathomless mysteries…

This is exactly what Brian did. He retired to his cabin and he began to ponder. And the first thing he pondered was how so many early authors had produced so many great works of literature before the days of creative writing courses. Because, as far as he knew, when these guys were busy knocking out what we now recognise as classics, there wasn't a single university in the land offering one of these essential programmes of tuition, and authors just had to rely on their own creativity and sort of make it up as they went along. It was one of the great unresolved mysteries of our time as to how they could possibly have done this. Well, Brian's pondering got him no closer to finding a solution to this puzzle, so he moved on – to consider the mystery of Fred Goodwin. More specifically, he wondered – not for the first time – why the cured skin of Fred Goodwin is now not on display in the Banking Hall of Shame, but in its uncured state, it still adorns its owner's well-cared-for body. It was a real and very annoying mystery.

Not so mysterious was Brian then falling asleep. It was probably that walk up the volcano – and his age. Indeed, he was still rather tired when dinnertime arrived, and he found himself unable to make much of a contribution to the evening's conversation. This could have augured well for Sandra, in that it might have meant an interlude in Brian's series of lectures on the nations of South America. But it was not to be, and as soon as they were both in bed back in their cabin, he started. And tonight it was the turn of French Guiana.

'OK,' he announced, 'as I'm sure you'll remember, Guyana is a relatively poor country, and Suriname – formerly Dutch Guiana – is a bit of a problem country. However, their neighbour down the coast, French Guiana, is actually the most prosperous place in South America, with a GDP per capita greater than anywhere else on the continent. And that's despite it having a very high unemployment rate. So, the obvious question is "why?"'

'To which the obvious answer,' interjected Sandra,

'is because it is an overseas Department of France, and it can therefore rely on all sorts of goodies and subsidies from the rest of France – and, no doubt, from all us other kind-hearted citizens of the European Union.'

Brian was taken aback. After all, Sandra had just stolen his lines. Nevertheless, he regrouped quickly, and asked his wife a question to which he doubted she knew the answer. Just to regain his position at the lectern, you understand. And the question was: 'Do you know the other two EU territories outside Europe that, with French Guiana, are not islands?'

'What!'

'Give in?'

'Brian!'

'It's those two Spanish enclaves in Africa: Cueta and Melilla.'

'It's also getting late…'

Brian acknowledged the warning and left the north coast of Africa to return to the north coast of South America. He did this with another question.

'Do you know what forms a large part of French Guiana's economy?'

'It must be the Guiana Space Centre. You know, the place that's now the European Space Agency's primary launch site. And it makes a really good launch site because by its being so close to the equator, the rockets it fires off get a little bit of extra velocity from the planet's rotation. Oh, and did you know that the space centre is such an important place, that there is actually a detachment of the Paris Fire Brigade stationed nearby to ensure its protection. Incredible, isn't it?'

Brian agreed. It was incredible – that his presentation had been hijacked. And by his audience! He was just trying to compose himself when Sandra then made another observation.

'You know they have occasional votes for independence in French Guiana. And the highest ever percentage voting for independence has been just 5%. Says a lot about their knowing on which side their bread's buttered, doesn't it? And, as I think you mentioned a few days ago yourself, it makes you think how other places might regard the opportunity of being a little less independent and a little more supported by somewhere like Europe...'

Well, that was it. Game, set and match. Brian could only grin and offer his wife a feeble sounding 'Yes. Errh, yes, it does, doesn't it?' Then he just grinned some more. And as he grinned, he thought, and what he thought was how on Earth did she know all that stuff? It was... well, it was another bloody mystery, another unsolved enigma to add to his tally for the day.

He felt even more tired than he had before dinner...

12.

Overnight the *Beluga* had sailed west from Puerto Villamil and then north and east around the bottom section of Isabela (i.e. clockwise around the seahorse's egg) to arrive at a visitor site called Punta Moreno. It had been a long voyage and a rough voyage, easily rough enough to overcome Brian's recently acquired sleeping habits, and on a number of occasions shake him from his slumbers. It was during one of these waking periods that Brian considered how he would be faring if he were not in a bed but in a hammock. He quickly concluded that he wouldn't be faring at all well. Just as he would be in a seaborne version of hell if he was having to make do not only without a bed but also without a shower, a washbasin, a loo and an adequate supply of loo paper. Yes, there was no getting away from it; being aboard the sort of marine transport used by Charles Darwin rather than being cosseted aboard a boat like the *Beluga* must have been more than dismal. And that was even before one had factored in one's 'unavoidable companions'.

A sailor on the *Beagle*, as well as having no bed and no bathroom facilities, would have had to endure for months the close company of a load of not necessarily sweet-smelling males and, for the same number of months, the absence of the close company of even a single female. It couldn't have made for a very attractive existence. Whereas, Brian not only had the company of his wife but the company of a group of people who were really very nice indeed – and, of course, who were always sweet-smelling. OK, it wasn't a perfect group, and to start with there was a bit of a language barrier with those in the group who made up the crew. Furthermore, for all his knowledge and application, there was also something of a *cultural* barrier with the guy who was acting as the guide in the group, Darwin. Then there were Shane and Shelly, who never quite bought into the whole 'group behaviour' ethic and also Bill and Andrea who were, for some reason known only to themselves, increasingly isolating themselves from the rest of the Nature-seekers. However, that still left the majority of these Nature-seeker members of the group in the 'first rate' category, and that meant for Brian and Sandra, ten other people on their *Beluga*-sized planet whose behaviour, attitude, generosity and general companionship were making their expedition to the Galápagos a really exceptional pleasure. No arguments had arisen. No cliques had been formed. No fights had broken out in the bar. And nobody had even taken exception to Brian's rants – at least, as far as he could tell. In fact, it occurred to him – while still on this comparison of life aboard the *Beagle* to life aboard the *Beluga* – that there were twelve people here who could probably stand (and actually enjoy) each other's company *almost* indefinitely, and if not indefinitely then for long enough for a voyage not just to the Galápagos but even to Jupiter. Hell, if he still remembered these thoughts in the morning he might even make a note to contact NASA.

He didn't. So NASA would have to plough on with its search for compatible astronauts for some time to come – and Brian could just get on and indulge himself in all those simply admirable bathroom facilities and thereby ready himself for another day in the company of his similarly admirable companions. Oh, and the day would start with a panga ride to Punta Moreno.

Brian wasn't quite sure what to expect here, but the first thing he encountered was a rather rocky approach to the chosen landing spot – and a 'new' bird. For here, sitting on the rocky shoreline, were not just some penguins but also some flightless cormorants. Well, these are very rare birds. They are endemic to the Galápagos and occur only on the west and north of Isabela and on the neighbouring island of Fernandina. In total there are no more than 1,000 breeding pairs and, in the recent past, this figure has been even lower, due principally to the impact of El Niño on their food source. Of course, what marks them out as particularly special among all the twenty-nine species of cormorants in the world is their inability to fly. Their life in the Galápagos has robbed them of this capacity, as it is a life that sees them never leaving the stretch of shoreline on which they were born (and therefore not in need of wings to fly to distant breeding grounds) and a life that involves their feeding very close to the shoreline – and underwater. Here their vestigial wings have no part to play, and it is their powerful webbed feet that provide them with propulsion, allowing them to get to where they want in order to catch octopuses, eels and other fish with their long and very effective hooked beaks. So, not a bad illustration of the operation of natural selection, thought Brian: an animal discarding what was not needed to best recognise the habits it pursued to best exploit its habitat. Even if it meant ending up with a name that somewhat insensitively emphasised nothing positive about this remarkable bird but just something it couldn't do.

Yes, Brian thought this was a bit mean. Or he did until he thought of 'penniless Greeks', 'brainless supermodels' and 'worthless bankers', when he then realised that sensitivity sometimes had to be abandoned in the interests of the essential-informative. Anyway, whatever this bird was called, it was still quite impressive, not only in terms of its evolution and its behaviour, but also in terms of its appearance. For the flightless cormorant is a big bird, weighing up to four kilograms (making it the biggest of all the cormorants) and it is black above and brown below and it has that long hooked beak and brilliant turquoise eyes. Not the prettiest bird in the world but, with the help of those stunning blue eyes, one of the most imposing.

Well, after this non-aerial avian opener, it was time for Punta Moreno itself, and that meant time for a rather challenging dry landing followed shortly thereafter by the realisation that Punta Moreno is essentially an expanse of barren lava. It was Santiago's Sullivan Bay, Mark II, albeit without Sullivan Bay's exquisite lava formations. Yes, Punta Moreno's lava was more 'fractured tarmac' in nature and not nearly as beautiful. However, within this huge jumble of 'tarmac plates' there was something that Sullivan Bay lacked, and this was a series of water-filled holes. They were the result, Darwin said, of the lava surface collapsing into lava tunnels that lay beneath, and they now constituted little oases in what was otherwise a tract of sterile rock.

The first of the oases that the Nature-seekers visited clearly had an underground connection to the sea, because swimming around in the clear-water pond at its centre were a couple of sharks! Those further from the shore could not boast the same class of tenants, but they did provide a home to an abundance of plant life and to chaps like pintail ducks, teal and common moorhens, which presumably meant that these oases also supported a healthy population of invertebrates – but fortunately no wildfowl-hunting enthusiasts of any sort.

Brian enjoyed this expedition, although he would have preferred it if there had been just a modicum of shade available (it had been fiercely hot for the entire two hours of the walk) and if at the end of the expedition there had been a ladder down to the pangas (the vertiginous nature of the descent into the inflatables threatened to turn what was supposed to be a dry exercise into a very wet one). However, Brian was never entirely satisfied, and he would soon have the opportunity to cool down properly – and by choosing to get wet. Because, when the Nature-seekers were back on board the *Beluga*, it was immediately time for another group snorkel…

This one was conducted just off the rocks of the shoreline – and, as Darwin had predicted, it was very cold. This was due to some local upwelling of cold water and it made the ambient water temperature so low that for the first time on this expedition, Brian regretted not donning a wet suit. He was in the minority of the Nature-seeker snorkelers who went about their snorkelling business in just swimwear and T-shirts and who, on this excursion into the ocean, divided their time between envying their wet-suited companions and shivering. Nevertheless the excursion was worth it. Not only was the cold water full of all sorts of fish and quite a few turtles, but within the rocks and the seaweed were a number of seahorses! These were not Isabela-shaped seahorses emerging from an egg (!) but real 'Pacific seahorses' (a name, Brian understood, that reflected their location and not their no doubt peace-loving nature) and they were a sort of orangey-brown, and at just three centimetres long, hiding within the marine vegetation, not that easy to see. Particularly by those of the group who were shivering.

However, they were seen, and they prompted a discussion back on board the *Beluga* concerning the odd appearance of seahorses in general, their even odder reproductive habits (which involve the male hosting the developing young in his front-facing pouch) and their incompetence when it comes to swimming. Yes, seahorses are probably the worst swimmers in the world, preferring instead to remain pretty well stationary, with their prehensile tails wound around something like a convenient bit of seagrass where they can then feed or choose to read the latest Stephen King at their leisure. In fact, Evan was able to illustrate just how poor they are as swimmers by revealing to the assembled company that the title of the slowest fish in the world is held by one species of seahorse known as the 'dwarf seahorse', which can manage a top speed of just five feet per hour!

The *Beluga* was noticeably faster. It demonstrated this directly after lunch when its captain took it north from Punta Moreno towards their next stop, a place called Elizabeth Bay. This bay was on the west coast of Isabela where it faces its smaller 'sister' island of Fernandina, and getting there would take a full two hours. Which meant that Brian and Sandra, from their windowful cabin, had a full two hours to observe the approach of Fernandina and, if they chose to, to brush up on their knowledge of Isabela. Brian but not Sandra chose this option, probably because Brian's interest in this giant island had been boosted by their earlier visit to Punta Moreno and probably because Sandra knew very well that her husband would, in due course, enlighten her on everything he'd discovered whether she wanted this enlightenment or not. How right she was.

Yes, ultimately he educated her at length on what he had established from his afternoon reading about Isabela, concerning its vegetation, its tortoises – and its goats. In the first place, he informed her, the island is so young that it does not display the various vegetation zones found on the older islands. This is because the lava fields, such as those at Punta Moreno, and the soils that surround them, have not yet developed all the nutrients required to support a varied flora – and the island has to make do with a rather simpler mix of plants. So it's a bit like a new Barratt housing estate where there's just laurel, Leylandii and grass. That said, not many Barratt housing estates come equipped with giant tortoises.

These chaps are more or less everywhere on the island, so much so that Isabela can claim to be home to more *wild* tortoises than any of the other islands. Furthermore, because these critters are not best equipped to negotiate really challenging terrain, the island's topography – and its volcanoes and lava fields in particular – have acted as barriers to their movement. Inevitably, and echoing what has happened on the individual islands in the Galápagos archipelago, this has led to the development of several different subspecies of tortoises on Isabela – and to Brian believing that there was yet another reason to regard the operation of nature as more than just little bit fascinating.

Then there are – or were – Isabela's goats, resilient little devils which had been introduced to the archipelago years ago and which on Isabela had grown to a population of 100,000. Not surprisingly, this had more than a minor impact on the ecology of the island, and in 2006 the National Parks Service and the Charles Darwin Foundation were obliged to undertake an eradication programme. This worked, since which time the island's elementary but natural vegetation has recovered and the endemic wildlife has experienced a general uplift in its mood. It was just a real pity, thought Brian, that so many essentially innocent goats had needed to get the chop. What's more, he thought, if they did have to go, wasn't it a pity that they weren't thought suitable to satisfy the demands of traditional Chinese medicine for an ingredient that would cure stuff like wheezing, impotence and night-time urinary incontinence. That way twenty million seahorses wouldn't have to be killed each year instead and several seahorse species wouldn't now be facing extinction. And frankly, extract of goat has just as much chance of being effective in stopping you wheezing, flopping and bedwetting as even the most exotic and expensive of seahorses. And it's a fucking disgrace that the rest of the world tolerates the practice of such diabolical nonsense when it means that seahorses will soon be joining that long list of other creatures that are all destined to disappear down that giant plughole of Chinese depravity.

Oh dear, he was at it again; getting all self-righteous about the behaviour of people who were probably unaware of the damage they were causing and were basically just very nice. Alternatively, they were all too well aware of the havoc they were wreaking, but they just didn't give a toss and were probably arrogant to boot. Which is why Brian made a promise to himself that he would never give up on his assault on all those practices that involve the misguided and totally unnecessary murder of so many creatures, no matter how futile this assault might be and how annoying it might be to all those who were called upon to witness and endure it. That said, he felt he could now do with some light relief, and he decided to provide himself with this by another dip into the pool of unsolved mysteries – starting with why the United Kingdom was still nominally united.

He got nowhere with this one, so he turned instead to considering why pistachio ice cream never really tastes of pistachios and why baked Alaskas are never anything like the right shape. He drew a blank here as well – inevitably – which is why he then wondered why anybody had ever thought that Turkey would make a good member of the European Union – or whatever was left of it – and why anybody had ever thought that oysters would make a good addition to the human diet. No. It was no good. All these mysteries insisted on remaining mysteries. As did the mystery of whether Bob Geldof had turned into an obnoxious pillock or had always been one – even as far back as the time of his one and only hit. So, Brian abandoned his contemplation of life's mysteries and instead had a brief nap. When he awoke, the captain was dropping anchor off Elizabeth Bay.

This is a large funnel-like and mangrove-fringed bay, leading into a peaceful lagoon, which is itself surrounded by a forest of red, black and white mangroves. It is a wonderful location for a spot of unhurried panga-borne exploration, and this is exactly what the Nature-seekers embarked on just minutes after the *Beluga* had moored. It then soon became apparent to all of them that as well as hosting mangroves, the bay provided a home to more flightless cormorants, to some brown pelicans, to some grey herons and some lava herons and even to some blue-footed boobies. There was also plenty of marine life here as well, and with their newly acquired swivelling skills, the Nature-seekers were able to make out the odd passing turtle and quite a few 'golden cownose rays', a species of eagle ray that hadn't been spotted before and one that is only distantly related to the golden raynose cow.

Darwin, as always, was busy providing his charges with all sorts of information about both the fauna and flora on show. However, when the two pangas left the bay itself and entered that 'peaceful lagoon', the didactic had to defer to the flora itself – and to the whole ambience of the place. It was indeed as peaceful as billed, not least because its clear, unruffled water was edged with some quite gigantic mangroves, and within the natural cocoon they created there was an abundance of peace – and something else, something that moved its ambience up from the simply tranquil to the simply sublime. And what this something was was, of course, the absence of so many things. Brian felt it – and relished it – straightaway: the absence of noise, the absence of crowds, the absence of haste and even the absence of dissent. And no traffic, no concrete, no litter, no dereliction, no protests, no smartphones and none of the other things that so often blight our lives with their intrusive and unwelcome presence. Yes, this ride into the lagoon of Elizabeth Bay would remain in Brian's mind as more an expedition into the realms of unblemished soothing calm than into the realms of an unblemished natural place. Although that wouldn't mean that he'd forget the size of those mangroves or his first encounter with a golden cownose ray...

Nor would he forget that he had a certain responsibility to provoke his Nature-seeker companions into some lively over-dinner conversation, and tonight he'd decided that he would discharge this responsibility by expanding on one of his thoughts from just yesterday. And this was the thought that a whole generation of humans is currently being infantilised by its embrace of hand-held technology. As regards how he would expand it... well, he thought he might just start by suggesting that the victims of this technology have neither the ability to navigate pavements without bumping into other pedestrians nor the ability to navigate life without the constant intervention of their parents.

However, in the event, he made a last-minute decision, and this decision was to be just a bit more charitable to the youth of today. He would not, after all, give them another bashing. Principally because they really were the victims and not the instigators of digital lunacy, and also because it just didn't seem fair to single them out. No. Better to have a go at society in general. So, soon after sitting down to the dinner table he invited his table companions to consider another topic completely. This he did by posing a question, and the question was: 'What do a number of growth industries in Britain tell us about the nature of our "national community"?' Then, inevitably, he proceeded to answer this question himself...

First of all, he listed some of the growth industries he had in mind. These included the security industry, the human rights 'industry', the asylum claims 'industry', the general claims industry, the interminable public enquiries 'industry', the deradicalisation 'industry' and the trafficking 'industry'. Then there was the convert-my-garage-into-an-insanitary-home-for-three 'industry', the crash-for-cash 'industry', the 'drain-covers-for-cash 'industry', the scam marriages 'industry', the abuse-of-postal-votes 'industry', and finally the plain old drugs industry. And what these burgeoning industries told us about our modern society, he suggested, was that there were now many people engaged in a whole raft of activities that were completely non-productive – or productive, but only for them and at our expense. His answer hardly gave much of an opportunity to anybody else to make a further contribution, other than to Sandra who suggested that he put a sock in it and then kept the sock in it until it was time to retire. This wasn't a bad suggestion, and if nothing else it reminded Brian that even though he'd been charitable to today's youth he hadn't provoked any lively over-dinner conversation among these older members of society – basically because he'd hogged it all for himself. However, it also reminded him of something even more damning of his own behaviour. And this was that just a few short hours ago he had been relishing the peace, calm and tranquillity of a truly unsullied place and, frankly, wasn't it about time he learnt not to sully the experience of others – particularly when they were going about their meals – with more of his ill-timed and ill-judged observations? Probably so. But that didn't mean he necessarily had to lay off bothering Sandra. Especially when he had a boster of a country to deal with – like Brazil…

Yes, he and Sandra were now back in their cabin, and Brian was preparing to deliver to his wife a monologue on what was South America's largest and arguably most narcissistically inclined country.

He began with some facts and statistics, pointing out that Brazil was easily the biggest sovereign state in South America, occupying 47.3% of the continental landmass and bordering every other country on the continent other than Chile and Ecuador. And in terms of both geographical area and population, it was the fifth largest country in the world and the biggest Portuguese-speaking country by far. However, this was just preamble, because the main thrust of Brian's lecture was to be Brazil's fascination with the body beautiful – even if this involved helping that body to gain and then retain some supposed beauty at any cost whatsoever.

'You see,' he said, 'body image in Brazil is all important. It is a part of their national culture. Particularly when, for Brazilian women, exposing as much of it as possible is almost *de rigueur...*'

'Ah,' interrupted an unusually engaged Sandra, 'so it's not what they'd choose...?'

Brian grinned.

'Very good,' he patronised. 'Because I think you're right. Far from the penchant for revealing one's flesh being a sign of liberation, it is much more likely that it is an act of compliance, a way of adhering to a set of preordained body standards that must be maintained with or without the help of pills, creams, potions, various suction devices or any number of surgical interventions.'

'Yes,' responded Sandra. 'I remember all those adverts for slimming creams when we were in Rio.'

'Well, they're still being used,' confirmed her husband, 'along with slimming tablets, slimming capsules, slimming coffees and slimming teas, "beverages that without fail will curb your appetite and melt away fat"...'

'But they don't.'

'No. They certainly do not. Which is why half of Brazil's population is overweight and 15% of it is obese. And why so many Brazilians, eager to fit into one of those microscopic bikinis – and adhere to the cult of the body beautiful – resort to surgical procedures. I mean, you would barely believe it, but Brazil has now overtaken the US as the world's leader for cosmetic surgery. And just to assure you that I'm not making this up, I've written down some statistics…'

At which point, Brian picked up a notebook by the side of his bed and began to read from its back cover.

'Yes. With less than 3% of the world's population, in 2013 Brazil accounted for 13% of all the world's cosmetic operations. And these included 515,776 breasts being reshaped, 380,155 faces tweaked, 129,601 tummies tucked, 63,925 buttocks augmented and 13,683 vaginas reconstructed!'

'Well, that's nice to know.'

'Yes. And because of that increase in obesity, liposuction is now the most popular procedure. With this, the surgeons are able to suck, sculpt and mould to their heart's content. In fact, they now have the use of one liposuction machine that is apparently able to extract as much as one gallon of fat per hour. And they have another machine with which they are able to suck out fat where there is too much of it and then reinject it back into cheeks, buttocks or breasts or indeed anywhere else that has begun to display too much in the way of unwanted sagging…'

'Well, that's definitely not nice to know.'

'So, anyway, Brazilians are just a little bit… misguided, and possibly more than just a little bit naive.

209

And all due to this weird worship of a body image that is either unattainable or unsustainable. And we all know about Brazilian waxing…'

'Quite,' interrupted Sandra. 'And on that note I think…'

'Mind, indoor tanning is outlawed,' reinterrupted Brian.

'Thank you, Brian.'

'Oh, and on a completely different tack, in 2004 the Brazilian government tried to sell an unwanted aircraft carrier on eBay – for £4 million – but they had to take it off because you're not allowed to sell military ordnance on eBay…'

'Brian…'

'And there are no bridges over the Amazon River proper.'

'Brian!'

'And a bite from *Phoneutria nigriventer*, otherwise known as the Brazilian wandering spider, can cause priapism in humans. Which, as I'm sure you know, means that their bites can cause some quite serious erections that can last for many hours and be really quite uncomfortable…'

'But they're not here in the Galápagos?'

Brian regarded his wife, who was now wearing an expression that fell somewhere between inscrutable, wicked and relieved. This was no great surprise. She had finally brought the latest of her husband's sermons to an abrupt and permanent end, and she knew it. So too did Brian. His intended postscript on the origins of Brazilian waxing being in Manhattan (in a salon operated by seven sisters from Brazil) and not in Brazil, would have to wait. As would that on all those who had read with glee that there might be some real promise in the exploitation of the venom of *Phoneutria nigriventer* – but not, of course, for its use as any sort of slimming aid…

13.

The overnight sail involved a short hop north as the *Beluga* tracked the west coast of Isabela to its next destination. It also involved Brian waking during this passage and his considering his past, a train of thought that had been originally triggered by his considering the *Beluga* and, in particular, its age.

It was Evan. During the previous evening's dinner he had been educating Brian and others on the vital statistics of the *Beluga* and on its construction. It was, he told them, a boat that was 110 feet long and it had a beam of 23 feet (which apparently meant it was 23 feet wide). It had a steel hull, two 530HP diesel engines, a generous total of three generators, and it had been built in Hamburg in 1968! Yes, this wonderful boat was also a venerable boat and it would soon be celebrating its first half-century. This was probably why it felt so solid and why it was quite easy to imagine that it might well go on for another half-century, if, that is, it didn't fall foul of some new environmental legislation – or an iceberg (which, if it stayed in the vicinity of the Galápagos, wasn't, thought Brian, particularly likely). Its age also explained why it looked so handsome; why it looked like a real boat and not like a tiny version of an ugly and vulgar gin palace of the sort favoured by such discerning folk as 'Sir' Philip Green. Yes, there was no doubt about it: its Hamburg designers had clearly been inspired more by the lines of a WWII German torpedo boat than they had by any of the design ethics of Gucci. And thank God for that.

Anyway, in the middle of the night it was the age of the *Beluga* that really captured Brian's attention and that then set him off along a tangent. And the tangent was a contemplation of what he, the Brian of the current age, had been like when he'd been the Brian of 1968, that year almost five decades previously when the *Beluga* had been 'born' into the world.

Well, he soon decided that all those years ago, he'd been a very different person. In 1968 he hadn't any wrinkles, any grey hairs, any missing hairs and not much in the way of reasoned views. It was, after all, a time in which he had yet to develop anything that could be remotely described as wisdom, and a time when he was still only a novice cynic. Indeed, it would be years before he would be ordained as a full-blown celebrant in the much maligned Church of Irredeemable and Deep-rooted Cynicism. And, of course, it wasn't just his cynicism that he hadn't got sorted out. Hell, back in 1968, he hadn't been aware that 'socialism is a bad thing' (and a bad thing whether you're a cynic or not), that liberalism is a well-intentioned but ultimately flawed political doctrine, and that human kind is all too human but not very kind. He also had not been aware that most things never turn out quite as bad as you think they will, that despite the mostly very disappointing nature of mankind, a surprising number of its individual members can be surprisingly good in all sorts of ways – and that olives really are one of the tastiest foods in the whole wide world.

Back in 1968 Brian would probably have slept through the night as well – without waking up and wasting his time pondering his past. Nor would he have woken feeling just a little bit tired in the morning because he had done this. Nor, for that matter, would he willingly have arisen at five o'clock in the morning for a six o'clock ride in a panga. In the first place he would not have been acquainted with that indecently early time back in 1968 and in the second place he would not have been acquainted with any sort of inflatable back then, let alone a confusingly named 'panga'. (Wasn't that something like a machete back in 1968?)

Well, tough. It was now 2016 and, as the *Beluga* was moored off the Nature-seekers' next visitor site, it was time to reconcile oneself to a very early rise and to get oneself into one of the *Beluga*'s two pangas. In short, it was time to visit Urbina Bay.

Now, Urbina Bay (or Bahía Urvina) has one particular claim to fame, and this is that as recently as 1954, it underwent a very uplifting experience. Yes, thanks to all the geological activity still in play in the western edge of the Galápagos archipelago, the whole area here was raised by up to ten metres. In fact, a further uplift of ninety centimetres took place in 1994. And these combined uplifts, apart from anything else, have resulted in an old landing dock becoming unusable other than at high tide, and the Nature-seekers therefore having to tackle another wet landing. This was onto a grey-sand beach, at the back of which was a roped-off VIP area, apparently for the exclusive use of Galápagos green turtles. Yes, these guys appear to have adapted to the uplifted conditions of Urbina Bay very rapidly, and now use their VIP area as an all-important nesting site.

For company they have both land and marine iguanas and a healthy population of giant tortoises. It was not clear to Brian whether any of these chaps are ever given a VIP pass, but he doubted that they would ever want one. The marine iguanas seemed content on the rocks that were a little further along the beach and the land iguanas and tortoises seemed content just to wander (very slowly) within the almost lush vegetation that lay beyond the beach. Here was where the Nature-seekers would be spending the whole two hours of their visit: on a trail that wound its way between the vegetation and a trail that would reveal evidence of the previously underwater status of the uplifted land – in the form of coral and pebbles. It would also reveal the previously living status of a singular tortoise – in the form of his now empty shell. Yes, according to Darwin, this poor old chap had decided to stop for a rest – on what he hadn't realised was a nest of fire ants. He had then compounded his error by not reacting to *their* reaction to his presence. That is to say, he hadn't moved away when they began to attack him, after which, having incapacitated him with their terrible bites, they eventually consumed him – entirely. What had clearly been a glorious period in the annals of fire ant history, with more available food than they could ever have dreamed of, was, for Mr Unreactive Tortoise, a bit of a disaster, and probably a painful disaster at that. Being struck by a meteorite would have undoubtedly been a better way to go.

Anyway, it was soon the Nature-seekers' time to go – to avoid the incoming seaborne invasion.

They had now returned to the grey-sand beach – and just in time. As Darwin had predicted, a new batch of visitors was now arriving. Not from a small boat like the *Beluga* or even from a boat twice its size, but from the *National Geographic Endeavour*, a boat that, whilst not quite the size of the *Titanic,* was vast. And that is vast in the sense of it being far too large to be let loose in the precious environment of the Galápagos with all its fragile and sensitive sites. It can host almost 170 passengers. That means that when it arrives at most of the visitor sites in the Galápagos, only a fraction of the passenger complement can be landed to enjoy those sites, while the others are obliged to go off kayaking or snorkelling or just to stay on the boat. Furthermore, even that fraction constitutes something of an expeditionary force when it is shipped to shore, and on this occasion quite enough of a 'threat' to encourage every last Nature-seeker to make it back to the *Beluga* as fast as he or she could. And the fact that there were more of those graduates in the art of voice projection within this expeditionary force – and children as well – was neither here nor there…

Back on the boat there was a breakfast to consume, and then, after some fairly unrewarding snorkelling, it was time for the *Beluga* to sail further north to a place called Tagus Cove. The trip there was uneventful other than it furnished the Nature-seekers with fine views of both Isabela and Fernandina, and it furnished a little flock of storm petrels with the opportunity to feed in the *Beluga*'s wake. These birds are remarkable. Although related to the great albatross, at fifteen to twenty centimetres in length, they are the smallest seabirds in the world. And easily the dantiest. You see, these are the chaps who appear to walk on water. Although, there again, they don't so much walk on water as flutter above it, while gently pattering its surface with their feet – apparently to create tiny eddies in the water that then drag particles of food towards them.

Brian and Sandra observed this behaviour from the back window of their cabin – a little group of petrels hovering and delicately 'pitter-pattering' in the disturbed water to the rear of the *Beluga* – and neither of them could really believe it. How, they thought, could such a diminutive bird survive at sea in the first place? And how could it possibly derive anything like enough nourishment by adopting the tactic of animated aerial paddling, especially when the aerial element of this tactic must have demanded so much energy? It was probably all done with mirrors, Brian suggested. And he also suggested that it would make his day if he could identify what sort of storm petrels were putting on the show. Were they white-vented storm petrels or band-rumped storm petrels? Or maybe even wedge-rumped (Galápagos) storm petrels? Oh well, whatever species they were, they were quite amazing – and all too literally incredible.

By the time the *Beluga* had arrived at its destination

of Tagus Cove, the storm petrels had disappeared. Maybe they didn't like graffiti. Even 'historic graffiti'. Yes, Tagus Cove is a flooded valley between two large volcanic cones and it makes for a dramatic anchorage. It also makes for a safe anchorage, as early visitors to Isabela in the shape of whalers and pirates were not slow to discover. Neither were they slow to leave their mark on this place, and the evidence of their being here is still extant in the form of some oversized graffiti: various dates and names plastered onto the rock walls of the cove and destined to stay there forever.

Brian thought that although this stuff was now described as 'historic', it was still an adulteration of a naturally beautiful place, and it amounted to no more than an act of desecration. However, it must also have reminded all those who saw it of the stupidity and carelessness of mankind – and of the recklessness of some of its members. How could it not, when one considers the risks those early matelots must have taken to enable them to leave their daubs on the rocks? They must, thought Brian, have been completely without fear. Or there again, he rethought, they might simply have ingested just a little too much rum. Not enough to hamper their writing skills but quite enough to suppress their appreciation of danger.

Anyway, despite the unwelcome decoration, after lunch Brian was quite content to spend his afternoon taking in the ambience of Tagus Cove and observing what went on here. Because quite a few things went on, not least because the cove now held no less than five boats, and one of these was that *National Geographic Endeavour*.

That meant that the cove had soon become filled with snorkelers and kayakers, and then a little flotilla of zodiacs had appeared, full of more of the *Endeavour*'s patrons and heading in the direction of 'Darwin's Lake'. This is a flooded crater at the head of the cove, which is accessed by a steep path, which is itself accessed via a (pirate era?) scary-looking landing stage, and then only when the swell of the water allows.

A squad of Nature-seekers had already taken on this challenge, and when they returned to the *Beluga* they reported that their expedition had been well worth it. However, they seemed quite unaware that by undertaking such an arduous excursion they had all missed out on the opportunity to enjoy an extremely juicy period of first-class indolence, interrupted only by the odd bit of people-watching and the odd glimpse of passing wildlife in either the water or the air. And Brian had to be honest to himself; the need for indolence could not be ignored, and neither could he break a habit of a lifetime and visit every man-made marvel or every natural wonder just because it happened to be nearby. Especially when it was excruciatingly hot and he had some preparatory thinking to do, preparatory thinking that would, in due course, be of benefit to his companions…

His thinking concerned autocrats. More precisely, Brian had devoted some of his indolence time to a consideration of a short list of current autocrats – some of the most reviled individuals on the planet – and in what ways they could be regarded as 'good'. When, ultimately, he had joined those of his companions who had made the mistake of sitting at his table for dinner, his plan was to enlighten them on the fruits of his thinking – and this despite Sandra trying to dissuade him from doing so. It was therefore right in the middle of the main course that the enlightenment commenced, and the first autocrat Brian had decided to deal with was Mr Zuma, the president of South Africa.

This guy, he proposed, may have proved to be the antithesis of his predecessor, Mr Mandela, but by spending all those millions of taxpayers' rands on his house in Kwazulu-Natal he had provided work for countless builders, countless electricians and plumbers and probably quite a few swimming-pool installers. And that was most certainly a good thing – for them. Furthermore, he had always sought to give a commendable degree of satisfaction to a whole string of female South Africans. And, maybe best of all, he had so trashed the reputation of the ANC that he will very probably have put South Africa onto a path of multi-party democracy, one that will ultimately see the current one-party dominance of the country removed for all time. And that would be a fantastic legacy of his time in power, and clearly a 'very good thing'.

Right. Well, Brian's table companions now at least understood what he was attempting to do, and this was to identify what might be regarded as the redeeming features of some of the very worst people in the world. It was, however, unclear whether they were entirely happy with this endeavour, but before any sort of clarity could emerge, Brian was into autocrat number two, a gentleman by the name of Mr Maduro, who has somehow managed to become the head honcho in Venezuela. Well, as far as Brian was concerned, here was somebody who was a fantastic role model for complete incompetents. If you hadn't managed to emerge from your schooling with any qualifications whatsoever, if you had a bit of a problem with words of more than two syllables and if subtraction was just not your thing, then never mind, because you could still become the president of an oil rich country – and make it poorer than you could possibly imagine. And if that's not a good thing about Mr Maduro's presidency, Brian didn't know what was.

Kim Jong-un of North Korea was next, and Brian's first point was that KJ might be something of a tyrant, but for virtually the whole of the world he was simply a source of huge amusement. Furthermore, he was a source of huge consolation for all those who have ever come away from a barber with a bad haircut – and for all those who have been putting on the pounds. Yes, there was a lot that was good about young Kim Jong-un, maintained Brian, and for that reason we should all be very grateful to him and wish him a long life and rather more luck with his missile tests than he is currently enjoying.

It was at this stage that Sandra suggested that three tyrants were quite enough for one evening, but it didn't work. John and Thelma spoke up in Brian's defence – for reasons unknown – and this was his licence to carry on. This he did with Mr Mugabe of Zimbabwe. This guy, Brian explained, was giving hope to a whole generation of geriatrics, people who couldn't govern their waterworks but, because of Mr M, now believed that one day they might be able to govern a whole country.

Oh, and Mr Mugabe was really good news for a host of other African leaders. Because no matter how crap they were, proposed Brian, they could all look incredibly competent and really well sorted when compared to old Uncle Bob.

Mr Erdogan was different. This president of Turkey might be a turkey of a president, Brian suggested, but he knew what he wanted and he knew how to get it. Furthermore, he wasn't a fool or an incompetent or an out and out loony. However, he was one of the grumpiest-looking people in the world, so much so that Brian understood that in many households back in Britain, 'doing an Erdogan' was now shorthand for being crotchety and crabby. And how can this convenient shorthand not be other than a good thing? So Brian proposed a round of thanks to this autocrat as well, before moving on to Xi Jinping, the president of China.

This guy, Brian argued, was very good news for the hair-dyeing industry (he apparently keeps an entire black hair-dye factory going – somewhere to the north of Shenzhen) and he has also been instrumental for a number of years in dispelling the fear of rigor mortis. So two plainly good things about this leader of the most populous country on the planet, and the third good thing about Xi, suggested Brian, was his impeccably accurate reflection of what it means to be Chinese – as in being inscrutable, contemptuous of foreigners, humourless, arrogant and more than a little lacking in individuality.

At this point, Brian wondered whether he should draw his encomium concerning tyrants to an end. He had begun to sense some restlessness in his audience.

But then he decided to do one further chap. And how could he not? How could he not praise the many good points of Mr Vladimir Putin? Because here was a leader who, by posing naked from the waist up on a horse, had made millions of gay men all around the world delighted beyond words. So, good thing number one, emphasised the preacher. After which the preacher put forward the view that in the same way that Mr Maduro was an inspiration for incompetents, so Mr Putin was the supreme inspiration for all those lacking height and even more so for all those who lacked the tiniest scintilla of charisma. Hell, he did it so well, Brian maintained. Expressionless for most of the time, and on those odd occasions when he tried to smile, it looked to all the world as though he'd just felt his colostomy bag overflowing and he wasn't at all pleased. So, no doubt about it. Despite the odd fault now and again, there was far more 'good' about this poor man's Yul Brynner than most people were prepared to concede.

Well, Brian's 'entertainment' didn't earn a round of applause at its conclusion, but nobody actually stopped talking to him after the event, and furthermore there was soon another distraction. It was Darwin baring his (Galápagos) soul.

For the last two weeks, Darwin had been an exemplary guide. He was extremely knowledgeable about every aspect of Galápagos wildlife, plantlife and geology, and he was always ready to share this knowledge with all his charges – whether asked to or not. He was also always concerned for their safety and he was unfailingly courteous and helpful. However, he 'switched off'.

When his guiding work was done, he tended to disappear into the bowels of the boat, only to reappear again for the evening listing sessions, at the end of which he would then brief the Nature-seekers on what they would be doing the next morning. Then he would be gone again. Socialising with the *Beluga*'s passengers did not appear to appeal to him, something that was rather underlined by the fact that he had never made any attempt to learn anybody's name. So, Brian was not alone on this evening in expecting Darwin to vanish at the conclusion of his listing and briefing business as he had repeatedly done before. But he didn't. He stayed on, and, much to the surprise of all the Nature-seekers, he addressed their assembled numbers (from behind the bar) on all that was wrong with the management of his cherished archipelago…

It started with a reference to that National Geographic behemoth seen earlier today, and his suspicions about how it and a sister ship had been given a licence to thread their way through the delicate environment of the Galápagos when he understood that similar operating licences had been withdrawn for their previous activities in the Caribbean and off the coast of Alaska. They were both very old ships, he said, even older than the *Beluga*. So, it seemed to Brian that what Darwin was suggesting was that not only were these two ships too big to be let loose in the Galápagos, but also that they might represent a potential threat if they encountered a mishap. And why would the authorities possibly allow that?

Well, maybe a clue was in Darwin's further comments of there now being just too many boats licensed to operate in the archipelago (a total of eighty-four) and their being obliged to follow a prescribed itinerary, supposedly designed to control their activities, but one that at the same time required them to steam backwards and forwards between the islands (as the *Beluga* had done) and thereby use far more fuel than they would in a simple circumnavigation. Yes, there was little doubt about it: Darwin was clearly suggesting that the Galápagos Islands were being exploited to the point of over-exploitation – for the benefit of… well, persons unknown who very probably were in mainland Ecuador and in positions of power. He underlined his point by then informing the Nature-seekers that the number of visitors allowed into the archipelago (which, of course, is a controlled national park) had recently been raised from 140,000 per year to 240,000 per year, and even this bigger figure might rise if plans for a 300-room hotel on San Cristóbal are approved. This, he believed, would see not only more and more people arriving in the archipelago, but more and more who were coming here to pursue non-Galápagos-type activities. That is to say that there was a real risk that the Galápagos would be developed as just another holiday destination – where one could swim, windsurf, sunbathe, drink margaritas and happily ignore the treasures of the national park. This was already happening. And it was already fuelling the increase in settler numbers in the Galápagos, as more poor Ecuadorians arrived to service the visitors' needs. And there was worse. There were now many fishermen, Darwin explained, who were equipping their boats with powerful outboard motors to enable them to be operated as taxis. Not taxis to necessarily take visitors to other islands, but taxis that would take visitors to out-of-bounds reefs. The natural environment of the Galápagos therefore faced the menace not only of more *Homo sapiens* and everything that entails in terms of more houses, more vehicles, more pollution and more filth, but also more active destruction of its natural wonders.

Darwin was pretty incensed. He made no secret of the fact that he thought those making decisions about the Galápagos did not have its best interests at heart but only their own personal interests, in the sense of how they might best benefit themselves. If not, why were they contemplating plans that would undermine the very essence of the Galápagos archipelago as a unique (and valuable) destination and not instead looking at ways to enhance the place – starting off by making it a national park that was as expensive to visit as some of those in Africa and elsewhere? (The current charge of US$100, Darwin maintained, was just far too low.)

Well, this was quite a sustained assault, and it clearly had an impact on all the Nature-seekers. At the end of it they were all looking either concerned or subdued. And as for Brian… well, he was feeling just a little bit distressed, and for three separate reasons. To start with, he had been really unsettled by the downbeat nature of Darwin's harangue. Hell, didn't Darwin know that the position of pessimist in residence on the *Beluga* was already taken, and Brian had no intention of giving it up? Then, of rather more import, there was the message in Darwin's address: that the Galápagos was been exploited and thus threatened like never before. And finally there was the confirmation of something that Brian had already suspected: that he and his companions on this boat were themselves part of the problem. They might be here to have a 'proper' Galápagos experience, but they were still adding to the pressures on this fabulous archipelago by just being here. Like any visitors they needed food, drink, fuel for their boat and all the other things that were required to keep them comfortable and safe and that could only be provided by adding even further to the burdens already borne by these islands. In fact, all in all, it was quite enough to make even an optimist pessimistic. And if you were the pessimist in residence... well, you'd probably want to deal with it in the only way you could: by retiring to your cabin and assaulting your wife with yet another discourse on a South American country – which, on this occasion, might also entail a reference to pants...

Brian started as he always did: with an assumption that Sandra would be in some way interested in what he had to say. So his opening remarks were made with confidence – and without any recognition of their potential impact on his audience.

'Tonight,' he said, 'I thought I'd say just a few words about Peru...'

'Just a few would be good,' responded his underwhelmed but resigned wife.

It was no good. He was never going to be dissuaded by such a poor attempt as that. And so he continued.

'Right. Well, Peru is famous for Machu Picchu, the consumption of guinea pigs and the origination of potatoes. However, I would like to make two points, and the first concerns potatoes...'

'Brian. We're on a boat in the Galápagos, and you want to talk to me about potatoes…?'

'Yes, but only to point out that over 90% of the world's presently cultivated potatoes are actually descended from varieties that originated in the lowlands of south-central Chile and which have almost completely displaced the formerly popular varieties from the Andes. Which means that Peru's claim to be the birthplace of a crop which now accounts for seventy-three pounds of the annual diet of an average global citizen is just a tiny bit suspect…'

'Give me strength…'

'Incidentally. Did you know that when they were first introduced into England, potatoes were considered to be so unhealthy and even potentially poisonous that the Society for the Prevention of Unwholesome Diets, otherwise known as SPUD (get it?), saw them as a real threat? In fact, they weren't that welcome to start with anywhere in Europe, with some people choosing not to eat them just because they weren't mentioned in the Bible…'

'Is your second point possibly just a little more interesting?' interrupted Sandra – with maybe only a hint of sarcasm creeping into her voice, and certainly not enough to be noticed by Brian, who happily ploughed on with point number two without further delay.

'In Peru, when the clock strikes midnight on New Year's Eve, you have to get out of your old underwear and into your new yellow pants without delay. And these will probably be pants that friends or relatives will have given you to ensure that you embark on the brand new year with all the good luck you will need.'

Sandra looked actually engaged – but suspicious.

'You're having me on?'

'No,' responded Brian emphatically. 'Google it, and you will see images of Peruvian street vendors in the run-up to New Year selling almost nothing else but men's and women's pants in various shades of yellow. Unless, of course, they're also trying to flog some red ones – for love – or some green ones – for money. But overwhelmingly it will be yellow.'

Sandra appeared at a loss as to how to respond to this alarming piece of trivia concerning the habits of pants-obsessed Peruvians. Brian, on the other hand, was pondering the fact that in 1968 not only did he know very little about the underwear preferences of anybody in South America – at New Year – but (sadly) he also knew bugger all about the underwear preferences of any of his contemporaries – at any time of the year at all.

Then they were soon both asleep – probably sooner than they would have been back in 1968...

14.

*T*he *Beluga* spent the night in Tagus Cove, and Brian spent the night sleeping. But not all of it. At around midnight he awoke to discover that he had thoughts of underwear on his mind. Specifically, he came to – just about – and realised that he needed to brood about the colour of his own underwear – which was invariably black. And if yellow was for good luck, red was for love and green was for money, what could black be for other than… well, death?! This wasn't a very welcome thought, and he desperately tried to think of something else that it might mean. However, he eventually gave up when all he could think of was total depression, total oblivion or… Guinness, none of which he was keen on at all. Instead, he decided that the colour of his underpants probably had about as much significance as the colour of his snorkel (which was black as well!) and he was finally able to drift back to sleep.

The next thing he knew was that it was the morning and that the *Beluga* was making a short journey west. Soon it had dropped anchor, and it was time for all the Nature-seekers to board their awaiting pangas and then to be taken to what was now the close-by island of Fernandina.

This is the most westerly island in the Galápagos archipelago, which means that it is the youngest and most volcanically active island of them all. In fact, it consists entirely of the uplifting and accumulated lava flows of the huge domed cone of Volcán La Cumbre, which have made it the third largest landmass in the Galápagos with a land area of some 248 square miles. Not surprisingly, for an island formed from a volcano that has erupted as recently as 2009, much of its surface area consists of only barren lava, and life here has only a tenuous foothold, mostly on its rocky coast and at places such as Punta Espinosa.

This was the Nature-seekers' destination: an area of the island on its northern coast that in 1994 was raised by between fifty and ninety centimetres to leave its small landing dock inaccessible except at high tide. No great surprise then that everybody in the party was completely wide awake by the time they had negotiated what was a rather challenging disembarkation onto some slippery rocks. And no great surprise that soon after this they had all realised that they had come to a very special place.

To start with there were marine iguanas – quite a few of them and all of them waddling over the rocks and towards the sea. Then there were more of them – hundreds of them – and these guys were either not waddling at all or just waddling rather aimlessly through the middle of a veritable horde of their kind. It was a mass of grey-black creatures carpeting an expanse of grey-black rock, and these creatures were only a little more animated than the rock itself. It was primeval-land – in monochrome – and it was spellbinding. Brian was completely spellbound, and so spellbound that he had to make a conscious effort not to tread on the 'wildlife', wildlife that was so numerous, so indifferent to the presence of visitors and so 'unwild' in its movements, that it would have been particularly easy to have 'put a foot wrong' – with probably some very unfortunate consequences.

Well, this had been an opener like no other. But there was lots more to come, kicking off with the appearance of a snake! It was, according to Darwin, a Galápagos banded snake, and it wasn't anything like as indifferent as its iguana neighbours. When it caught sight of its Nature-seeker observers, it was off like a shot – leaving the stage clear for a couple of sea lion pups and an octopus. The pups were eager to make it to a rock pool for a swim; the octopus to make it to a crevice in another rock pool, probably for the sake of its survival.

As the Nature-seekers then strolled further along the rocky shore, there were suckling sea lions, non-suckling pelicans, lots of Sally Lightfoot crabs, plenty of lizards, a few oystercatchers and blue-footed boobies – and a noticeable number of flies. If that was not enough, there was more than one lizard who was exploiting the rather inert characteristics of the iguanas by using their heads as a lookout point – and one iguana who had taken his inertness to the ultimate degree. He had clearly climbed up to the top of a piece of recumbent driftwood and there he had simply expired, his dried-out carcass now looking like a member of Lord's, somehow overlooked at the end of the last game of the season and now turning into a pavilion-end mummy. It's what they did, according to Darwin (the iguanas, not the members of that august club). Apparently, they couldn't always derive enough nourishment from their undersea diet and they just ran out of fuel – sometimes at the top of a piece of driftwood.

Yes, there was no getting away from it. This place shouted not only 'primeval' but also 'a-bloody-hard-life-primeval', and this characterisation of its essence was reinforced in spades by the sight of a turtle dragging itself ashore for a bit of a warm. It looked incredibly hard work and the turtle looked incredibly resentful. Maybe, thought Brian, he was resentful not just because of the energy he'd had to expend in hauling himself out of the water but also because a nearby lava heron had needed to expend no such energy in catching and swallowing a fish, one that was nearly as big as itself. The heron had obviously had in mind to eat something that would keep it going for days – and to reinforce even further that 'bloody-hard-life-primeval' nature of this patch of Fernandina. Yes, this place was very definitely all about primitive, primordial, perilous and pitiless, with maybe a soupçon of slightly alien thrown in for good measure. And it was certainly unique.

Brian was sorry to have to leave it. But after Darwin had rescued the octopus from its crevice in the rock pool – which had now drained completely – it was time to go. Shortly thereafter, when the Nature-seekers were back on the *Beluga*, it was then time to snorkel, with the object of observing some of those marine iguanas having their elevenses under the waves. However, none were observed, and the Nature-seekers had to make do with observing their companions feeding on another one of

Pedro's lunches. As they were doing this, the *Beluga*'s captain was taking his craft further north – past rafts of delightful phalaropes – to a place called Punta Vicente Roca.

This is on the tip of the Isabela seahorse's nose (remember?) and it consists of some simply gigantic vertiginous rocks and a display of volcanic plumbing – in the shape of exposed volcanic pipes. It appears that at some point in the past there had been a rather sizable nasal collapse, and this failure in Isabela's proboscis has produced the most dramatic of cliffscapes – and an intriguing place off which to moor and an intriguing place to be explored with the aid of a panga…

Accordingly, both pangas were soon in the water: one carrying a clutch of Nature-seekers kitted out with lifejackets, the other with Nature-seekers kitted out with just snorkelling equipment. Yes, for this latter clutch (which included Brian), this excursion was to end in the water. Even though, from Brian's perspective, the water looked somewhat less than inviting. This was because it was rather opaque, rather turbulent and it had as a backdrop a towering rock face, the sort of backdrop that emphasised the piddling insignificance of the pangas' passengers and the folly of any of those who were planning to take to the water. Nevertheless, that was for later. Right now there was a slow-speed navigation to undertake – close to those towering rocks and not that far from some of the local wildlife.

On the cliff face itself there were frigatebirds and blue-footed boobies. On rocks jutting out of the sea below the cliff face there were (more) marine iguanas.

And in the sea itself there were both sea lions and fur seals. (Brian could now tell them apart.) These were all to be welcomed. Indeed, they were deserving of a much more enthusiastic reception than what appeared as Brian's panga made it around a headland and what Darwin revealed would be their ultimate destination before they embarked on their snorkelling. Because what appeared was a ruddy great sea cave. And we are talking here about a Premier League-type sea cave, an enormous arched portal in the side of a cliff, with beyond it just darkness and beneath it… well, a rather worrying swell. Brian scrutinised it with interest and not without a good deal of trepidation.

No matter. Both pangas were soon approaching it. And, before he knew it, his was at the very mouth of the cave, and Darwin was pointing out boobies…

It was remarkable. Here he was, with eight other souls, bobbing about in a small rubber inflatable with rather too much animation – on the lip of a watery black hole – and it was time for a spot of impromptu birdwatching. And quite right too. The boobies (and they were blue-footed boobies, sharing some rock ledges with some brown noddies) were only a few feet above their observers and, as usual, completely unconcerned at their presence. That said, Brian did think that on this occasion they were showing a modicum of interest in their visitors, and he immediately put this down to their desire for just a little more 'spice' in their lives. After all, he speculated, if one was destined to spend one's life sitting on a rock ledge, flying over the sea and occasionally diving into the sea, there must come a time when you crave just 'something more' in your life. Even if that something more is provided by a gang of flightless creatures that regularly drift past your ledge, totally ignoring your desire for privacy as well as your inherent booby rights for a peaceful and undisturbed existence.

This speculation then got the better of him, and he was soon considering whether these boobies – and the noddies – had their very own version of that childhood game of *I Spy*, involving, of course, the use of their very own *I Spy Passing Bobbers* book – complete with appropriate scoring. It wasn't long before he was then trying to imagine what might earn them points, and the first idea he came up with was that any of the bobbers that weren't middle aged – other than the recognisable guide and driver, of course – would allow them to clock up maybe five points apiece. Extensive tattooing of bobbers would also furnish them with five points, as would any display of extensive areas of sunburn. Then there would be an awkward display of cleavage – either at the front or the back – which would be worth fifteen points, and an adornment with a ginger moustache, which would be worth twenty. But to get that rare fifty-pointer, the boobies and noddies would have to clap eyes on either genuine dreadlocks or a genuine hijab, two sights that Brian suspected may never have been witnessed here ever. Then he stopped thinking about their *I Spy* game completely, because his panga was now on its way into the cave, and thoughts of potential perils and the potential for survival began to overtake him.

It was very disconcerting. The water in what was revealing itself to be a gigantic cave was not at rest. It was… undulating. Significantly. The swell outside appeared to be magnified within the confines of the cavern, and both pangas were now not just bobbing about but they were really heaving. Fortunately none of their passengers were, but this experience did put Brian in mind of a rubber duck. Not of a rubber duck in a bath, but of a rubber duck in a tank full of water, one that was being carried on the back of a poorly sprung truck over a poorly maintained track at an inappropriate speed. It was 'interesting', but not that interesting that Brian was sorry when it came to an end, and had only the prospect of snorkelling in cloudy, 100m-deep water to distract him…

He felt smaller – and more vulnerable – than ever. Especially when Darwin warned him and his fellow snorkelers that, as they would be swimming just below the vertiginous cliffs, it was quite possible that they might experience a torpedo. Not a submarine-launched torpedo, but a torpedo travelling at speed vertically in the shape of a diving booby. Oh, and then there were the jellyfish. And, of course, the lack of any worthwhile visibility.

So… it felt more like an element of SAS training than a regular snorkel, and Brian saw only the jellyfish (as well as feeling their sting). He was therefore fairly pleased when it was at an end and it was time to make it back to the *Beluga*, there to join Sandra and the other more sensible Nature-seekers who had all chosen to stay dry. Except, that is, for one…

Yes, as the *Beluga* came into view on the other side of the headland, two things became apparent. The first was that the *Beluga* was on the move – to collect Brian's panga as it approached and to expedite their departure from Punta Vicente Roca – and the second was that aboard it Pedro and Abel were pointing to something in the water. Wow! It had to be a sunfish. It was so large. And Darwin had told them earlier that this was a good place to see them. Excitement mounted in the panga as it then made its way to where this huge beast was making a commotion in the swell. And this excitement built right up until it became apparent that it wasn't a sunfish, but that it was Shane! Unbelievably, he had gone for an unscheduled swim, but had not told the crew, and the *Beluga* had weighed anchor and started to sail off without its overlooked and now marooned Californian. Well, a vote was taken on board the panga, and by a wafer-thin majority it was decided that it should proceed towards him and pluck him from the water. But only on the condition that its passengers were not required to stifle giggles or refrain from shaking their heads as they pulled him aboard. What a plonker. And what not a sunfish.

Anyway, the captain had made such a prompt start because he had before him a seven-hour trip. He was on his way to Santiago, and this meant a passage north and then east around the northern coast of Isabela and then south-east down towards his destination. It also meant, within just a very short time of setting off, yet another crossing of the equator – and more cocktails with eggs. Fortunately, things then got rather better. In the first place because a school of dolphins was found – and then another school – and then there was the Nature-seekers' first ever sighting of a giant manta ray. It was almost inevitably at a distance, but it was definitely one of these spectacular creatures and it was relished by all those on board. And then the *pièce de résistance*: another marooned Californian! But no. It wasn't a Californian; it was a *Mola mola* or, in other words, an ocean sunfish, known for its huge size and its frequent confusion with bathing Americans. Again, it was at quite a distance, and all one could see was its fin. But all the same. What a thing to behold. Brian had been reading up on these chaps only recently, and he was soon busy telling Sandra that the *Mola mola* is the heaviest bony fish in the world and it can weigh up to an enormous 1,000 kilograms – which is about the same as ten Shanes… Although, there again, it doesn't look like ten Shanes; it looks more like a fishhead with a tail. And another interesting fact he had to impart to her was that the sunfish manages to achieve this huge size on a diet of mostly jellyfish – and wouldn't it have been great if one of them had been around during Brian's recent snorkelling expedition? If there had been, he would not now be nursing those itches on his legs. But anyway, there was one further fact that he felt Sandra had to know. And this was that the sunfish is fantastically fecund, in that the female of the species can produce more eggs than any other known vertebrate – up to 300,000,000 at a time. Which is more, pointed out Brian, than were used in those cocktails earlier on.

It was at this stage of his presentation that Sandra blocked its continuation by changing the subject from *Mola molas* to gin and tonics. Didn't he think, she suggested to her husband, that now they were in the northern hemisphere again it might be about time for a couple of these northern hemisphere drinks before dinner? Well, this was a dastardly clever ploy, because she obviously knew that Brian would remind her that gin and tonic was a drink that originated in the British East India Company and it could therefore hardly be described as a northern hemisphere drink. However, he did concede it was a drink of the Tropics, and as they were still very near the equator and hence about as much in the Tropics as one can be, an investment in a couple of gin and tonics would not be out of place. So job done. Brian's *Mola mola* dissertation terminated and the bonus of a nice G&T before dinner. Perfect. All she needed now was Brian to behave himself over dinner and then, after dinner, to forget that he had not yet lectured her on Paraguay…

Well, the G&T was fine. However, dinner wasn't quite as silky smooth. And this was largely because Brian had sneaked his soapbox in again, and he mounted it even before the main course had arrived. Oh, and his subject for tonight was 'the purpose of life': what could be the object of us humans living on this planet for three score years and ten – or indeed for rather more? Well, he initiated his assault with a question, asking all those around the table what they thought might be the purpose of life. But in doing so he had neglected that his audience now knew him very well and they therefore knew how to respond. Thelma was first and she suggested to Brian that the purpose of life was to remain seated for as long as possible, but that not many people knew this. Brian was somewhat taken aback by this, but not as much as he was when Josh then announced that the purpose of life was to be a witness to its purposelessness – and to appreciate the amazing diversity of cheese. In fact, Brian was so dumbfounded that he barely took in Mandy's assertion that the purpose of life was to give some sort of purpose to the act of procreation, rather than leaving it as being just an extremely enjoyable process.

These responses should have knocked that soapbox from beneath his feet. But of course they didn't. They simply energised him, and caused him to respond with a series of pseudo-philosophical explanations for the purpose of life, all of which he then shot down as soon as he'd introduced them, before he then ended up with the conclusion that life had no purpose other than to be lived. As well and as enjoyably as one could – without causing too much harm. In fact, this conclusion was a little hurried, as Sandra had, without a great deal of discretion, let it be known to her husband that she and the rest of his table companions were losing the will to live, whether there was a purpose to their living or not. And he would do very well to switch to 'mute' just as soon as he could. This he did, and only when he and Sandra were back in their cabin did he disengage mute and re-engage vocal. Yes, Sandra was to be unlucky again. Not only had his behaviour not been flawless over dinner, but he had also remembered that he had a list of lectures to complete. And this last one – on Paraguay – wasn't just fascinating; it was also rather long…

He started, as he so often did, with a question.

'Sandra,' he asked, 'do you know a great deal about Paraguay?'

Sandra, who was sitting up in bed, ineffectively armed with a book, answered promptly and honestly.

'No,' she said. 'I don't.'

She could have added that she had a pretty good idea that Paraguay would feature as a lecture topic this evening. But that seemed unnecessary, and anyway, Brian had what he wanted: an admission that Sandra was just as unacquainted with Paraguay as are most people in this world, other than Paraguayans. Therefore he responded immediately – and gleefully.

'Yes. Well, you're not on your own. You see, Paraguay has something of a reputation for being... well, rather low profile and more than just a little bit insular. In fact, there was a guy called Augusto Roa Bastos, a Paraguayan novelist, who once said that Paraguay was an island surrounded on all sides by land. And then there was some US satirist – I think it was P. J. O'Rourke – who said that Paraguay was nowhere and was famous for nothing.'

'A little bit harsh,' observed Sandra.

'But true. I mean, it is pretty well famous for nothing and as for being nowhere – and being an island surrounded by land – well, that's got more than an element of truth as well. It is landlocked, and it is ringed by Argentina to the south and south-west, Brazil to the east and north-east and Bolivia to the north-west...'

'Yeah, but you could say the same about Switzerland or Austria or any number of landlocked countries. But you wouldn't say they were nowhere – and islands surrounded by land...'

'No. Because, unlike Paraguay, they haven't pursued isolationism and protectionism for their entire history.'

Oh dear. Sandra had unwittingly primed her

husband's address without really trying. And now he would launch into it. Probably with a few 'national facts' to start with and then with an amplification of those references to isolationism and protectionism. She just knew it. And, of course, she was spot on. Even about the 'national facts'.

'Right,' he started, 'I suppose it might be a good idea if, to begin with, I told you that Paraguay lies on the banks of the Paraguay River and its capital is Asunción. And Asunción is home to a third of the country's population of seven million souls. Oh, and it's probably not true that on early maps, Paraguay was called "Parrot", in memory of a parrot called Frank, who was first befriended and then eventually eaten by the earliest Jesuit settler in the area...'

'Well, that's reassuring to know,' observed Sandra.

'Nor that Frank was homosexual... You know, as in "parrot gay"...'

'Brian...'

'Yeah. OK. Isolationism and protectionism. And a history of authoritarian dictators who maintained these policies right up until quite recent times. But why?'

'I thought you were going to tell me.'

'I am. And it involves my telling you about a most remarkable man. Nay, a unique man, a gentleman who went by the name of José Gaspar Rodriguez de Francis, and who was the guy who ruled Paraguay from 1814 right through to his death in 1840 – which made him the very first dictator of this country – and from what I'm about to tell you, incontestably its most exceptional and most influential – at least in terms of his extraordinary legacy.'

'I'm all ears.'

'Right. Well, to start with, José was not your normal common or garden dictator. On the contrary. He was somebody who had been deeply influenced by the ideas of the Enlightenment and latterly by what had been happening in the French Revolution. Accordingly, he was disgusted by the class system that had been imposed on Paraguay as a colony – which essentially meant a Spanish caste system where your status was decided by your colour and your birth with, not surprisingly, those with the whiter heritage being granted the higher status. And he desperately wanted to replace this inherited system with what he saw as a utopian society based on Rousseau's 'Social Contract'. This was all about recognising that monarchs were not divinely empowered to rule, and that only the people, who are sovereign, have that all powerful right.'

'Oh...'

'Yes, this Social Contract stuff is all very interesting when you look into it. And the bit I particularly like concerns something called "the state of nature" – which is a set of hypothetical conditions under which people might have lived before societies came into existence – and the view that in many societies people are now in a state that's much worse. You know, than in the state of nature.'

'Can't argue with that,' offered Sandra. 'But you do seem to be drifting just a wee bit off the plot...'

'Ah, yes,' admitted Brian. 'And to return to the plot, José reckoned that to create his utopia he first had to break the power of the Spanish establishment – by greatly reducing the power of its resident representative in the new independent Paraguay: the Roman Catholic Church. And that's exactly what he did – by passing various laws. Only that was just the start. Because he then forbade colonial citizens (the high-caste whites) from marrying one another and allowed them to marry only blacks, people of mixed parentage or natives. And in this way he completely broke the power of the colonial elites and created a genuinely mixed-race society. So much so that in modern-day Paraguay, over 95% of its population is *mestizo* – or mixed race.'

'Blimey!'

'Yeah. Quite a thing, eh? Although given that his utopia was all about freedom and being released from various forms of slavery, being told who you could and couldn't marry might represent something of a minor contradiction...'

'But he did it...'

'Yes. And he did it by keeping at bay any outside influences – and setting in train this national embrace of isolationism, which remained the hallmark of the country right into modern times. Helped to no small degree by Paraguay losing 5,000 square miles of its territory to Argentina and Brazil in the 1864-70 Paraguayan War, along with up to 70% of its population – through disease or the war itself.'

'I see.'

'Yeah. Well, anyway, going back to old José, you have to admire him not only because he was able to mould a nation – through his imposition of some fairly draconian marriage arrangements – but also because he was refreshingly honest. I mean, the title he chose for himself was 'Supreme and Perpetual Dictator of Paraguay', a title, I might say, that as far as I know, was not adopted by any of the successive dictators of that country, nor by any of the many other tinpot despots that South America as a continent has since had to bear.'

'So how is he regarded in Paraguay now?'

'Good question. Because despite imbuing Paraguay with a tradition of autocratic rule that lasted until 1989, he is seen as a national hero. Oh, and despite his idealism inevitably morphing into ever more arbitrary and despotic rule...'

'Oh.'

'Yes. It's always the same, isn't it? No matter how well intentioned they are to start with, sooner or later it all starts to go pear-shaped. And with old José, it was no different. I mean, he ended up ruling through ruthless suppression and, with the help of a secret police force, through what might be called random terror. He also outlawed all opposition to his rule and executed anybody that plotted against him. And then he went completely bonkers...'

'How?'

'Well, when he implemented the death penalty – which was applied increasingly frequently – he insisted that all executions were carried out on a stool under an orange tree outside his window. And to save bullets, most victims were bayoneted, and then their families were not allowed to collect them until hours after the event, just to make sure they were dead.'

'Lovely.'

'He also, apparently, kept a ledger of all the women he'd ever slept with, and he sired quite a few illegitimate children. He declared prostitution a decent profession when he discovered his oldest illegitimate child on the game outside his house. He became paranoid about being assassinated and slept with a gun under his pillow. And on top of that he then instituted a rule that nobody could come within six paces of him, and if he went out riding, trees and bushes that could conceal assassins would have to be uprooted, and pedestrians would have to prostrate themselves before him as he passed.'

'Uhmm, but I bet he sang along to the national anthem and he knew how to dress properly,' suggested Sandra. At which point Paraguay's history, Paraguay's first dictator and Paraguay's national psyche were all abandoned in favour of a transient consideration of Britain's current would-be *El Supremo*. And then both Brian and Sandra fell asleep.

15.

*B*rian and Sandra awoke to find the *Beluga* back in the southern hemisphere and moored off Santiago, and Brian found that he felt like an out-of-date taramasalata. In fact, he felt really grotty and in no condition to participate in the morning expedition. This was to a visitor site called Puerto Egas, a place that promised a smorgasbord of rock formations, grotto-like formations, tidal pools, fur seals, marine iguanas, oystercatchers and whimbrels. Anyway, Sandra was not similarly afflicted. So, while she joined the other Nature-seekers on a panga ride to this new display of Galápagos delights, Brian remained on board – and applied himself as best he could to drafting his speech!

Yes, just because he had misbehaved himself again the previous evening with an unwarranted harangue about the purpose of life, his companions had conferred on him the 'honour' of delivering a thank-you speech to the crew before he and his companions sat down for tonight's dinner. This was... well, less an honour and more an exercise in prodding the brain into action when all the brain wanted to do was to coast along without any demands made on it at all, other than maybe entertaining the odd fantasy about Joanna Lumley or Sigourney Weaver – just to keep things ticking over, you understand. Well, coasting and fantasies would have to wait. He could not disappoint his audience, and after breakfast when his fellow passengers had set off for Puerto Egas, he dragged himself from his cabin and up onto the sundeck, and there he composed…

It proved a draining exercise, and when Sandra and the others returned, it took all the energy he retained to show any interest whatsoever in what they had seen and then the use of his reserve tank of energy to make it through lunch. The afternoon, he soon decided, would be spent in his cabin, recharging his batteries as much as possible so that he stood any chance at all of being able to stand and deliver – his speech – as required.

For the other Nature-seekers, it was different. There was yet another visitor site to be… visited. And this was Isla Bartolemé. This is the small island off the east coast of Santiago, which faces Sullivan Bay (the site of all that wonderful ropey lava that the Nature-seekers had walked across eight days before). It was advertised as quite a place; a small island equipped with a flight of wooden steps that lead to the island's summit and what is supposed to be the most photographed view in the entire Galápagos. It was therefore somewhere that all those Nature-seekers who were not either indisposed or just plain indolent were keen to visit, and it wasn't long after lunch before two pangas, each with a full complement of anticipation, had set off from the Beluga in the direction of Bartolemé. Unfortunately, it wasn't long after this that the two pangas returned – with no anticipation any more but with just a cargo of very damp passengers. The sea had proved far too rough. Although the pangas had been able to approach the stone landing at the foot of that flight of steps, they had not been able to use it to discharge their cargo. The sea had been much too choppy and the swell much too large, and the Nature-seekers had had to return to their boat with no outstanding photos but with just wet clothes. Such is the nature of nature, and such is the nature of the end of holidays…

Yes, tomorrow would see the Nature-seekers returning to Baltra Island and from there they would fly back to Ecuador, and although some of them would then go on to the Ecuadorian Amazon, it would be the end of their expedition to the Galápagos. So it was all running down, and that aborted trip to Bartolemé just seemed to underline it. Certainly, in Brian's mind, this visit to this wonderful archipelago had essentially run its course. Although, there again, he still had that speech to deliver.

Well, in the event, he was able to revive himself just about enough to make a decent job of it, even though it involved some not quite simultaneous translation… Of the locals, only Darwin and Abel were able to understand his English, and therefore, after a short burst of narrative, Darwin would step in to provide a translation of what had been said. This worked pretty well, other than when Brian had chosen one or two idioms that were clearly not in common circulation among English-speaking Ecuadorians, and he then had to help Darwin out. But anyway, British/Ecuadorian relations were in no way dented, and at the end of the presentation Captain José and his crew all looked just about as pleased as they

would in the morning when they all received their tips…
And nobody mentioned Julian Assange.

Well, with the speech delivered, Brian was still feeling slightly below par. So he excused himself straight after dinner and retired to his cabin where, before Sandra joined him, he'd decided he would review his time in the Galápagos and attempt to decide what were its high points and what were its low points. This is what he did, and this is what he eventually decided…

First on the list of high points was the Beluga. It had been difficult to find fault with: a beautiful, streamlined vessel, with more than adequate accommodation, a more than competent crew and an offering of food that was more than any of the Nature-seekers had expected. Yes, this tiny boat had become a very cherished home from home, and it would leave Brian with an enduring affection for a life on the waves – just as long as Pedro was there with him.

Then there was the Galápagos archipelago. And where could he start? Maybe with its natural beauty or maybe with its other-worldliness. Or maybe with its unique complement of animals and birds who, despite what we have done to so many of their cousins around the world – and to so many of their ancestors – still seem able to accept us as harmless visitors and amazingly don't regard us as a threat. And what a complement! Comical and charming blue-footed boobies. Splendid and literally magnificent frigatebirds. Ponderous and possibly pensive giant tortoises. Primeval and not in the least bit pensive marine iguanas. And then all those creatures of the sea: all those perspicacious sea lions and fur seals, all those colourful fish and sinuous rays, all those lumbering turtles – and all those absolutely fabulous sharks. Yes, even though they couldn't be classed as Galápagos endemics, the sharks Brian had seen both in the water and from a beach might prove to be the most memorable creatures of all. And without a doubt, the single high point of this trip, which was head and shoulders above all the other high points, was that hammerhead shark off the Devil's Crown. When Brian had entered the water there and found that he was alone except for a twelve-foot-long marvel of nature just a few feet below him, he had been catapulted into another world, a world of true wonder and a world that encapsulated what all this nature stuff was really all about: enchantment, even enthrallment – and something that can only be called genuine spirituality.

Anyway, returning to this world, it was at this stage of his musings that he remembered that he had shared it for the past two weeks with a group of other people who clearly needed to feature in any list of high points for this holiday. With a couple of New World exceptions – and a couple of self-isolating exceptions – they had proved themselves not just good company but outstanding company – and eminently 'normal' company, in the best sense of the word. They had shown humour, kindness, tolerance (for Brian's interminable lectures), forbearance whenever this was necessary – and a degree of enthusiasm that was no less than inspiring. In fact, Brian was inclined to give them ten out of ten. Even if they might not all have reciprocated this score. And even if they might not all necessarily agree with what was on his list of low points for this expedition.

Now, Brian normally conducted these end-of-adventure reviews by starting with the bad bits and then concluding with the good bits. However, for this Galápagos adventure, it had to be the other way around. Partly because of the nature of the bad bits and partly because of his own complicity in one of them in particular.

Anyway, the first bad bit/low point of this expedition to the Galápagos was its inevitable lack of freedom. By its very nature, it was impossible to simply land and then walk where one chose, and although it would have had appalling consequences if one did this, it did make for a very constrained and a very regimented 'adventure'. Indeed, so much so, that 'adventure' didn't feature at all, and it could often feel as though one was on a guided school visit – with Mr Darwin, the teacher, in control. Brian had given this aspect of the expedition a lot of thought, and had almost decided not to put it onto the low-points list at all. It was, after all, unavoidable and he'd known all about the restrictions imposed before he'd come. But it could definitely not be regarded as a high point – from the perspective of somebody who had been fortunate enough to roam around other parts of the world almost unhindered. So, he had put it down as a negative, even after recognising that when snorkelling, he hadn't felt constrained at all. And certainly not in the company of that hammerhead shark…

OK, second low point, and a much more serious low point: the inhabited areas of the Galápagos and the behaviour of the inhabitants. This was a tricky one, because Brian was not poor, he wasn't a landless peasant from Ecuador and he wasn't a fisherman or farmer who had a big family to feed. Whereas most of the people living on the Galápagos Islands seemed to fall into one of these categories, and during their lives they had failed to accrue the precious middle-class concerns for the environment and the world in general that Brian and his companions had. Accordingly, they seemed indifferent to the impact they were having on such a priceless manifestation of nature – whether on land or in the sea – and they were equally indifferent to the scars they were inflicting in the form of their settlements and their scruffy farms. Brian had known for a long time that people had lived on the Galápagos, but before he had come here he had not been aware of quite how many of them there were or of quite how callous they were in their attitude to their surroundings.

Of course, this assessment of the Galápagos residents was a terrible generalisation, and there were many people – like Darwin – who held a very different view of how the islands should be treated and how the islanders should behave. But they were clearly not in a majority and their ranks were unlikely to be swelled if the 'authorities' had their way and more and more visitors were brought to the islands. And this pressure being exerted by this burgeoning number of visitors led Brian to the final low point on his list – and to the part that he himself played in it.

Yes. In sailing around the Galápagos archipelago, one cannot fail to notice that one is rarely on one's own. Occasionally one is, and on other occasions one may be moored at a visitor site with just one other vessel. But commonly there are three, four or even five boats lying off a popular site, and some of these boats, as already reported, are not the size of the Beluga. Some are double its size. Some are four times its size. And a couple are absolute monsters. All these boats contain visitors and inevitably all these visitors, as well as representing a direct threat to the environment in terms of their sheer numbers, represent a much bigger threat in terms of what is needed to support their visit. And this is because most of what they need can only be provided by people who live on the Galápagos – and, not surprisingly, breed on the Galápagos. Quite simply, nature tourism in this archipelago risks undermining the very nature on which it is currently based – because of its demand for the permanent settlement of residents. And whilst great efforts are being made to ensure that this risk is minimised, it is going to become a monumental struggle when the 'authorities' seek to exploit the archipelago further, even to the extent of promoting 'regular' holidays as well as eco-holidays. More and more permanent residents will arrive. More and more babies will arrive. And more and more of the land in the archipelago will be 'zoned', grabbed or otherwise screwed up in order to meet their demands for housing, food and even recreation. It's what happens. It's what happens everywhere in the world. And, it can now be reported that it is happening in what might be regarded as one of the most precious environments in the world. And that's not precious as in middle-class precious, but precious as in magnificent, astonishing, sublime and *unique*.

If that wasn't bad enough, Brian was inescapably complicit. By coming here with Sandra, he had required food, drinks, a boat, fuel for this boat, a panga, fuel for the panga, a supply of napkins, toilet paper, cleaning products and no doubt many more things that he was unaware of. And none of this stuff appeared out of thin air. It had to be ordered by people, brought to the archipelago by people, warehoused by people, distributed and delivered by people, and all or most of these people lived here in the Galápagos – in one of those less than salubrious settlements that were still growing apace. Yes, there was no doubt about it. He was guilty as charged. And whilst he would not be fined or incarcerated for his felony, he would feel genuinely guilty and certainly more than a little uncomfortable that he had come to this place – and had enjoyed it so much…

But what could one do? How could one come to these conclusions without coming here? How could one realise one's folly before one committed it? And what was the alternative? To eschew the archipelago entirely and so starve it of the funds it needs for its conservation work? Or maybe just empty it of its residents and seal it all off? Neither of which alternatives had much to recommend it and neither of which was in any way practical.

Well, it was at this point that Brian thought he had probably over-reviewed his experience of the Galápagos, and however guilty or otherwise he felt about coming here, it would make no difference. The archipelago would thrive or suffer despite what was going on inside his head. And anyway, he could hear Sandra returning to the cabin now, and it had struck him earlier in the day that he had omitted from his review of all those

South American countries one very important 'country' indeed: that other archipelago off the coast of the continent which went by the name of the Falklands. So, lucky Sandra. She had a bonus to come. And he knew a great deal more about the Falklands than she'd expect. Including the fact that its environment might not be quite as fascinating as that of the Galápagos, but thanks to its history and its present minimal human presence, this environment was not really under threat. Neither was it under threat from too many visitors.

Which, thought Brian, might mean that Sandra would not only receive a lecture on the Falklands this evening, but also an invitation to consider it as their next destination! A balance to their visit to the Galápagos, or an atonement or a penance. Call it what you will, thought Brian. But it would be perfect. Even if it lacked boobies, the *Beluga*, the *Beluga*'s complement of passengers, giant tortoises, Pedro's food, mockingbirds, Darwin's lectures, oversized calderas, colourful iguanas – and hammerhead sharks.

Although, there again, without that one hammerhead shark off the Devil's Crown, it couldn't, Brian admitted to himself, be entirely perfect…

By the same author:

Brian's World Series

Brian on the Brahmaputra (with Sujan in the Sundarbans)
A Syria Situation
Sabah-taged
Cape Earth
Strip Pan Wrinkle (in Namibia and Botswana)
Crystal Balls and Moroccan Walls
Marmite, Bites and Noisy Nights (in Zambia)
The Country-cides of Namibia and Botswana
First Choose Your Congo

The Renton Tenting Trilogy

Dumpiter
Ticklers
Lollipop

Light-bites

Eggshell in Scrambled Eggs
Crats
The A-Z of Stuff

www.davidfletcherbooks.co.uk